MY EVERY BREATH

A BECOMING US NOVEL

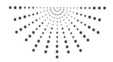

BRITTNEY SAHIN

EMKO MEDIA

My Every Breath

By: Brittney Sahin

Published by: Emko Media, LLC

Copyright © 2018 EmKo Media, LLC

Second edition © 2019

This book is an original publication of Brittney Sahin.

Editor: Carole, WordsRU

Proofreader: Joy Editing

Proofreader: Lawrence Editing

Cover Design by: Mayhem Cover Creations

Image License: Shutterstock

Paperback ISBN: 9781947717039

eBook ISBN-13: 9781947717015

❀ Created with Vellum

1

CADE

"YOU COULDN'T THINK OF ANYTHING MORE ORIGINAL THAN A strip club?" I glance at my brother, the perpetrator of this cliché bachelor party, as a smirk stretches across his face and meets his eyes.

Jerry, the groom-to-be, smacks my brother in the chest and winks. "He's a smart man." He flicks his wrist, motioning for our group of five to head toward the dance stage.

It's three-tiered and glittery like a birthday cake. The dancer's leg curls around the pole as the candle on top.

"Come on, bro. You need to lighten up."

I exhale through my nose and look to where a woman wearing only silver stilettos gives a guy his own personal show.

"Why this place, though?" Strands of green beads dangle like partitions between the booths around the outer rim of the club, and the Irish flag is positioned on nearly every wall. This isn't our typical hangout.

Corbin directs his attention to the blonde dancer with her ass up in the air on stage. "It was Jerry's idea. Maybe he didn't want to be recognized."

"No one should recognize him here. Well, other than maybe a few criminals he put behind bars and are now out on parole."

"He's a homicide detective. Let's hope none of those assholes are back on the streets," Corbin says.

True. "Just try and stay out of trouble, okay?" I warn.

"Hey, I haven't gotten arrested even once this entire year."

Laughing, I tip my head back and squeeze my eyes shut for a moment. "It's January sixth." Having friends like Jerry has had its perks for my brother.

"What? That counts for something."

Corbin hasn't managed to tame his wild side yet. Maybe he never will.

"Come on. Tonight is for Jerry." He casually strides through the crowd toward the stage, already reaching into his pocket for his wallet.

I need a drink if I'm going to survive tonight.

I head to the bar and move a stool out of the way so I can remain standing.

The bartender takes a shot of whiskey straight from the bottle, then fills a glass to the brim. He slides it to some guy a few feet away with a thick neck displaying a tat of a serpent darting through the eye hole of a skull.

"Jack and Coke. Light on the Coke," I order a minute later and turn toward the stage while I wait.

I honestly don't have anything against strippers. A lot of them are dancing to pay their way through college. I respect people who work hard. Period. But this particular blonde on stage isn't doing anything for me. And I assume she's wearing a wig. The almost-white hair reaches the small dimples on her back, and every time she bends over, it slips out of place.

At the sound of a glass sliding behind me, I start to pivot, but I stop dead in my tracks at the sight of a woman walking through the crowd, heading my way.

My gaze slides over her, assessing. She's in a classy black, fitted dress that hugs her body but isn't too tight. It falls just above her knees, showing off her long, tan legs. Legs that go for fucking miles.

The lighting is shoddy, but she still looks pretty bronzed for this time of year.

But Jesus, it's her eyes. They're narrowed as if I'm not someone she expects to see here.

Yeah, I feel the same about her.

The closer she gets she sucks me into her orbit almost to the point where I don't feel in control. And I'm always in control, so it rattles me.

She stops in front of the bar and tips her chin up, her beautiful pouty lips tightening.

"Your usual, love?" I hear the guy ask, a faint Irish accent evident in his voice.

Her eyes land on mine, but it's only long enough for me to catch sight of the color. A gorgeous hazel.

She shifts a barstool out of the way and remains standing like me.

Her fingertips drum on the counter as if annoyed or impatient. The color of her nails matches her black hair.

I can't help but eye the small angel wings tattooed on the inside of her wrist when she reaches for whatever the bartender is offering her.

There's something eerily familiar about her, but I can't quite place it, which is strange for me. My memory is crazy. I remember the play-by-play of every moment in my life. Important and useless information is stored in my head, even when I try to forget it. So, there's no way I know her, right?

"Ahem."

I inhale her scent as I drag my gaze up. She smells like freshly cut orchids, the kind my mother always had in every room of our summer home.

"Is there a problem with your eyes?" Her dark brows go inward as she lifts her cocktail. "Perhaps you should change your focus to the stage." She tilts her head that way.

"Say that again."

"Say what?" Black eyeliner wraps around her almond-shaped eyes, making her irises appear lighter.

She's unbelievably stunning. What the hell is she doing in a place like this?

"Say anything." I take a swig of my drink, the warmth hitting my chest. "I like your accent. I can't quite place it, so I need you to talk a little more."

She surprises me with a smile, flashing me white teeth. "Well, you're in an Irish club, so . . ."

I shake the drink in my hand, knocking the cubes around. "Your accent is not Irish. Not even close. Although, if you've been hanging out in this bar"—I raise my glass—"maybe some Irish has rubbed off on you."

Her lips purse for a moment. "I'm from Brazil."

"But . . .?" I smile, enjoying myself a hell of a lot more right now than I was five minutes ago.

"I'm half-Irish."

"Portuguese and Irish, huh? It makes for one hell of a combination."

"One point for you." She lowers her tumbler and sets it on the counter. "At least you know I speak Portuguese."

"I didn't realize I was collecting points."

A small chuckle escapes her lips, but her hand immediately darts to her mouth, covering it.

"That will be the only point you get."

She starts to turn, but I touch her forearm, and she stops moving.

"What's your name? Do you work here?"

She faces me again, and I release my hold. "No, but I can introduce you to a dancer if that's what you'd like."

"Not interested." I take a step forward, and she takes one right back. "Your name?" I ask again, my voice deepening, my intent clear.

I want this woman in every way possible. I've known her for a few minutes, but Christ, I need her on her back and in my bed, pinned beneath me.

She's probably only in her mid-twenties, which is way too young for me, but right now, I can't seem to care.

"My friends call me Gia, but I'm not available, Mister . . .?" Her palm presses to the counter.

"King," I say. "But you can call me Cade."

She rolls her tongue over her teeth, which is entirely too damn distracting. Her eyes sweep over my black dress shirt before settling on my mouth. "Hm."

"Are you married? Have a boyfriend?" I have one rule: I don't get involved with anyone who cheats. My father's string of affairs left a bitter taste in my mouth, and as much as everyone assumes I'm like him, I'm not.

I watch the movement in her throat as she swallows, her gaze cutting up to my eyes, and although I sense confidence in those irises, fear is overshadowing it.

"I'm not the kind of woman you want to get to know, Mr. King." The tone of her voice changes as my last name edges off her tongue.

"Shouldn't I be the judge of that, Gia?" I'm saying her name like I know her, like I already know the curves of her body, the way her hip feels against my palm, and the touch of her tongue in my mouth. But there's something about her, and

5

it's not just her looks; there's something beneath the exterior that I need to get to know. Now.

"Walk away from me. Please. I'm the wrong person to hit on." There's a slight tremble to her bottom lip as she talks, and it has my hand rushing to cover hers that rests on the bar.

"Gia, I don't know who you are, but that's something I'd like to change." In bed. Preferably sooner, rather than later.

She's looking at the bartender instead of me now. The man tips his head to the right.

Her eyes widen, and she retracts her hand from beneath mine, stumbling back a step in the process. "I have to go," she says in a rush and brushes past me.

"Do yourself a favor, mate. Don't pursue her." The bartender refills my glass but leaves out the Coke.

"Who is she?" I ask without touching the tumbler.

He leans forward, crossing his arms, and his green eyes find mine. "She's like a pot of gold at the end of a rainbow: un-fucking-attainable," he says, exaggerating his accent.

He straightens and pulls on his red beard before wiping down the bar counter.

I ignore his comment—or maybe it was a warning; who the hell knows?—and turn around to see where Gia hurried off to.

The place isn't all that busy, and most people here are either crowded around the center stage or tucked away in private booths. Of course, even if the place was packed I doubt she could ever go unseen.

She's standing alongside an empty table twenty or so feet away, and she's with some guy in a suit.

He's clutching her forearm, tight enough that even from where I'm standing I can tell something isn't right.

The guy jerks her toward him, and her palms land against his chest. When she steps back, she looks my way for one fleeting moment, and then he urges her by the elbow to walk with him.

I start in their direction as they head toward the back of the club, unable to think twice about it.

There's one thing I have zero tolerance for, and that's abuse. My father smacked my mom one time—well, once that I know of—when I was eleven. I stood stupidly, frozen in place after seeing it happen. I should have done something. But I couldn't get myself to budge. I may not be my mom's greatest fan, but no woman should ever be hit.

This woman from the bar is no exception, and I'm getting the feeling something shitty is about to go down.

"Yo, you good?" Corbin swoops in front of me from out of nowhere.

I don't want him getting mixed up in anything. That's the last thing he needs. "Bathroom."

"Jerry got himself a private room. Just meet up with the rest of us at our booth near the stage."

"Sure." I nod, my body on fire, worry drilling through me.

Once Corbin's back is turned, I head to the hall where Gia disappeared.

"Please, let me go."

It's her voice. The accent . . .

But the hall is empty.

There's only one door and it's cracked open, so I shove it inward without thinking.

The guy in the suit has her pinned to the wall near a desk, his palms pressed over her shoulders.

I enter the room and hiss, "Back away from her." My heart pounds and climbs up into my throat.

He looks over at me. "And who the fuck are you?"

"Who the fuck am I?" A humorless laugh floats from my

lips, and I start at my sleeves, rolling them to the elbows, exposing the tattoos I normally hide on the inside of my arm.

I cross the office with slow and purposeful strides. The need to hit the son of a bitch is overpowering right now. "I don't think you want to find out."

Another strange sensation of familiarity crawls up my spine and splinters out, but it's not like the feeling of a good whiskey as it spreads warmth through my chest—no, it's more like the woozy feeling from too many shots of bad tequila.

What the hell is wrong with me? Why is this son of a bitch, and even Gia, giving me the feeling of déjà-fucking-vu?

"Are you the arsehole who was hitting on my woman at the bar?"

"Your woman?" I snap back to the present, to the prickly sounds of this man's Irish tongue grating on my ears. "Sounds to me like she isn't yours at all." I've always liked the Irish, but this bastard is leaving a bad taste for the country in my mouth.

"She's for sure as hell not yours." His jaw is tight, a slight tic in his cheek.

I glance over at Gia. She tugs her lower lip between her teeth as she studies us.

I'm standing a few feet away from them both, waiting to see if the asshole will make a move.

He cocks his head, and his green eyes tighten to thin slits. "Do I know you?" A long finger stabs at the air.

Yeah, the feeling is mutual.

"I do, don't I?" He taps the side of his skull.

"I'm pretty sure you and I don't hang out in the same circles."

My arms loosen at my sides in anticipation, but he doesn't look like he's ready to charge at me yet.

"Gia, come on, let's go." I hold my hand palm up, offering her the chance to leave, but she doesn't even flinch.

She stares at my hand like she's in a trance.

"Are you that ballsy that you think you can waltz out of *my* club with *my* woman on your arm?"

"She's not yours. I thought we cleared that up already." My body remains ready, poised for action, as he strides my way. "She comes with me and no one gets hurt."

God, I feel like I'm in some bad action flick right now.

He stops moving, leaving a few feet of open air—more like tension—between us. He rubs his thick beard as his eyes focus on mine. "I think you know as well as I do that if you even try to walk out of here with Gia at your side, you'll end up with a body full of bullets. And since you walked through a metal detector to get in the club, you're not packing heat."

"I'll take my chances."

"No." At the sound of Gia's voice, my attention sweeps over his shoulder to her. "Leave, please." She's got a gun in her hand—aimed at me.

"It's okay. I'm trying to help." I keep my voice low and smooth, trying to calm her. Why the hell is she pointing that thing at me?

The guy smiles. "Told you she was my woman."

"Go." She removes the safety, her elbows locked, her arms stiff. There's not even the slightest bit of a tremble.

"Please, put the gun down." I try one more time, not sure how the hell this situation turned out like this.

The guy continues to observe her with a hint of a smile on his lips, not saying anything.

"Go!" she cries again, and I note the break in her voice.

Why is she doing this? And how the hell can I leave?

But she's not giving me much of a choice.

"I'll be seeing you around," the guy says as if he really means it. But none of my plans include ever dealing with this son of a bitch again.

I finally start for the door, guilt clawing its way through me one inch at a time.

I check my impulse to steal one last glance at her before leaving.

2

GIA

"Where's your entourage? You're not normally alone." I'm still holding the gun, but it's pointed at the ground now.

"The boys are on a job."

Slight tremors scrape down my arm, like needles pricking my fingertips. I know this isn't my moment—my moment to run. I need to be patient. Shooting Rory isn't part of the plan, even if I'd like to kill the bastard right now.

And so, I lower the gun and set it on his desk.

Rory's eyes flit from the gleaming metal up to me.

Hopefully I bought Cade enough time to get away before Rory does something stupid like chase after him.

I didn't have a choice but to grab the gun Rory keeps in his bottom drawer, acting like I was on his side. I can't let someone else get hurt because of me. It's happened too many times.

"Should we resume the conversation we were having before that asswipe interrupted us?"

I hiss too low for him to hear. "Nothing has changed. I don't want to be with you."

Before Cade blasted into the room like a tornado—a sexy storm—Rory was making his usual attempt to get me to sleep with him.

But tonight, he didn't want to take no for an answer. He was jealous when he saw me at the bar with Cade. I don't normally make the mistake of talking to another guy like that.

"I'm tired. I'd like to go home." I start for the door, hoping he won't say—

"No."

The one word I didn't want to hear, and it's enough to make me stop in my tracks.

His heavy footsteps from behind have my skin crawling.

A hand trails down my arm as he presses up from behind and shifts my hair to one shoulder. His hot breath is at the shell of my ear.

"Rory." His name is more like a plea from my lips because I have to walk such a fine line between appeasing him and standing my ground—just enough to try and keep him at bay without infuriating him.

"The only reason why I don't bend you over and take you on my desk right now is out of respect for your father." He nips my earlobe. Bile rises in my throat when he jerks me around to face him. "But you better believe my patience is wearing thin. You either get on board with the idea of being with me and soon, or I'll take matters into my own hands."

I curb my urge to remind him that my father would kill him if he ever forced himself on me—consequences be damned.

My dad might be a ruthless hitman, but he'd walk through hell and back for me, which is something I've learned over the years.

A large hand slides up my chest. He forcefully grips my

chin, holding my eyes with his. I try to swallow back the desire to spit in his face.

He's breathing harder. The want in his eyes is there, the violence storming in his irises, thick and heavy.

He deliberates, but releases me and steps back, raking a hand through his dark hair before turning away. "Be sure Malcolm takes you straight home."

The tension starts to drift from my shoulders, working its way down as I try to reclaim a sense of safety and walk toward the door.

"Gia?"

I pause and look back. "Yeah?"

"What was the name of that wanker?"

My spine bows at his question. "He didn't say."

"Are you lying?"

"No, of course not." And he should believe me after the stunt I pulled with his gun.

He can't hide the cool smugness that's taken up residence on his face since I obediently sided with him. He's relishing in the win.

But, it was a small price to pay to keep Cade safe. "Good night," I mutter and head out into the hall.

I start to close the door all of the way but hesitate.

Something inside of me says this might not be over, and so I listen through the crack, waiting for what I'm worried might happen next.

"I need a favor after you drop Gia off at home." He must be on the phone talking to my driver. "Pull the surveillance cameras from the last thirty minutes and get me a name on the guy who was talking to Gia at the bar. He's familiar, and I want to know why."

3

CADE

MYA'S LIPS TWIST AT THE EDGES AND HER EYES WIDEN FROM the shock of my recent statement. "Can I quote you?" She lifts her pen and starts writing.

"No." My mouth tightens and I lean back in my desk chair and study her.

She's gorgeous. Long, strawberry-blonde hair, dark brown eyes, tan skin, and amazing curves.

But I can't make a move on her.

She's not only a journalist but my friend's daughter.

I need to get laid, though. I reach for my phone, remembering Lydia texted me right before Mya came into my office ten minutes ago.

Lydia: Are we on for drinks tonight?

Lydia's the perfect friend with benefits. Reliable, noncommittal, and never jealous. She knows how I like it in bed and never asks for more than sex. She's not clingy or after my money. Hell, she's richer than I am.

So, yeah—the perfect woman. Just not someone I want to marry. And she's not eager to run to the altar either.

It works for us.

I consider replying to Lydia's coded text for fucking, but tonight might not be the best night for it, even though I've developed a serious case of blue balls since meeting Gia.

Gia's beautiful on an entirely different level than any woman I've met, but I need to get her out of my head after what happened at the club.

Thinking about a woman who pointed a gun at me is a waste of time.

I set my phone back down when I notice Mya's eyes skate down my chest before settling on my hands.

Her cheeks turn a little pink when she realizes she's been caught.

She's shy. Too innocent for me.

"Mya, the only reason you're here is because your dad is one of the only decent judges in this city, and he called me last night requesting this last-minute meeting with you. I never take interviews, but he asked, and so—"

"Wait! What?" She taps the notepad against her thigh. "I thought I got this interview on my own. I hate when he interferes."

I cock my head, studying her. "Have you ever heard of me giving an interview before?"

"No."

I lift my palms. "Any more questions, then?"

"Yeah. Why did you and Veronica break up?"

"That's old news." The governor's daughter—the engagement I never wanted—is another reason I'm not looking to get serious with anyone in the foreseeable future.

My father strong-armed me into being with her for business purposes since he views relationships as marriages of opportunity. But as soon as I kicked him out of the company, I ended things with Veronica. I can't say she was too upset about it. She knew I didn't love her and never would.

"And you haven't answered the question since you split." She straightens in her seat, taking on a greater air of confidence.

"And I'm not about to start."

"Are the rumors true, though? Can you at least answer that? Are you really screwing all of New York?"

"Only the good half," I mutter.

She starts scribbling on her pad.

James, my publicist, is standing in the doorframe of my office, and he's glaring at me. "Don't write that shit down."

Mya looks over her shoulder at him and stops writing.

"Sorry I'm late. Any questions you have about the company should be directed to me," James says while approaching the desk, his forehead creasing with anger—probably at me for starting the interview without him.

He's my go-to for fixing shit, and my love life is the kind of shit he's been dealing with lately. My brother is the one normally in the public eye, but ever since he left the business and I took over as owner and CEO, the media has been all over my case.

Manhattan is known for being a rumor mill, and my sex life is front-page entertainment news.

Can't a guy get laid without social media needing a play-by-play?

"Come on." James flicks his wrist, motioning for her to stand.

Her gaze moves over her shoulder and across the room to someone else instead.

Corbin. Looks like my brother decided to make a rare appearance today.

"Uh, one last question before I go." She clears her throat

and redirects her attention to me. "What were you doing with Jerry Chase at a strip club Friday night?" She reaches into the bag at her side, retrieves her phone, and slides it across my desk.

My jaw tightens at the image of Jerry, Corbin, myself, and the guys in front of the club. "How much do you want for that?" I can feel the tic in my cheek as I clench my teeth. "And were you seriously following me?"

I stand and come around my desk before I know it. I've been wound tighter than normal ever since meeting Gia, so adding this to the mix is not the right damn time.

"Easy," Corbin says as James snatches the phone off my desk.

"Why would Jerry go to a place like McCullens, unless it was for work? I didn't see him escort anyone out in handcuffs." Mya rises and holds her hand out, palm up, requesting her phone back from James. "That's obviously not my only copy."

After James hands it to her, she shoves it into her purse. Then she looks me square in the eyes, not a speck of intimidation evident. Maybe I had the judge's daughter all wrong. Maybe she's not so timid. But she should be fucking terrified, because I'm hanging on the edge right now.

"So, you were following *Jerry*?" This doesn't piss me off any less. Jerry's a good guy, and a damn workaholic. He doesn't need this shit right now.

Corbin comes up next to me and wraps a hand around my forearm for a brief moment, urging me to back down. He can probably tell by the gruff sound of my voice that I'm losing my temper.

Her brows pull together in defiance. "Answer my question first."

Who the hell does this woman think she is?

A judge's daughter. I release a breath and step back.

"It was a bachelor party," Corbin answers for me as I go to the wall of windows and press my palm to the glass, looking down at the city while it continues to roar to life as if some little journalist didn't just fuck up my day.

So much for doing friends favors. It clearly bites you in the ass.

"How much for the photo?" James repeats my earlier question.

"Not for sale." She sputters out a response fast, and I can tell she's going to be trouble.

"Everyone has a price," I say casually and tuck my hands in my pockets.

"Even you?"

She's got me there. Now that my father isn't in New York —the only person who has ever been capable of pulling my strings—no, I can't be bought. But I'm an exception to the rule.

"Why'd you go to that club?" Mya asks.

I drag up images of Friday night, and with the memories comes the aching familiarity in my gut again.

When I face the room, James is eyeing me, giving me that *don't say shit* look he's mastered so well over the years. He had to work for my prick father before me—so he's familiar with these kinds of situations. And he's one of the few people who aren't afraid of me, which is good. I need someone to call me on my shit when need be. It's a rarity, but still . . .

"We. Went. To. A. Strip. Club," Corbin says slowly, enunciating each word to be a dick.

And she's not fazed. "But why *that* one? There are plenty to choose from."

"It doesn't matter," I interject, my patience paper thin. "If you want to keep your job, I'd suggest you not share that image with anyone else."

I surge forward and come to an abrupt stop in front of her, so close I can smell her flowery scent.

She sucks in a deep breath and holds it. Good. She's finally scared.

I grate out, "Back off whatever story you're working on. Leave Jerry alone. And do yourself a favor: find a nice cushy job writing reviews for movies or something. It'll be better for your health."

"Did you know that club is run by the Irish mob?" she continues to press.

Her question strikes me hard. And now I know why she's really here. It has nothing to do with me or Jerry. This should ease my frustration, but it doesn't.

Irish mob.

Gia.

Fuck . . .

"There's still an Irish mob in New York?" Corbin glances at me and then back at the eager reporter. "Thought that was a Boston thing."

Her shoulders sag. "Well, there is, but it's different now. They're not like the Westies from Hell's Kitchen. They're more modern and a lot wealthier."

"Honestly, none of this matters right now." James arches his shoulders back and lifts his chin to gain another inch. "You need to leave."

I'm not exactly shocked to learn the asshole in the suit is a criminal, but hearing it right now is like a punch to the gut. What the hell is Gia doing mixed up with the mob?

Mya looks at me for a moment as if I'll be the one to save her, to offer her a chance to stay longer. Good fucking luck with that.

"We'll pick this up another time, then." A puff of air escapes her lips and she leaves.

"Jesus," Corbin says under his breath before dropping onto the couch by the bar. "She's hot, though. Maybe I can get her number."

"She's Judge Vanzetti's daughter. You know, the one who dropped the charges against you last year for that illegal race you were in."

"No shit?" Corbin smiles. "Well, she doesn't look anything like her father."

"You think I better call her dad? Let him know his only child could end up at the bottom of the Hudson if she's looking into the mob?" James asks, scratching his graying beard.

"No. It's her life." Guilt has my stomach twisting at the possible thought of something happening to Mya, though. "Shit. I'll call him."

"Okay, good. Try and stay out of trouble." James heads for the door. "That goes for both of you." His words hover in the air even after he's gone.

"Why are you here?" I eye my brother, waiting for him to lay some BS on me.

"Heading to Vegas for a race, and I wanted to let you know." He shrugs.

"Like, warning me you might need to be bailed out of jail?"

Why does he have to be an idiot and do this shit? I mean, word is he's one of the best streetcar racers out there, and so I know he'll be fine . . . well, *fine* is a broad term, but damn it, I can't keep him out of prison forever. And his racing is going to give our sister an ulcer one of these days.

"I'll be good. No worries." His attention deflects to my assistant standing in the doorframe with a folder in hand.

"Not now," I bark, too much edge to my voice.

She immediately turns away, closing the door behind her.

"I thought you were turning over a new leaf and trying to be less of a douche at work. You know, less like Dad."

Dad.

A word that rarely passes between us.

My heart grows thick, hardening like my arteries are clogged, as I think about my father and the shit he put us all through.

It still kills me that even to this day my brother and sister don't really know the real me. Of course, I'm not even sure who the hell I am anymore.

But ever since I took over the business, we've been trying to build a relationship again, to start fresh. I'm trying to do better at being less of a dick to the people in my life.

I've had walls up for so long, though, I'm not sure if I can really ever let anyone in, which is why I stick to my pseudo-relationships. No personal questions, nothing too intimate, no opening up old wounds by dissecting feelings.

And no matter how much my mother has tried to stay in my life, even though I don't want her here, and no matter how much I try to allow Corbin or my sister into even one corner pocket of my mind, it's hard.

Walls. Ten feet high. Thick and concrete.

We don't do emotions in this family, Dad once told me when I tried to talk to him. *We do money.* Yeah, that's the fucked-up shit he'd say to us kids. I was eight when he spoke those words, and I never opened my mouth about my feelings again after that fantastic heart-to-heart.

I drag my attention back to my brother who is staring at me, waiting for my typical asshole response. "And I thought you were supposed to stop screwing the grad school therapists the courts keep assigning to you whenever you get your ass in trouble." The mere mention of my father is like a cool whisper through my veins, making all my organs fucking freeze.

"Hey, at least they're not undergrads." He smiles. "Cue eye roll . . . Yup, there it is." His mouth broadens even more as he approaches my desk.

"Get out of my office," I grumble.

"Sure, as soon as you tell me what the hell is going on with you. You've been high-strung—well, more than normal, since Friday night. You ever gonna tell me why we had to bail like a bat out of hell from the club—a club that's apparently run by the mob?" His brows rise as he braces the desk, attempting to bait me into a conversation we both know full well won't go far.

I swallow, tightening my grip on the cell I just picked up, clutching it like it's a stress ball.

"You got that look, man." He pokes the air.

"What look?"

"When we're at the gun range and you're focused on a target, or when you've seen a woman you decide you"—he pauses to use air quotes—"have to have."

He shoots me a grin as if he's pleased he's cracked me, that he's figured me out.

"You look determined, bro. You want to tell me what's going on?" He glances left, then right, and shrugs. "Because I don't see a woman, and I'm pretty sure you don't have a pistol hidden in your desk. Plus, there's no bull's-eye in here."

I crack a smile. "You so sure about that?"

I do have a target in my mind.

Well, targets. Plural. One I'd like to screw, and one I'd like to shoot. But neither will happen, so . . .

He chuckles. "I don't know. Something is off with you."

I shake my head. I can't have this conversation right now. "Just go win your race, okay? And don't fucking die."

He wraps a hand around the back of his neck, eyeing me. "Go."

"Fine." He salutes me, just to be an ass, and leaves.

Once the door is closed, I scroll through my contacts to the judge's number but decide I need to make another call first.

After a few rings, the line connects.

"Everything okay?" Jessica answers, getting right to it.

"Yeah. The company is fine." She handles our cyber security, but she's also my sister's best friend. She's not one of my greatest fans, but right now, that doesn't matter. I need a favor.

"So, why are you calling?"

She's never been one to fake pleasantries, which I like about her.

"I need to hire you for a job. Probably need one or two guys. Whatever you think."

"Uh, okay."

"I need you to follow Mya Vanzetti. She's a reporter."

"And why am I tracking a reporter?"

"She's the daughter of a friend, and it looks like she's trying to break a story on the Irish mob. Look into a strip club called McCullens." I listen to her tap keys, taking notes.

That's all I'm supposed to say. I want to look out for Mya because of my friendship with her father—and because it's what a decent human being would do. And I've been trying to be a better person. Really, I have.

But there's part of me that wants to know more. More about Gia.

"Anything else?"

I hesitate, something I rarely do. I usually know what I

want, and I do it without qualms. "There's a woman," I finally say. "Her name is Gia, and she's somehow connected to the club. See what you can find out."

"She a dancer?"

"No."

"Anything more to go on than that?"

"About five-five, dark hair to her mid-back, and classy-looking. Skinny, but with curves, you know—"

"Cade."

I look down at the desk and grip my temples with my thumb and finger. "She's Brazilian and Irish," I add.

"Anything else? Like, is she a C or D cup?" A hint of a smile slides through the phone.

"Funny," I grumble . . . but probably a C. Maybe a D. Whatever she is, she's fucking perfect. "Just call me as soon as you have something, okay?"

"Yeah, okay."

"Is Luke available?" He's her brother, a former Navy SEAL, and they run the business together. Aside from their "on the books" company, they run an underground PI firm, protecting and rescuing people. Basically, they're exactly who I need right now.

"No, he's been on an assignment overseas for the last month."

"Well, make sure whoever you have on Mya is armed." I end the call before Jessica can make any snide comments and piss me off.

I settle behind my desk and stare at the computer screen. There's a sudden itch to my fingers, a desire to go online and try to learn more while I wait.

I try to convince myself again this is all to protect the daughter of a friend . . . that this has nothing to do with Gia.

4

GIA

I CAN STILL TASTE THE SALT ON MY TONGUE. IT'S AS IF THE tide is roaring in and the sand is between my toes. The sun lights up the horizon as bursts of color explode in the sky, and the Christ the Redeemer statue looks over the city—protecting it.

My home. Rio de Janeiro.

The flame of the candle on the table sways as I stare at it as if I can see my life on the beach in that little dancing red and orange strip of color.

I try to hang onto the good memories, so the bad ones won't haunt me right now.

I'm not sure if Brazil can ever be home for me again, after what happened there ten years ago. But I don't see how New York can ever be home, either, not with Rory and my father here—not with their death-grip hold on me.

I glance down at my phone, thinking about the man I met last Friday as I swipe my finger across the screen, unlocking it.

I pull up my last Google search, making a mental note to

delete my browser history before I get up from the dinner table.

I zoom in on the image—Cade King.

I'm not going to lie. He takes my breath away. He's the first man to ever do that, so it means something.

Brown hair with a slight wave to it, dark scruff, almost turquoise eyes, and don't get me started on his body. Not overly bulky—just the right amount of muscle.

But my attraction to him is only skin-deep. I know any profound connection with someone is impossible.

"Who is that?"

Layla is over my shoulder, arms crossed, looking right at my phone.

I flinch, exit the webpage, and flip the phone over as if I'd been caught looking at porn. "No one."

"Sure doesn't look like 'no one' to me. He's hot." Layla comes around in front of my table and slides into a chair opposite me. Her long, red nails tap on the wood, and I know she's waiting for more from me. But what can I say to her? She's Rory's cousin. I might consider her a friend, but blood is thicker. I can't take the risk.

"Busy night?" I ask and nervously glance around the restaurant, hoping for a distraction.

She shrugs. "The norm for a Monday night." Layla manages the family restaurant, which serves Italian food instead of Irish. She wasn't born in Dublin like Rory, and she seems to have less of an obsession with all things Irish. I wish she'd break free from the family, but I highly doubt she would, even if Rory let her.

"How's Johnny?" He's her latest boy toy. She goes for men at least ten years younger.

Instead of answering, she starts to reach for my cell.

I chuckle and rest my hand on my phone before she can

get it. "You bored of him already?"

Her brows dart inward. "What's up with you? You're extra jumpy. Got your period?"

I think about saying yes because I can't exactly say, *Well, your cousin might kill a man I just met.*

"Oh, fuck. Hang onto that thought. Rory just walked in." Layla is on her feet before I have time to process her words.

I quickly open my phone and delete my last web search.

"You should have told me you were having dinner here tonight. I would have joined you." Rory's words sail through the air from behind and slam into me like a metal two-by-two to the spine.

I don't bother to face him. I can't stomach the eye contact.

When his hand wraps over my shoulder, a not-so-gentle squeeze, I shut my eyes and pray to God to burn this man alive where he's standing.

Unfortunately, there's no smell of sizzling flesh.

"Wait here. We'll have dessert after my meeting." A puff of air hits my neck.

I finally glance over at him as he heads to a booth on the other side of the restaurant and settles across from Van and Creed—two of his main guys.

I've been doing my best to keep an eye on Rory since Friday to see if he'll make a move on Cade, because I know that once he has his sights set on someone it's game over.

Cade's in danger for trying to be a good guy.

I take a sip of my soda and remain discrete as I observe them.

Van, the younger of the two, slides a tablet across the table to Rory. He's pointing to something on the screen, and Rory is nodding. He likes what he's hearing.

"So." Layla is back at the table, positioning herself in her previous seat. "Is Rory still trying to get in your pants?"

My shoulders sag, and a major unease burrows its way into my stomach.

"Too bad my uncle isn't around anymore to keep you safe from him."

I never thought there'd be a day when I wished Richard McCullen was running the mob again.

As soon as Rory took over the family business, I lost one of my two protectors. Rory's dad had a soft spot for me, and he kept all the assholes at bay. And my dad, well, he still thinks of me as the fifteen-year-old he brought to New York from Brazil.

"Did you visit Richard last weekend?" I change the subject because any conversation involving Rory will only get me in trouble.

"No, I couldn't. He was in the hole."

"What'd he do to get thrown in solitude?"

"Who knows." She motions for one of the servers to come to the table. "Vodka and cranberry."

The young kid, probably only sixteen, nods and hurries off. Layla might be a saint compared to Rory, but she's still intimidating as hell to most people.

Her green eyes pin mine, and her red-painted lips spread into a deep grin. "He's serving three life sentences, so I guess he doesn't give a damn."

Fifty-seven days since Richard McCullen was sentenced to life.

Fifty-seven days since I've had to dodge Rory's increasingly aggressive advances.

How much longer can my father keep him away from me? Rory runs this part of town like the newly crowned king of an empire, and he is one. The power he wields over the city scares the hell out of me.

His father was controlled and even-tempered. He usually only hurt people who were involved in rival mobs. He wasn't a saint by any means, but Rory is dark. He's violent for the sake of violence.

He's the devil, and he's trying to claim my soul, but I'll die before I let that happen.

I glance over at Rory's table, and he's still talking to Van and Creed. Rory's lips are curved up at the edges, and his brows are darting inward, his jaw tight. He has "the look." I've seen it more times than I wish to count—it happens when he's excited . . . He looks like the Joker in *Batman*—a kind of screwed-up excited. He's about to hurt someone, maybe even kill.

Cade.

My stomach twists.

"I'm not feeling great. Gonna head home," I sputter in a rush.

"So, you do have your period? Thought you were off." She smiles.

"Uh, yeah." I rise. "See you later." I don't even take two steps before I feel Rory's gaze on me, and so I stop. "Sick," I mouth and touch my stomach for dramatic effect.

He narrows his eyes in suspicion, but then Layla blurts, "She's got her period." Yeah, she's never been shy, even in front of customers at her own restaurant. Me, on the other hand . . . warmth travels up my neck and floods my face.

But it works. Rory nods and returns his focus back to Van.

My heartbeat nearly tramples my lungs as it pounds in my chest. I'm about to make a possibly dangerous move.

A move that could impact the plans I have set in place to escape this life.

But I can't exactly let a man die because of me, can I?

5

CADE

"Thanks for meeting me so late for drinks. I think I spend more time in my office, signing papers, than I do in court." Tony Vanzetti raises his tumbler to his lips and takes a sip. His gray-blue eyes follow our waitress as she walks past the table, and his gaze slides up her long legs to the hem of her black skirt. "What's it like to be young and single?"

"What?" I grin, his question catching me off guard. "I thought things were good with you and Meryl." Thirty years of marriage isn't easy to come by these days. He usually brags about how good he has it at home during our poker games.

"Things are perfect." He sets his drink down on the little table.

We're about two blocks from my office, sitting in a lounge that has a retro feel to it. I've never been here, but apparently, the judge is a frequent guest. It's a gentleman-only kind of place, but without strippers or cigars.

"But . . .?" I wait and clasp my hands in my lap. I haven't touched my drink yet, and I'm not really in the mood to. It might be late, but I need to swing back over to the office later for a call with a company in Dublin I'm trying to acquire. It'll be morning for them soon.

"Perfect can be boring," he says, dragging his words out as he looks up at another waitress now standing at his side. She places a hand on his shoulder and bends forward, pressing a kiss on his cheek.

"I don't even know what boring feels like, but I'd like to give it a try one of these days." Maybe on a beach in Bali.

"It must be nice to have women drop their panties for you in the blink of an eye," he says once the waitress is gone from his side.

Tony is showing a side of himself I've never witnessed before, and I'm not sure I like it. I had this idea of him in my head, and it's getting shattered right now. Honest, hardworking, faithful . . . you know, father-like . . . and maybe I hoped a few good ones existed since mine was shit. But now I'm wondering which server he's screwing. I glance around the room. The blonde by the door? Maybe the redhead behind the bar?

"So, about your daughter."

He rubs the stubble on his jaw and leans back in his seat. "So, which mob is Mya after now?"

Now? "The Irish mob down in the Clinton neighborhood."

His eyes narrow, but he doesn't look as surprised as I expected he'd be.

"I get that she's a reporter, but I'm worried she's going to get herself in trouble," I say.

"Why couldn't she have gone to law school like I wanted?" He shakes his head. "She had to ignore me and go to Syracuse and get that damn degree in communications. And now look at her—she's working for one of the best papers in the country. But what's the point, if she ends up killed?"

"So you'll talk to her?"

"Yeah, but it probably won't do much good. Maybe I can convince her to take a vacation, though." He blinks a few times. "She's stubborn. Always chasing down the next big article."

I guess he's used to this, but if I had a daughter, I'd probably lose my mind with worry every day. This city can eat someone alive.

I start for my drink, suddenly in the mood for the liquor now, but my hand falls back into my lap before I can lift the glass.

I lean forward a little, trying to make sense of what I'm seeing. "Uh, could you excuse me?"

"Yeah, sure."

I rush to my feet and exit the club.

Did I hallucinate her? Because I thought I saw—

My heart slams against my ribcage at the sight of Gia's long dark hair whipping over her shoulder as she peers my way right before disappearing around a corner. "Wait!" I take after her and yell, "Gia, stop!"

But she doesn't.

I pick up speed and continue to pursue her. And then she finally stops dead in her tracks, and I nearly knock her down.

"We have to keep moving," she sputters, out of breath.

"What? Why?"

She faces me, then looks over my shoulder and down the street. "They can't see me here with you."

"Who?" But she grabs my hand, taking me by surprise, and I follow her, not sure what the hell to think or do right now. All I know is the woman I've been thinking about for the last few days is now with me—and clearly scared.

35

"My office is up there. There's a delivery entrance. No one will see us." I point ahead, and she nods.

I scramble in my pocket for the keycard and note the movement of her eyes, left to right.

Once inside, she falls to her knees. She's shaking. I crouch down and touch her cheek. "Jesus, you're freezing." Her lips are somewhat purple, and her face is like ice. "Let's get you to my office and get you warm."

I help her to rise, and we head to the back elevators. I pull her against me as we ascend and wrap my arms around her, rubbing her back, trying to increase her body temperature. I've wanted my hands on her since we met—but I didn't expect it to be like this. Soothing. Comforting.

No, I had other images in mind—and all of them included my hands on her while she was naked. Maybe tied to the bed.

But, shit—I need to forget those thoughts.

Right the fuck now.

"I-I'm s-sorry," she says as her teeth chatter and her words vibrate against my chest.

"Don't talk right now."

When the doors part, I scoop her into my arms without thinking. Her eyes flutter shut as she slings her arms around me and nuzzles her face to my neck.

I hurry to my office, and without letting go of her, I swipe my card by the door to unlock and open it.

The lights automatically flick on, and I place her on the couch.

I grab an extra blazer from the closet behind my desk and wrap it around her shoulders. "A thin leather jacket won't cut it during the winter."

She forces a smile. "I wasn't really thinking clearly. Thank you, though."

I drag a hand down my jaw as I assess the situation.

I left the judge alone without an explanation, and I have a conference call starting soon . . . but shit, none of that matters right now. Because the woman that's been running through my mind is now sitting before me.

"I didn't mean for you to see me. Not yet, at least," she says after a minute, her voice calmer now, her lips turning pink again. "I wasn't following you. I was tracking someone else."

"Tracking?" I sit next to her. "Care to explain?"

Silence swallows the room, and yet, the gravity of the moment, of her being here, isn't lost on me. Something is seriously fucking wrong.

Her shoulders slope down as she fists the material of my jacket in front of her chest. "You kind of pissed off the wrong guy last Friday night."

"Yeah, Rory McCullen." I haven't heard back from Jessica, but it was only earlier today that we talked on the phone. I gave in and did my own research, matching Rory's face to a name. Not exactly rocket science, since the club is called *McCullens*.

"So . . . you know." She lowers her head, staring down at her lap, at the buttons beneath her polished nails.

I nod and reach down, tipping her chin up, needing eye contact.

Her face is warmer now, her temperature normalizing. "But what I don't know is what you're doing involved with a man like him. Since you're not a dancer at the club . . ." I wait for her to finish my sentence.

"I'm sorry, but I have to go. If my bodyguard finds out I'm not at home, and that I'm here, it won't be good. For either of us." She removes the jacket and sets it next to her, but when she stands, I touch her wrist.

Her eyes linger on my hand for a moment before drifting up to meet my eyes, and then she slowly settles back down.

"Who were you following?"

She rolls her lips inward briefly. "After my driver brought me home, I snuck out and took a cab back to the restaurant where Rory was at and followed two of his crew. They led me to you."

I raise a brow. "I didn't see anyone."

"They were in the bar. Right behind you."

I take a moment to process her words. "Why are you suddenly worried about me?"

"I-I don't want you getting hurt because of me."

I almost laugh. "You pointed a gun at me and kicked me out of the club just a few days ago."

I'm greeted by silence, yet again. She's afraid to answer my questions. The fear flows up her spine and spreads across her face.

"He may have killed you if I didn't do that," she finally says.

"Well, I can take care of myself." I scratch the back of my head. "How'd you know someone was going to come after me?"

"I overhead Rory talking about you after you left Friday, and I wanted to make sure his guys weren't going to hurt you."

This time, I do laugh. I don't mean to be a douche like Corbin loves to call me, but what the hell was she planning on doing if two gangsters came at me?

I eye her, wondering if she's packing heat. She's in tall brown boots, which cover dark leggings, and there's a cashmere sweater that hangs to her quads beneath the leather jacket—I highly doubt there's a gun tucked somewhere beneath it all.

"This is serious," she murmurs and rises to her feet.

I take a step toward her, but she stumbles, almost falling right back onto the couch behind her.

I shove my hands in my pockets and study her, trying to figure out this mystery of a woman. "So, what was your plan? If you were coming here to warn me, why'd you run?"

"I-I didn't really have a plan. I don't want anyone else killed because of me, but then I freaked when you saw me."

There's a somber look in her eyes—the look of a person who has suffered an unbelievable amount of pain in life.

"'Anyone else'?"

She turns away from me instead of answering, and so I rest my hands on her shoulders. She flinches at the contact and my hands fall back to my sides.

"I appreciate your concern," I begin when she still doesn't say anything, "but I'm more worried about you right now than myself."

"You don't need to be worried." She spins around so fast she bumps into me, her hands landing on my chest, and I can't help but seize her wrists. I'm barely holding on, not wanting to scare her, but I also can't get myself to let go.

She drags her eyes up to meet mine, her hands still pressed to my dress shirt. She swallows as her lips part a fraction of an inch.

"It doesn't seem that way. It looks to me like you're terrified."

"I really need to go." Her chest slowly rises and falls, but she keeps her eyes on mine. There's so much intensity there. So much fucking depth.

"So, that's it? You come here to warn me, then run off into the night? You've done your part, and now you can be on your way?"

"You make it sound—"

"Like what? The truth?"

She moves away from me as if she doesn't want me to read her—to see the truth in her hazel irises.

She heads to the wall of windows, folding one arm under the other as she peers out the glass.

That's my signature move of avoidance.

I come up alongside her, press a palm to the glass, and look out at the New York night. The city is glowing and alive, and for the first time in a long damn time, I feel alive, too. It's been a while. A long fucking while. But there's something inside my chest, and it's like a slow burn splintering throughout my organs and lighting everything on fire.

"Tell me why you're really here," I say and continue to stare out the window.

This city never lies. It absorbs everything and will spit the truth right back in your face when you least expect it.

I'm still waiting for it to happen to me.

"I told you."

"No. Some part of you came here because you want my help." I step back from the glass and wait for her to follow suit, to fight my words.

Fear might rule part of her life, but she's also bold. I saw it Friday night, and when she faces me right now, I see it in her eyes. Like me, there's a fire inside of her, too.

"I don't need anyone's help. I've survived this life for ten years."

"Survived?" I rub my jaw. "Is that what you want from life? Just to survive?"

She leans her back against the window. "I don't have much of a choice."

"And I'm trying to give you one," I say through gritted teeth.

"And what would you expect in return for helping me?"

She pushes away from the window, her eyes darting to mine as she shifts her sweater off her shoulder, showing me the top part of her black lace bra. "Sex?" She swallows. "Do you think I'll screw you?" Her voice is harsh and bitter like the cold New York nights.

"No, Gia. I'm not a fucking monster." I'm trying not to be, at least.

"Then what is it, Cade? Why help me? You don't know me."

"Can't a person do something for someone without wanting anything in return?"

She shifts her sweater back in place and murmurs, "Not in my world." She starts past me, but I turn and grab her wrist. "I just need you to help me get home unnoticed. After that, I never plan on seeing you again. I warned you, so now, you're on your own . . . like me."

"You can't ask me to do that."

"Do what?"

"Leave you alone." I mean it, too. I'm invested now. In her health. Her life. My brother is right about one thing—once I've made up my mind about something or someone, it's all bets on the table. And I'm showing my cards right now.

I might be emotionally closed off to people, but that doesn't mean I'm going to let this woman get hurt if I can do something to help.

A flash of hesitation passes over her face. "Don't get involved with me. Look where it's gotten you so far. Any more time with me will only get you killed."

"And what exactly will happen to you if I let you walk out of my life without a second thought? What will this son of a bitch do to you?"

She shirks free of my grasp, and I let her, because I'm not

41

like Rory. I won't keep my hands on a woman if she doesn't want me to.

I move, giving her some space.

"Is there a way out of here for me? I need to get home before anyone realizes I'm not there."

Back to avoidance.

I contemplate my options, but locking her away in my office until I can figure out a way to keep her safe isn't going to fly.

"I'll have my driver pick us up in the garage. No one should see us," I say, but I'm nowhere near done with this conversation—she just doesn't know it yet.

"Thank you," she says.

Twenty minutes later, we're sitting in my limo, and Gia is positioned across from me, her eyes outside, observing the city as it blurs by.

I raise a glass to my lips and swallow the shot of whiskey, unable to take my eyes off of her, and it's killing me that a woman like her—hell, any woman—should be living in fear.

When her eyes catch mine in the glass, she rips her gaze away.

"Please, be careful," she says in a soft voice. "Rory doesn't give up."

"And neither do I." My grip tightens around the glass as my other hand clenches into a fist in my lap, my eyes falling shut.

How has she dealt with the guy for ten years? Ten fucking years.

"I know what you're thinking." Her accent thickens. "I *will* get away from this life."

And why don't I believe her? Why do I feel like I'll see a picture of her dead body on the front-page news someday?

The mob.

No getting out.

Not alive, at least.

My eyes open at the rustle of material. She's lifting my blazer from her lap, holding it out to me, and I catch sight of the angel wings on the inside of her wrist as the jacket sleeve slides up a little.

I almost shut my eyes again as a memory—a recognition of some sort—tries to resurface. It's like a thin veil has dropped over my mind, taunting me with only fragments, a puzzle to figure out.

"We're here, Mr. King," my driver says after opening the glass partition.

I had instructed him to park around the block from the location Gia gave me. Hopefully she won't be noticed. And as far as we could tell, we didn't have a tail.

But before she leaves, there's something I still need to know. "How'd you get involved with Rory in the first place?" I finally take my jacket from her, and she reaches for the handle.

"My father," she says before getting out and closing the door.

And it's in that moment everything comes to me.

The memory of her from my past . . . it blankets my mind, wrapping around my head like a tight bandage. It cuts through me to my very soul, if I even have one.

"Jim, I need you to follow her and see what apartment she goes to. Don't let anyone see you."

I grab my cell from my pocket so I can call Jessica as soon as Jim has information.

I can't be too late to help.

I need eyes on Gia. I need her safe. Alive.

I screwed up eight years ago. I can't do it again.

6

CADE

My sister never comes to my office. She hates the place. She considers it the Seventh Circle of Hell. And I don't blame her. My father made her a prisoner of this place.

He chained us all to the family name and business. I'm just the only one who decided to stay. Did I ever have a choice but to become married to the business, to the life, though?

He started bringing me to the office when I was home from boarding school every summer. I even had my own briefcase, although, when I was younger, it was mostly stashed with Twizzlers.

Grace sits on the sofa next to her husband, Noah, and I realize she's nervous about something. Or maybe excited. I haven't mastered my sister's tells yet. I need to work on that. Or even better, I could just ask, do that whole communication thing I've heard about.

"So, what brings you here?" I sit across from them, but I become distracted by thoughts of Gia. I can almost smell her sweet, but not too sweet, perfume, even though she hasn't been here since Monday night.

45

I've been getting regular check-ins from one of Jessica's men about her, and every time my phone beeps from a text, I'm worried he's going to give me bad news.

Owen, whom Jessica tasked to be on the team, is a good friend of Noah's. He was a Navy SEAL, too. Actually, I'm pretty sure everyone who works with Luke and Jessica are former military. Owen normally works down in Charleston, where he also owns a tavern, but he's one of the best guys on Jessica's payroll, so I requested that he fly up yesterday, since Luke is out of the country.

Thanks to one of Jessica's contacts at TSA, she found out that Rory's not in town, and his flight won't get back until Friday. At least I know Gia has a few days to breathe before that asshole comes home.

But I need to focus on my sister right now—on the sudden paleness of her skin.

Noah wraps a hand around the back of his neck and eyes Grace.

Something is off with her.

"What's up with all the extra security?" Noah asks when Grace still doesn't speak.

Yeah, I need to talk to Noah about that, but I'd prefer to do that without my sister within earshot, especially since she looks—

Grace is on her feet before I can finish the thought, and she's heaving into the trash bin by my desk.

Noah's at her side, and he's rubbing her back.

"You sick?" I go to the bar and grab a bottle of water and paper towel.

The color has returned to her face now. Actually, it's more like a glow.

She wipes her mouth and tosses the towel in the trash. "Not sick in the normal sense of the word." She takes a drink.

"Sorry about your trash. Apparently, morning sickness is not always in the morning."

Morning sickness? "You're pregnant?"

Noah's hand slides over her stomach.

"How? When?" I rush a hand through my hair, smiling. "I don't need to know the *how* part. Sorry."

She laughs.

I'm not good at this, but shit, I go up to her and pull her in for a hug. And then Noah and I do that one-armed manly kind of hug thing where it's more like a *good job* kind of slap on the back.

"How far along?" I ask, once I've tied up the trash and given it to my admin, who deserves another bonus now.

"Four months." She smiles and sits back down. "But there's more."

"What?" I ask, nervous.

"We're having twins. Boys." Noah grins. The man couldn't look fucking happier, and I don't blame him. He's already a father from a previous marriage, a great one from what I hear, and he's the kind of guy who could probably have ten kids and keep his sanity together.

How can I ever be a father after the role model I've had?

"But the doctors need to keep a close eye on me. I have placenta previa. They said it should correct itself, but I need to be extra cautious."

"Placenta what?" I ask.

"It's not a huge deal, but whenever there's more than one baby, plus this issue—you gotta be more careful."

"So what the hell are you even doing in my office right now? You should be in bed!" I snap, not meaning to, but I don't want anything happening to her or the babies.

"I'm okay. I promise. I was hoping to tell Corbin, too, but

he texted me that he's in Vegas." She frowns. "Another race?"

I want to lie because she doesn't need the stress. "Yeah," I finally admit.

"Oh. Well, I haven't told Mom or Dad yet, and I, uh, don't know when I will." Her lips tighten. She didn't invite our parents to her wedding since they were opposed to her even dating Noah. I can't say I was exactly enthusiastic, either—but I was dead wrong about him.

I'm wondering, though, if Grace will let them know about her pregnancy.

Mom pops into New York every few months. She mostly stays in L.A. with her younger boyfriend since our parents split. And Dad's in Paris with someone a third his age, the last time I heard. They still haven't even gotten divorced. Maybe they won't. Who knows? Who cares?

"I won't say anything to anyone, but, do you mind if I have a word alone with Noah?" I ask.

She smiles. "I should freshen up, anyway."

Noah squeezes her hand and she leaves the office, pulling the door closed behind her.

"So?" Noah tucks his hands into his pockets.

I go over to my desk and press my palms to it, trying to find the right words. "I need you to take Grace out of the city. And you should probably take Lily, too." It'll be tricky to work that out with his ex, but if something happened to his daughter because of what I'm planning to do, I wouldn't be able to forgive myself.

"What the hell are you talking about?" He's at my side before I know it, waiting for some kind of response, some sort of explanation that makes sense.

"I'm sure everything will be fine, but I don't want to take any chances, especially with Grace pregnant. You need to get her to some safe place with a good doctor to keep an eye on her."

"Slow down a second." His hands are raised in the air between us, his eyes narrowing.

I arch my shoulders back for a moment. "I pissed off an Irish mobster last week, and I'm about to make shit worse," I say this as casually as I can without alarming him, but I'm pretty sure there's no way to sugarcoat my words.

"Are you kidding?" He shakes his head and drags in a deep breath.

"Have I ever been one to make jokes?"

"Right." He grips the bridge of his nose, and my eye catches the titanium band on his finger.

"I have Jessica and Owen helping me out, but I'd feel better knowing that Grace isn't in the city in case anything backfires."

"You want to tell me what's going on?"

"Probably better if you don't know."

"You need backup?"

I know he's capable, but . . . "I'd rather know you're protecting Grace and Lily."

He nods. "I've gotta figure out how to get them out of here without scaring Grace."

I hate this. I hate that I'm putting him in this situation, but what choice do I have? "I'm sorry, man."

"Yeah, okay. Keep me updated." A quick smile flashes across his face. "And try not to die. Grace wouldn't like that."

"Will do."

* * *

"WE HAVE EVERYTHING IN PLACE, BUT WHO KNOWS HOW

long this will all take to go down. It's a little different from our normal jobs," Jessica says.

Kidnappings. Protection. Even terrorism. Why not add *organized crime* to the résumé?

"Still hard for me to believe all of this started because you went to Jerry's bachelor party." She cringes. "The idea of Jerry and some stripper . . . ugh."

Jessica is friends with Jerry's fiancée, so I guess I can't blame her for getting offended.

"This kind of stuff happens at bachelor parties." I smile. "What? Women don't get stripteased?"

"No comment." She chuckles. "But, I don't know. Jerry is such a straight-edge good guy. Can't picture it at all."

"Yeah, well, how about we discuss what you've found out since we last talked, instead."

"Got it, boss man." She winks at me before holding the tablet up between us.

A picture of Richard McCullen, Rory's father, appears on the screen. Long silver hair, tied back, green eyes like Rory's, and a hardness to his face—he's got the look of a man you don't fuck around with, but he's not in power now, so he's the least of my concerns.

"My guy at the bureau said someone gave them a goldmine of dirt on Richard. Too bad they didn't manage to lock Rory up, too."

"You were at the Feds' office?"

She lifts a shoulder and flips her blonde ponytail to her back, batting her eyes for dramatic flair. "What can I say? I can charm myself into any place."

She probably can, too. She's gorgeous and one of the smartest women I've met in my life. Right now, I'm thankful her business also handles cases like this one.

"I take it we don't know who snitched on Richard?"

"I checked the witness list from the trial. Whatever the Feds got didn't come from any of them. I'm sure they'd be at the bottom of the Hudson if it did, anyway."

"True."

"I thought you'd find this interesting, though." Jessica brings up another image. "This is from last night."

I zoom in, trying to grasp what I'm seeing. "What the hell is Mya doing with Gia?"

"Figured that was her based on your description." Gia and Mya are standing side by side in front of what looks like art easels.

"Where was it taken?"

"Every Tuesday and Thursday, there are art classes at a school in Brooklyn. It looks like Mya and Gia are enrolled. Mya was a late add. Seven weeks ago."

"Yeah, that can't be a coincidence." I shake my head.

"That's about the same time Richard got locked up, too."

"I'd better talk to her father again. Mya's definitely going to get caught in the crossfire, otherwise." It's hard for me to believe Gia would give information to Mya, though—or to let anyone help her if that's what she's doing.

"You sure you want to do all of this for some woman you don't even know?"

"And are you really asking me that? Isn't this what you do—save people?"

"I do, but you . . . well, this is kind of unexpected."

"I've made up my mind."

She lifts her shoulders. "Okay, then."

Knowing Jessica, she won't press for more, which is something else I like about her. "I talked to Noah, by the way. He's taking Grace and Lily out of the city."

"Good. If anything happens to them—"

"You'll kill me. I know."

She nods. "So, you ready for tonight?"

I stand and rub my palms down my face. Memories of my past are clawing to the surface. "She's going to say *no* again. She'll probably shoot me herself, but I'm going to try. We have a narrow window before Rory is back."

"Okay. My team will be in place if you need an assist."

I'd like to toss Gia over my shoulder and make her leave with me, but I'm hoping it won't come to that. "Anything on her father yet? Or a last name on her?"

"Not yet. The name she used to register for the art class was fake."

"Yeah, okay. I figured."

Five minutes after she leaves, the doorbell rings.

I check the peephole.

This isn't the best timing, but Lydia's on the cleared security list, so I'm not surprised she managed to get up here without my being notified.

I open the door and lean against the interior of the frame.

Her lips twist into a seductive smile as her green eyes land on mine. "I thought I'd surprise you." She reaches into her pocket and pulls out a pair of fuzzy leopard handcuffs.

A week ago, my balls would have instantly tightened, my cock stiffening . . .

But not today.

"You going to let me in?" She dangles the cuffs. "I'm cold. I don't have anything on under this jacket," she says in a soft voice.

This is typical of Lydia. Showing up like this. I think she watches too many chick flicks; otherwise, where does she get these cliché ideas?

I haven't had sex in a week. A week isn't long to most people, but I don't usually go more than a few days.

This can't happen, though.

"I'm sorry. Not a good time."

"Oh." She swallows, her cheeks turning rosy, and she shoves the cuffs into her coat pocket. "Is someone here?" She takes a step back. "I'm so sorry. I should have called first."

And this is why I like her. She isn't going to go batshit crazy on me. She won't act jealous. She won't question me.

"Sorry," I say again, allowing her to hang onto her foregone conclusions.

She takes a step forward and presses up on her toes to kiss my lips.

"Good night."

"Call me when you're free." She smiles and leaves, and I wonder if I'm making a mistake.

Being with Lydia is easy. It's safe for my walls. Working my ass off at the office and screwing women with zero emotion is what I know how to do best.

Why complicate shit?

But it doesn't look like I have a choice. I want a woman who's probably as untouchable as Rory McCullen. And even though I can't have her, I'll do my best to make damn sure he can't, either.

7

GIA

"HOW'D YOU KNOW I LIVE HERE?" I REACH FOR CADE'S ARM and try to yank him closer and out of the hall.

I maintain my grip and look up at him. He's a lot taller than me. Six-foot-two, probably.

It takes me a second to remember what the hell I'm doing, because I can't seem to remove my hand from what feels like steel beneath my palm.

"You do want me to come in, right?" A slight smile tugs at the corners of his mouth as his brows rise. "Maybe we should shut the door?"

"Yeah." I stumble back and retract my arm. Once we're both in, I lock up and secure the chain in place. It's my only protection, flimsy as it is, from Rory and his men.

I turn around to find Cade moving farther into my apartment.

He's in light-colored, fitted jeans. His ass looks . . . well, it's distracting.

I tuck my hair behind my ears and try to rein in my sudden hormones that are equivalent to the one time I bumped into Derek Jeter when I was eighteen.

My dad's a diehard Yankees fan, and it's one of the only things we've ever really found common ground on.

What is wrong with me? I need to focus. Rory's out of town, but that doesn't mean his guys aren't watching me.

"Why are you here?" I move to stand in front of him, my heart pounding.

"Nice place."

"Not as nice as yours," I can't help but say as my arms cross.

"So, you know where I live too, huh?"

"Looks like we've been Googling each other," I joke, surprised by my ability to tease, given the situation.

Another smile stretches across his face, and it does something funny to my chest: a weird sensation grips that organ of mine known as the heart. It's been a long time since I've felt emotions there, besides pain and sadness.

When I notice his gaze dropping to my sketchpad on the couch, I try to get to it before him, bumping into the side table as I do so, but he's too fast. "Give it to me." I hold my hand out like an impatient five-year-old.

He starts to flip through the pages as he holds it above his head, too high for me to reach.

Who's the child now?

"Are you a fashion designer? These sketches of women are great. They look sad, but . . ."

I push up on the balls of my bare feet and try once again to snatch it from him, but his eyes cut to mine, narrowing. My breath gets stuck in my throat.

It's already the second wave of desire that's hit me since he showed up tonight. I stand flat again and my thighs squeeze.

He finally hands it back to me, and I stare down at the veins on the top of his hand.

"I have friends in the industry. I could show them your work."

I pull myself out of my daze and shake my head.

I tuck the notepad beneath the cushion on the couch as if that will deter him. I don't let anyone see my drawings. My art classes are different—they're for a purpose—but these sketches are part of me, of my past.

I head over to the wet bar on the other side of the room to pour myself whiskey. I don't normally drink something so strong, but I need to shut down the little vibrations that are rocking through my veins and making my heart pump so much faster.

When I turn around, I nearly spill the amber liquid all over his shirt, not expecting him to be so close.

"When did you move to the States?"

"Ten years ago," I say softly.

"And you've been under Rory's control since you came?" His eyes narrow as if he's processing it all.

"Something like that."

I hand him the drink, realizing it'd be rude not to offer him something.

He nods his thanks, and I face the bar again.

At the touch of his hand on my hip, I brace the black marble counter with both palms.

My eyes close at the feel of his hand there, but it doesn't feel wrong.

It feels safe.

I know that's weird. There's a guy I barely know in my place, and he has his hand on me, and yet, I want to press my back to his chest and let him put his hands wherever the hell he wants to.

"Your English is damn near perfect," he says into my ear,

his breath like a hot whisper across my skin, making me flushed and warm.

"Why only *near* perfect?" When I face him, his hand drops, my body cooling from the loss of his touch.

"I like your accent, you know that," he answers, avoiding my question. He takes a sip, and I focus on his lips. Full lips that have me wondering how they'd feel against my own.

I forget my drink and go over to the window to close the blinds. "I was raised trilingual. My mother spoke Portuguese, Spanish, and English, and so she made sure I did, too."

"Smart woman. And where's your mother now?"

I lower my forehead to my palm when the last memory I have of her floods my mind. My body trembles and my skin pebbles.

"Gia, are you okay?"

I have no idea how long I've been quiet, but when I look up, he's standing before me, observing me with concern in his eyes. And it looks genuine.

"Can we just get back to why you're here?" I swallow the pain. I stuff it down inside to where I bottle everything up— everything that matters—so Rory and his people can never touch it, never get to the real me.

"I'm here to help you. And don't worry, no one saw me come up." He squints as if the sun is in his eyes, even though it's dark out and the blinds are shut, closing the silver moon from our view.

He sets the drink down by the couch, and his fingers rest on his jacket zipper. He looks at me as if waiting for permission to remove it.

I nod and go past him before rooting myself into the oversized suede couch. I hate this couch. Rory bought it. Well, Rory bought everything here. Everything except me. When his father was officially sentenced, Rory convinced my dad I needed to move closer to the club for safety reasons. He never explained more than that to me, and I wasn't given much of a chance to protest the move.

Cade sets his jacket on the leather chair near the window, and my gaze skirts up his exposed forearms. He's in a black tee, even though it's too cold out to be wearing short sleeves. "I didn't expect a man like you to have ink." There's a tattoo of a lion on its hind legs with fire encircling it. The ink expands from his wrist up to the inside of his elbow.

Without realizing it, I brush my fingers over my own tattoo.

The muscles in his jaw clench as he glances down at his arm. He releases a breath and sits down next to me. "So, I'm not allowed to have tattoos?" His hands settle on his thighs, and the veins on his forearms have me tucking my bottom lip between my teeth. Maybe I should have let him take on Rory. Rory usually has his men do the heavy hitting, and I don't doubt for a moment that Cade could knock Rory down.

Of course, that would have put an even larger target on Cade's head.

"No," I finally say, "not when you're a millionaire businessman."

"Mm. Maybe I have layers, like you."

I'm sure he does. And if we weren't living in two different worlds, maybe I'd like to get to know what's beneath the surface. "You really shouldn't be here." I pull my attention up to his face, and my heart palpitates.

One look from him, one touch—it does something to me. It's not just that I'm not allowed to be around him . . . it's something else that's throwing me off, that's shattering my normal composure. I've learned over the years to deal with a lot of men. Powerful, brash, arrogant, strong, successful . . .

all kinds. But I've never had a reaction to someone like this before.

"I know I shouldn't, which is exactly why I am."

"Your cryptic talk isn't helping."

He smiles. And for some stupid reason, I smile again, too.

But then the moment is gone, and my hand curls into a fist in my lap as I try to grind out the words I need to say without allowing too many emotions to rush to the surface too fast. He needs to understand what he's doing—how dangerous this really is for him.

"The first time I ran away from this life, I was only sixteen." My eyes flutter shut as my skin tightens on my forehead, giving me a headache. "I barely knew how to drive, but I stole a car that belonged to a friend of my father, and I headed for Poughkeepsie. I was on the Taconic Parkway when I hit black ice. The car spun in a circle, and I bounced off the guard rails. I thought I was going to die."

The feel of Cade's warm hand over my closed one has me stilling for a moment.

"Somehow, I only came out with a broken arm and a few scratches." I finally look up, and he's staring back at me. "But the next time I ran away my broken arm wasn't from an accident."

His thumb slowly moves over the top of my hand, and the gentle stroke does something to soothe me. "My father sent someone to find me, and the guy was more brutal than that car accident."

"Jesus, Gia. Your father was okay with that?" His voice is deep, almost silky, and it glides over my skin, cascading like a rush of water pouring over me, and then right through to my very core.

"No. Dad killed him when he saw what he did to me." I'll never forget the moment when I was dragged through my dad's door. The guy was an idiot for having the balls to hurt the daughter of one of the most notorious and feared hitmen on the East Coast.

But when I entered my dad's home—I wasn't in tears because of the pain. No, I was crying because I was back. Back to the darkness. The dark, inky oil of my life.

One bullet to the forehead, and he was gone in the blink of an eye. "He shouldn't have died because of me. Shamus wasn't a good man, but still, his blood is on my hands. If I hadn't run away . . ."

"Don't say that." Cade scoots closer and pulls me against him as if I'm someone special, as if I'm someone important to him. And for some reason, I let him. I let him wrap an arm around me, and I press my cheek to his chest, hearing his heartbeat.

I haven't had anyone care about me since I lived in Brazil. My father is good at keeping me safe—more like imprisoned—but he's never shown real emotions. I'm not even sure if a killer like him is capable.

So, the affection from Cade, a stranger, is confusing. But I hang onto the moment for as long as possible, because moments of safety are so rare. "The third time I ran away, Rory came for me." I'm not sure if I can keep talking, if I can expose my past, my secrets, my life.

"What'd he do?" There's a hint of anger that vibrates through his words and chills me.

"Well, he, uh, brought me back to the city and put me in some room at their underground casino. I thought I was going to die, but it was even worse." I secure a deep breath and let it out. "My best friend, Chinara, was chained to a chair in the room and blindfolded. She was my only real friend. And Rory nearly killed her, while forcing me to watch. His guys held me back while I struggled, trying to get to her. I was powerless to stop it."

"Fuck." Cade slowly pulls away and finds my eyes.

I didn't realize I was crying.

If I froze every tear that's fallen over the years, I could make my own icy pond. Maybe even a lake.

"I never talked to Chinara again after that. I can't care about people; if I do, they'll get hurt." I gaze deep into his eyes, to make sure he truly understands what I'm saying.

"And when I run again, I have to make sure I'm not leaving any bodies behind, including yours, which is why you shouldn't even be here right now."

He looks up at the ceiling for a moment in thought before his eyes cut back to mine. "I want to help you."

I almost laugh at the absurdity of his words as I stand. "Did you not hear anything I said?" I heave out a deep breath. He's not making this easy. "Do your family and friends know you have a superhero complex?"

My knees are weak as I head to the kitchen. I take a sip of water then spin around.

He's casually leaning inside the doorframe of the kitchen entrance, watching me.

"Do you fasten on a cape at night and go crusading around, saving young women?"

His long legs swallow the distance between us, and he stops shy of me by a foot or so. "I wouldn't look good in tights."

I don't know about that.

His head angles, his eyes hold mine, and I'm done. I'm lost in that sea of blue.

"You, um . . ." Shit, my heart is beating so damn fast I can't even talk. Not in English, at least. "You should really go." I manage to string the words together, even though my pulse is climbing and I feel a squeeze of pressure, a tingling between my legs.

"Tell me something," he says and steps even closer. Too close. All I can smell is him now.

"What?" I ask, almost breathless, as my nipples harden.

"If I could give you a way out, where no one gets hurt, would you take it?"

I raise a brow, wondering why we're talking hypotheticals—because that's all this is. There is no "no one gets hurt" way out. I have a plan, but even then, I have no idea how it will play out when it's time. If the time ever comes.

But maybe with Cade's help . . .

"Humor me."

"Of course I'd want out."

He edges back a step, giving me space to breathe. Thank God.

"Then I'll be in touch soon."

I open my mouth to protest, but I can tell my words won't go far with this man. He's stubborn and determined, and I have no idea why he wants to interject himself into my fight.

I can't seem to get myself to tell him *no*, anyway. The wheels of my mind are turning as I formulate potential outcomes of what might happen if he does, in fact, get involved.

It's selfish of me to consider accepting his help, though.

He nods as if satisfied by my lack of response and turns away. He grabs his jacket from the living room, and I trail behind him on our way to the foyer.

Once standing in front of me, the back of his hand skates down my cheek. "I'm not going to let anything happen to you, but I need you to tell me one thing."

"What?"

His hand falls from my face. "How's your dad connected to the McCullens?"

"He's, um, one of their hitmen. The very best."

There's no physical response. No increased look of worry. It doesn't make sense.

"Would he ever hurt you?" His eyes narrow. "*Has* your father ever hurt you?"

"No, he loves me." In his own messed-up kind of way—in the way only a killer could . . .

He looks like he wants to reach for me again, to touch my face or my arm, but he holds back. His eyes say it all, though. I've seen the look before.

Guilt. But from what? Why?

I should be the one feeling guilty right now, for accepting his help.

"Here's my number, if you need me before I get to you."

I take the business card he's holding and simply nod goodbye.

Everything is surreal right now.

I lock up once he leaves and slowly sink to my knees. My fingers smooth over the bold script on the card: **CADE KING.**

Can I really let him put everything on the line for me?

Can I trust a stranger?

I pull my knees to my chest and hug them as if I'm fifteen again, hiding beneath the trap door in my house—listening to the sounds of heavy shoes above my head.

Listening to my mother scream.

8

GIA

STREAKS OF SILVER DRIP DOWN MY CANVAS, MIXING WITH THE black and dark gray watercolors at the bottom. I don't know what the hell I'm doing right now. I can't concentrate.

"The colors are all wrong, Gia." Darya scrunches her brow, leaning forward to get a better look at the canvas.

"What do you suggest?" I set my paintbrush down on the palette and place it on the stool.

"Your paintings are always so dark. So morbid. You need to do something with color. You need vibrancy in your life."

I can still hear glimpses of Russian in her voice, even though she does her best to hide it.

"I thought painting was about feelings—and *these* are my feelings." I remove the apron and clutch the material tight in my hands, then scan the room for about the twentieth time. I don't think Mya is showing up. She would have told me if she wasn't coming, though. Something isn't right.

"Of course art is about emotions, but—" She cuts herself off and shakes her head. "I'm worried about you." She brings a hand up and rests it on my shoulder, giving it a gentle squeeze. "Do you want to talk?"

This isn't the first time my art instructor has tried to get me to spill my thoughts, but isn't that what the art is for? Why dilute paint with water? Why pour my heart out to a woman who's not much more than a stranger?

"No, but thank you." Darya will never know the real me, and probably, no one ever will.

"I need to clean up and get going. But, um, did Mya mention she'd be missing class tonight?" I loosen my grip on the apron when she lifts her hand from me.

"No, she didn't. Maybe she's sick?"

"Yeah, okay." I nod, but unease rushes up my spine, and the need to get out of here has me cleaning my supplies in a hurry.

"Have a good night," Darya calls out as I make a beeline for the door.

I don't respond because my mind is elsewhere. I focus on the empty hall, checking left and then right, making sure I'm alone. I head to locker 524 and fumble with the lock and open it.

A heaviness lifts from my chest at the sight of a burner phone within the locker. I check the cell and notice a message.

Not wanting to waste time, I call the voicemail. "Gia, I found something! We're close. Keep this phone. I'll be in touch soon."

Oh. My. God. Finally.

My heart speeds, and a mix of excitement and fear claims my body, taking hold as I replay Mya's words over and over in my head.

I tuck the phone away in my purse and close the locker.

When I get outside, the car is parked out in front of the school, where it always is, but my driver isn't waiting outside the car like normal.

I open the door and jerk back a step as if burned when I see who's behind the wheel.

"Hi, love."

He's not supposed to be here. He's not supposed to get back until tomorrow. And since he's here right now, it can only mean one thing: I'm screwed.

"Surprised to see me?" Rory cocks his head to the side and jerks it a little, motioning for me to get inside. When I don't, he adds, "We don't have all night. Get in."

He positions the rearview mirror once I'm inside so he can see me. "You left class early."

"Mm hm." I look out the window, trying to remain as calm as possible.

"Tell me something. Did you really think you could run around this city without me finding out about it?"

I stiffen, my gaze finding his. "What are you talking about?"

"Monday night. When you ran off to see Cade King . . . did you think I wouldn't find out? You don't breathe unless I know about it." He makes a *tsk* noise. "And when he was in your apartment last night, did you fuck him?"

"What? No camera inside my bedroom?" I hiss, unable to control my anger. "You don't watch me when I shower or sleep?"

I should try to backpedal, to make some excuse instead of further angering him. What the hell is wrong with me?

"You'd like that, wouldn't you? You'd like for me to be watching you while you touch yourself—when you fantasize about me fucking you."

I look out at the Hudson as we cross the Brooklyn Bridge, and my fingernails bite into my palms.

"You lied to me Friday. You knew who the arsehole was

and didn't tell me, and now I want to know why. Who is he to you? Have you met him before?"

I glance back his way, noting how his fingers are wrapped tight around the wheel and his voice is pitched higher than usual, like he's on something, maybe coke. The glow of the city lights dances across his face.

I decide silence is my best bet, and so I close my eyes, but I know wishing myself out of this conversation won't actually work.

"Someone like Cade might be useful to me, so I want to know what the story is with him."

"Useful?" This has me opening my eyes fast. "Useful how?" Bribery, money laundering, foreign purchases . . . I can think of a few things, but there's no way in hell someone like Cade would do business with Rory.

Rory doesn't know that yet, which could play to my favor. Buy some time.

"Why don't you just tell me what the fuck is going on between you two instead?"

"I didn't tell him anything about you. Relax."

Rory's acted cagier than normal ever since his dad was sentenced, and I have to assume he's afraid of winding up in the cell next door.

Wouldn't that be nice?

"I don't believe you." His eyes are focused back on the road. "I looked into him. A rich arse like him would go after easier tail. But we'll talk more about this face-to-face at your place. I don't trust you, Gia. Not anymore."

Did he ever?

I lean back against the leather as he drives, knowing I should be more scared, that my skin should be crawling with unease, but Mya's message tonight gave me too much hope—and I'm high on the possibilities of what she might find.

MY EVERY BREATH

Of course, I need to be able to get away, and even if Cade wants to help me, Rory's never going to let me out of his sight again.

But I have to find a way.

Once we're at my place and in front of my door, he uses his key and then shoves me in so hard I fall to my knees. If he's being rough with me, then he's not too worried about my father, but I'm not in the right state of mind to internalize that information right now.

I slowly rise to my feet, a burst of adrenaline shooting through me as I think about the last ten years of living a caged life. I wish I never hid ten years ago when they came for my mom and me. If I hadn't, at least I wouldn't be here now.

I loosen my jacket and take it off, feeling suffocated by it, and toss it to the floor, facing him head-on, as if I can actually stand up to him.

And for a moment, it feels good.

Euphoric almost. I push my chest forward with confidence as if I'm in control.

He rubs his jaw, a smirk spreading across his face. "Ohh. You're looking to fight me, eh?"

Well, that wasn't my exact intention. I never learned to even throw a punch, and now I'm wondering why not, given my life.

His laughter fills the air and slides under my skin, making me sick. "There's only one way this would end." His face is only inches from mine now as he adds, "With you pinned beneath me."

His breath touches my skin, and I look up at him.

He grips my chin, his jaw locking tight, and I press my hands to his chest, trying to push away from him, but his other hand secures around my back, pulling me closer.

"You can't fight me, baby, so don't bother trying. Instead, be a good girl and tell me what the fuck you told King."

He releases me, and I drag in a breath. "You think I ratted on you, is that it? Why would I tell him anything?"

I need him to believe me if I'm going to have a chance in hell at getting away.

"King beefed up his security at his office and home. Military-grade. He wouldn't do that for no damn reason."

"Maybe you scared him at the club Friday."

"Then why the hell did he risk his neck by seeing you again Monday?"

"I wanted to see him, not the other way around. I don't want anyone dying because of me." Sometimes the truth is easier to hide behind.

"Little late for that." He scratches at his throat, shaking his head. "Maybe if all you did was spread your legs for him, this situation would be easier to deal with . . . well, for you, at least, but I'm betting it's about a lot more than your pussy."

He reaches between my thighs, and I smack him right in the face on instinct. The slight sting against my palm feels good. It was almost worth it.

He throttles my throat a second later and shoves me against the wall. He's squeezing so tight, I'm seeing stars.

"Tell me what I want to know. You have five seconds, love."

It's hard for me to think, to focus, to find a way out of this.

I'm losing oxygen, and my eyes shut. The fight in me is dying.

And then I hear a noise. A voice, maybe.

Before I know it, I've fallen to the floor, dizzy. Everything is blurry.

"Well, now I don't have to look for you."

"I'm right here. I'm ready."

Two voices.

One is Rory's, but the other . . .?

I blink a few times and drag my gaze up the length of a pair of jeans, to a familiar black fleece jacket.

Cade.

He's here.

"You think you can really walk in here and point a gun at me?" Rory's voice is smooth, almost casual.

Cade's eyes connect with mine for a brief moment before I lose my focus again.

I try to stand, but my knees buckle, and I collapse back to the floor.

"Did you know that, in Gaelic, *Rory* means *Red King*? So —the two of us standing here—king to king. Face to fucking face, yet again." He laughs. "Tell me, mate, why are you constantly trying to protect this woman? Is she worth it? Is her sweet arse worth dying for?"

My vision is almost normal now, so I look back up at Cade.

"Come on, you're coming with me," he says with a steady voice.

And unlike at the club, I'm not going to disagree.

"I told you before, you can't walk out the door with her. So why the bloody hell do you think tonight is any different?" Rory takes a step closer to him, and the familiar sound of a safety being removed registers in my ears as I finally stand.

Cade extends his hand but keeps his other arm locked straight, prepared to shoot Rory. Is it bad that I want him to? That I want to see this man bleed all over my carpet, the ugly burgundy carpet Rory had installed in here?

"This time, I came prepared." Cade's brows stitch

together. "Why don't you call the boys you have parked outside and see if they answer?"

I allow Cade's warm hand to grasp mine, and he pulls me around behind him, offering his body as a shield.

I peek around Cade to see what's going on.

Rory's hand slips into his jacket pocket and he pulls out his cell. His eyes remain on Cade as his mouth tightens. I assume no one is answering.

"You shouldn't have come home from your trip early, McCullen. You should have stayed in Boston. But since you did return, now I have the pleasure of seeing your face when I take Gia away from you."

"You won't get far, mate. I'll send every guy I have after you. Or better yet, I'll sic her father on you. That motherfucker will shred you."

My stomach folds in on itself at Rory's words.

I want to close my eyes and go to that place in my head where I like to escape. It saves me when things become darker than I can handle.

"You think you have people in your corner?" Cade tips his head to the door, and I think he's signaling for me to go to it, so I edge back a few steps, and he walks backward with me. "Well, I've got a whole hell of a lot more people in mine."

We're about to run, aren't we?

Oh God.

"I-I can't leave yet." I move around Cade and his eyes become thin slits—confusion there.

"Change of heart, love?" Rory smiles, triumphant.

"Gia," Cade rasps.

"I need something." Slowly, I move Rory's way, terrified he'll grab me, but Cade edges closer, keeping the gun on him.

"Don't even think about reaching for your pistol," Cade warns. "I won't hesitate to fucking kill you."

My heart is beating so damn fast I can barely breathe as I move past Rory, fully aware his eyes are burning a hole in my skin.

Before I can second-guess myself, I rush to the couch, lift the cushion, and grab my sketchpad. "Okay," I say under my breath as I walk past Rory, keeping a few feet of distance between us.

I nod at Cade as I crouch down to grab my purse off the floor by the door—I need the burner phone, too.

"I'll be seeing you soon," Rory says as I hurry out of my apartment, and then Cade slams the door shut behind us.

"Go," Cade yells and motions for the stairwell at the end of the hall, knowing Rory will be fast on our trail.

And it's barely three seconds before plaster explodes from the wall at my side.

I glance back, and Rory aims his gun my way, his eyes holding mine.

I'm frozen in place, waiting for him to fire, for this all to end.

But he doesn't kill me.

No, he wants me alive.

Cade grabs hold of my arm and tugs me into the now-open doorway.

As we make our way down the stairs, more shots ricochet off the metal railing, and one almost hits Cade.

"Get in the car!" he shouts once we've made it out of the building.

There's a black Range Rover at the curb, and I jump inside as Cade follows suit.

"We've got heat," he says to the driver when I see Rory exiting the building.

Rory gets two shots off as we speed away, but they don't seem to cause any damage.

"You okay?" Cade's hand is on my thigh, but he's looking out the back window, and so am I.

Rory's still there with a phone to his ear. But he's not chasing after us, at least.

I lose sight of him as we round a corner.

"You're going to be fine," he says and hands over his gun to the driver. He unzips his jacket and shirks it off.

Shit, he did get hit. I thought the bullet missed him.

I drop the sketchpad and my purse in my lap and move my fingers to his arm, where blood trickles down his bicep.

"How bad?" The driver looks back at Cade.

"The bullet only grazed me. I'm fine." He looks down at my purse. "If you have a phone on you, turn it off so he can't track us."

My hand is shaking and slicked with his blood, but I tuck it in my purse and turn off both of my phones, not wanting him to see I have two.

"Why are you really doing this?" I ask a few minutes later when my heartbeat normalizes. I still can't quite wrap my head around all of this.

I need to know the truth. I need to know if he can get me where I need to go.

His lips part as he looks away for a brief moment.

When his light eyes return to mine, he says in a low voice, "Because I should have helped you eight years ago, and I fucked up . . . so now's my chance to make things right."

9

CADE

GOD, THIS ENTIRE NIGHT HAS BEEN A WHIRLWIND.

Jessica only called a few hours ago to let me know Rory was back early from Boston. We had to bump up our plans. Thankfully, I had just received word from Noah, letting me know he had my sister and his daughter safe and far away.

We've been on the highway for about three hours now. We ditched the Range Rover as planned in Jersey, and we're in an inconspicuous minivan that has a *BABY ON BOARD* sign dangling in the back window. And no, we didn't steal the car. Jessica is just super thorough in her prep.

I still haven't opened up to Gia, despite her twenty-something attempts to get me to talk.

It's a conversation that can't be had in a damn car, though.

She fell asleep a little while ago, giving me some air to breathe—to think through everything that went down.

She's stretched out in the back, her hands tucked beneath her face, and I'm upfront now with Owen.

I never believed in fate before, but there's some part of me that thinks I was meant to see Gia again. Is it possible I can make amends for my past, for my fuck-ups and failures?

For the shit I did at my father's orders, and for the stupid shit I did all on my own?

I'm working on changing, but just because a lot of that is in the past doesn't make it disappear.

"Did your guys kill Rory's men or just knock them out?" I've been hesitant to ask this question since we jumped into the car, but I'd like to know if I'm responsible for murder.

Owen swipes a hand through his dirty blond hair. "I wish we could've slit their throats, but no, man—we kept them alive."

I scratch at the gauze on my shoulder. It's becoming itchy, and I want to yank the damn thing off.

"How's your arm?"

"It's fine," I grumble.

"First bullet wound, I take it?" Owen looks at me out of the corner of his eye, a slight smile pulling at his lips.

"Yeah, a first."

"You could have let me go in and get her, ya know."

I was in a goddamn gun battle with an Irish crime boss tonight. In what world am I now living? How did I go from a board meeting yesterday morning to this? "She wouldn't have gone with a stranger." Hell, I'm pretty much a stranger, too.

"But you're paying us a lot of money to back you up."

True. But it's worth it.

"This is a lot for someone you barely know," Owen says after a few minutes of silence pass. "Based on what I know about you from Noah, this doesn't really jive with your image."

"Well, whatever my sister has told her husband is probably fairly accurate, but she also doesn't know me that well."

"Really?"

I nod, and my gaze flicks to the window. There's nothing

but trees and darkness outside. We didn't want to take Route 95 and drive through the busy cities, so we're taking a major detour.

"So, looks like we're beginning to scratch the surface to find the real you, man." He smiles, but God, he has no idea.

It's more like we're about to break the motherfucking ice.

* * *

"GOOD NEWS OR BAD?" I ASK JESSICA AS SOON AS I ANSWER her call. It's almost six in the morning, and I took over driving for Owen three hours ago so he could rest. Gia woke up once to go the bathroom two hours ago, but she fell asleep shortly after. Or she's pretending to doze to avoid conversation with me, which suits me just fine. I'm not nearly ready to open up yet.

Shit. Open up . . . it's something I never thought I'd be doing.

"As far as we can tell, Rory hasn't sent anyone after you guys yet." Jessica is tired. The exhaustion is evident in her voice. She's probably been up all night, like me. "And the bad news is we lost track of Mya."

I almost hit the brakes at her words. "Are you shitting me? Don't you have the best guys working for you? How'd a petite blonde slip your men? And how the hell did she know to slip them?"

A crackle comes through the line from a deep puff of air. "One of my guys was following her yesterday, but instead of going to her art class, she went to the airport. We lost her there. He didn't have a ticket to get through security."

"Have you—"

"Already reached out to my man at TSA. Well, I tried, at

77

least. He hasn't gotten back to me yet, but when I know something, you will."

"Maybe her father managed to send her on vacation to get her off the story." At least she'll be safe. Well, hopefully.

"Is that your friend?" Gia's sleepy voice sounds from behind, and the hairs on the back of my neck stand. "Is Rory following us? Did they send for my dad? He's their number one. You're probably his new target."

There's a casualness to her words. Her dad's a killer, but she almost talks about it like we're discussing where to go for dinner. I guess when you're in that life long enough, it becomes the norm.

I look back over my shoulder at her. She's sitting upright now. Her hair is disheveled, her eye makeup smudged, and yet, she looks unbelievably stunning. She has that just-fucked look—and I can't help but feel my body tighten at thoughts of—

No . . . I can't cross that bridge. I won't let myself. I can't even think about her like that. But it doesn't mean my cock understands.

Morning wood without the sleep and while driving. Just fucking great.

"What's your father's name? We can try and locate him."

"He's like a ghost. Good luck with that," she mumbles.

"Name," I say again.

Her shoulders sag. "Pierce Callaghan."

"Can you give me an address?" I ask.

She rattles it off after I've placed Jessica on speakerphone.

I press the phone back to my ear. "You got that?"

"Yeah. I'll be in touch. You near the first hotel yet?"

"About five minutes away, actually." I catch Gia's eyes in the rearview mirror. She's staring off in a daze, as if in disbelief about all of this. Hell, I am, too. I'm supposed to be having a meeting with a manufacturer this morning. Well, that won't be happening. But how long will I be able to put my life on hold?

I end the call a minute later and stow the phone back in my pocket. "How are you?"

"I'm not even sure," she says softly. "How's your arm?"

It doesn't hurt anymore, so I almost forgot I got hit. "I'm fine."

Owen shifts in his seat, but his eyes remain shut, and so I look back at her in the mirror again, adjusting it to better see her. "Why'd you need that sketchpad?"

She reaches for it and smooths her fingers over the leather exterior.

The car drifts into the other lane, and I yank the wheel back over. I need to stop looking at her, but having her in the car with me is probably equivalent to driving under the influence. She's distracting. This is entirely new to me. Women don't make me act like this—out of control.

"It's important to me," she finally answers. "So, um, what's the plan?"

Deflection.

My specialty.

We're going to get nowhere fast if we're too much alike.

"My friend is working on setting up a safe house until we can figure this all out. We're going to make our way to Florida over the next few days, and then we'll see where she's sending us."

"A safe house? Like a prison?"

I check the mirror again, noticing her breathing increase, her chest swell.

"Not a prison, just a place to keep you—"

"Safe," she finishes. "But still, I can't be pinned up somewhere and just wait."

"It won't be long. We're going to get this all squared away soon. I promise."

"You can't promise anything. You don't know Rory like I do. You don't know my father." There's desperation in her voice now. Fear. I can't say I blame her. "I've been like a prisoner for ten years. I didn't leave one life just to be a prisoner in another."

My jaw tightens. I wish I had more answers for her, more to say, but this has all happened so fast. "The end goal isn't to keep you locked up."

"Then what is it?"

"It's to give you your freedom. To shut Rory down."

"How?"

I pull into the hotel parking lot and park the car. "Gia—"

"We're here?" Owen cuts me off, and maybe that's for the best right now. "Shit. I didn't realize I fell asleep." He straightens and unbuckles.

Soon after, we check in and head to the rooms.

"Owen's staying across the hall," I say once we're outside our room.

"And you?" she asks.

I hold the keycard in front of the small black box and wait for the green light. "I'm staying with you."

"With me?" Her brows arch.

Owen rests a hand on her shoulder. "I'm going to call the team and get a few more hours of shut-eye. Holler if you need me." He winks at us before hoisting a bag over his shoulder and opening his door.

"There are two bedrooms separated by a living room," I say once we step into the suite. "It's not exactly the Four Seasons, but we're in a rural area, so we have to make do."

Her lip tucks between her teeth as she scans the room, and her shoulders tremble as if chilled.

"Okay. Well, you should rest," she says a moment later.

"No, I'm good. Someone needs to stay awake, just in case."

"Let it be me," she offers as I slide the safety chain in place.

"No." I face her.

Arms fly up across her chest again, and this time, it's in defiance. "Sleep," she says in a husky and ridiculously sexy voice.

"Gia," is all I say as I lift the duffel bag and walk past her to one of the bedrooms.

She follows me, and I drop the bag on the bed and unzip it.

"What is that?"

I smirk and hand her a stack of clothes. "What do you think?"

"Did you really buy me lingerie?" She angles her head while studying me, holding on to a pair of red lacy panties I'd very much like to see her model for me. And at this point, I'm so damn tired I don't have the energy to scold myself for the thought.

But Christ, I'm not used to being good. I'm used to going after who and what I want. It's the only way I've ever known. Well, minus those six months I was engaged. For those six-months . . . I was a caged animal scratching at the walls, dying on the inside. Being with a woman you don't care about or have a physical connection to . . . not my finest time.

The closest I came to love was my senior year at Stanford when I dated Samantha, a wild redheaded tattoo artist. She's the reason why I got ink.

I swallow, choking back the sudden pinch of emotion in my chest. It's an uncomfortable thing—feelings.

"My friend thought you'd want a few things," I finally say after blinking away images of my past, of the woman I once lost. "She went shopping for you. There are toiletries in the bag, too."

"I guess you really were prepared, huh?" She drops the underwear back on the bed and wets her lips.

"Yeah." I zip the bag once it only has my things in it. "Sleep," I echo her command right back at her.

"You're not going to give up, are you?" She frowns.

"Never." I step closer to her, but her legs bump against the bed and she falls back.

She peers up at me beneath her long, dark eyelashes. "Well, I'm stubborn, too. And I've been taking orders for ten years, so I'm not going to back down either." And with that, she pushes right back up and stands before me, challenging me. And my heart begins to knock around in my chest, harder than normal. The desire I don't want pricks my body like a sharp magnum tattoo needle.

"Then we're at an impasse." I rest both hands on her shoulders and lower my head to look into her eyes.

She sighs. "Sleep in this bed while I take a bath. Lock the bedroom door and put a chair in front it. If someone tries getting in, the noise will wake you, right?"

Yeah, sure. Sleep in the bed while she's naked and getting wet in the adjoining room. That's a brilliant fucking idea. But I keep my mouth shut because I've been awake for twenty-four hours straight, and exhaustion is settling in and seeping through my bones. "Fine," I grumble. "But how long of a bath are we talking?"

"When I'm done, I'll relax on the couch," she says,

pointing to the loveseat by the closed window within the bedroom.

"Fine." I lock up but don't feel the need to do more than that. Then I go around to the other side of the bed and kick off my shoes before sitting down. "Don't go drowning on me in there."

A triumphant smile appears. I have a feeling she isn't used to getting what she wants—unlike me.

"Cade?"

I look over at her as she rests her hand on the master bath doorknob.

"Yeah?"

"You ever going to tell me what happened eight years ago?"

I shut my eyes, my core tightening. "I'll try."

"You're going to need to do much more than try," she says in a soft voice and then slips into the bathroom.

10

GIA

I WAKE UP. MY BODY'S TENSE.

It takes me a minute to digest where I am.

Free from Rory, from my father, but for how long? Will I really be able to get away?

Will I finally be able to find my mom?

My legs drop to the floor, and I look around the room.

How'd I end up in the bed? After the long bath, I wrapped myself in the hotel robe and rested on the couch.

I remember watching Cade sleep, feeling odd about being in the room with him while he slept on the bed. His long legs had been stretched out, his hands clasped on his lap, his sleeves rolled to the elbows, showing his ink. I almost went over and brushed back the lock of hair that had fallen across his forehead.

I must have fallen asleep, and he put me here—but where the hell is he now?

I tighten the knot on my robe, run my fingers through my damp hair, and go to the door.

When I push it open, I stumble back a step, surprised at the sight before me.

Cade is shirtless and in black sweatpants, with his back to me. The coffee table has been shoved to the side of the room, and he's kicking the air.

The curves of his biceps flex when he drops to the floor next, supporting his entire body with only his arms, keeping the rest of his weight off the ground.

My hand rests on my collarbone as I lean against the doorframe and watch in awe as this man lowers himself to the ground before hopping upright a moment later.

His body is like a work of art—why couldn't he have been one of the nude models I got to draw last month?

He grabs a small hand towel off the couch and turns to face me while swiping it across his face. He's not startled at the sight of me, and his breathing is controlled for someone who worked up that kind of sweat.

"What was that?" I approach him.

He tosses the towel, grabs a bottle of water, and comes back in front of me. "Jiu-jitsu."

"Brazilian?" I grin.

"Yeah." He smiles back.

"I'd like to learn some self-defense moves. Maybe you could teach me?"

"Now?" He sucks down nearly the entire bottle, and when he smiles again, his eyes smile, too. God, the man is sexy.

"Well." My lips twist as I contemplate what to say next.

He tips his head forward and takes a step my way. "Learning while in that robe might not be the best idea." His voice is deeper, more guttural than normal, and I can hear it —the desire flowing through his words.

The way he's observing me, too, it's as if he's conflicted about something—pensive and tense. Like he wants to grab me and make me his.

Is it bad that I almost want him to? What would that be

like? To have a man like him take me? Even for one night? My cheeks heat as he scratches the back of his head. "How long have you been studying?"

"I've been practicing martial arts on and off since I was a teenager. My father made my kid brother, Corbin, enroll when he was eight, and Corbin wouldn't do it unless I did. Dad thought it would teach my wild brother some discipline. That didn't exactly work." He half-laughs. "But I ended up liking it more than him."

"Oh, yeah?"

"I have to practice even more now to keep up with all of it, though, because I'm so damn busy with work."

"Yeah. I mean, it must be hard to compete with the younger guys, now that you're so much older," I tease.

He takes one step, swallowing the short gap between us. He's so close the sheen of sweat on his chest makes his muscles gleam as trickles of light spear through the semi-open blinds in the room.

"I'm, what? Nine or ten years older than you."

"Mm. You're not supposed to ask a woman her age."

His eyes narrow, his face growing taut and serious. "I wasn't asking."

I inhale as the back of his hand touches my cheek, and he holds onto my eyes as if he were designed by the heavens above to study me for all eternity. I wouldn't mind that. "So, uh, what are you trying to say?"

"You're just too young."

"Too young for what?" I raise a brow, challenging him.

This tension between us, this feeling of lust I'm not used to—I need it to go away. But there's a part of me that wants him to make me forget about the last ten years of my life.

I'm too close to finding my mother.

Too damn close.

And so, I step back, which has him dropping his hand.

He clears his throat. "I need some air. And a shower. I'm going to send Owen over to keep you company for a bit."

Don't look down. Don't look down.

But I do it. It's like saying *don't see blue*. That's all that's there. And damn if Cade is going to have blue balls based on the massive size of the erection he can't seem to hide.

"Um, yeah, okay," I say, embarrassed.

He turns, roping a hand around the back of his neck, the veins thick on his arm. God, there needs to be a picture of Cade on social media with the hashtag: #veinporn.

"Change before Owen comes," he says over his shoulder while walking to his room.

"I don't do well with commands." Or, more like I don't want them, now that I'm nearly free. I won't classify myself as free until I know Rory and my father can't get to me anymore.

"Unlucky for you—neither do I." He shuts the door behind him, and now that he's out of sight, I can finally breathe.

I peer around the room, thinking about trying to imitate the moves I saw him do. I hate feeling powerless.

I should have helped you eight years ago. Cade's words come back to mind.

Helped me how? How would our paths have ever crossed? Eight years ago, I was seventeen and forced to work at—

My hand goes to my mouth as a memory pops into my mind like the crackle of a sparkler.

No . . .

Cade would have never been there. No, it's not possible.

A man like him?

He's a CEO. Why would he ever be caught up in my world?

But my stomach starts to pinch tight and my shoulders sag as a memory unfolds, one that includes Cade. I think it was him. It was a long time ago, but still . . .

Maybe everyone's a potential target for being pulled into the McCullens' world. I thought Cade was different.

I guess I was wrong.

* * *

"So, the guy has a gun, and he's hanging on to the hood of my buddy's car, yelling at us to drive—says that he's being chased."

I take another swallow of the vodka from the mini bottle I'm holding and swipe at the drop of liquid on my lips, waiting for Owen to continue.

He stretches his legs out in front of him and smiles. "I was under direct orders not to get into any shit while I was there, so I called the cops."

"You—be good?" I can't help but laugh. I've been chatting with Owen for two hours now, listening to his stories, and so, I've learned this man is a beacon for trouble.

"Hey, I tried." He holds his palms up in front of him before running one hand through his disheveled, longish blond hair.

"Well? You can't leave me hanging. What happened?" I blink a few times as I realize the alcohol is going to my head now. I'm not sure how many little bottles of liquor I've drunk. Owen thought it'd be a good idea for me to relax. He brought me food and then raided the minibar after Cade had sent him to babysit.

"So, I tell the cop about the gang banger on my car, and

the dude says, 'assess the situation and call us back.' Can you believe that shit?" He shakes his head and grabs his soda. "Yeah, I assessed the situation all right."

"Do I even want to know what happened?" I slide off the couch and sit on the floor next to him.

"No, you don't."

A smile lights his face, and his hazel eyes shine even more than normal. He has a lot of the color wheel going on in his irises: hints of blue-green with gold flecks and traces of nutmeg brown.

"Well"—I think back to my life in Brazil, and an all-too-familiar pain settles inside me—"I guess that's Rio for you."

"Brazil is nice, though. You miss it?" He finishes his drink and then reaches for an Oreo.

How does he eat like he does and stay looking like that? I'm pretty sure he's met my daily caloric intake in the last twenty minutes.

"Yes, I do. My, um, mother and I lived in a place outside the city. The community was small and tight-knit. We all kept to ourselves until—" The last memory of my mom comes to mind, and I can't keep talking. Fresh pain seeps inside of me.

She was taken because of me . . . because they wanted *me*.

"You ever think about going back?" He arches a brow and wipes the crumbs off his jeans, and I'm pulled back to the present and out of the nightmare of my past.

"Only every hour." But not for the reasons he probably thinks.

My lips purse together, and I finish off the rest of the vodka, needing to dull the pain.

"All that alcohol, and you still look tense. I guess my plan to loosen you up failed." He shrugs. "I'd offer to massage you, but that'd be fucking awkward, and I don't really feel like going head-to-head with Cade since it seems to me he's into you." He smiles.

Like Cade, he has a great smile. "Into me?"

"Well, yeah. I've never known a man to do what he's doing for a woman unless he's either getting paid or helping family out. You know?"

I swallow his words and save them for later in the day. Maybe I need to have another drink, even though I'll probably be married to the toilet later. I'm kind of a lightweight.

But before I can push up to stand and head to the minibar, there's a knock at the door.

"It's me." Cade's rich voice carries through the door. He has the card to come in, but Owen has the chain fastened in place for extra security.

"Coming, man." He shoots to his feet and lets him in.

My palms find the floor, but my knees are too weak to stand.

Shit. I'm drunk, more so than I thought.

Cade eyes the empty bottles on the floor by my legs, and then his gaze sweeps to my face. "You've been drinking?"

Owen scratches the back of his neck as if guilty. "Not me, but Gia needed to relax, so I thought—"

"What? You thought it'd be a good idea for her to get alcohol poisoning?" Cade heads my way and kneels down next to me. He collects all the little blue bottles and tosses them into the waste bin. "I've got it from here."

"Sure." He's not fazed by Cade's deep, slightly threatening tone. "I'll be across the way. We'll be leaving early tomorrow, so be sure to get enough sleep."

I finally get to my feet and start for my bedroom once Owen is gone. I'm pretty sure I'm not walking straight, but as long as I can make it to the bed without needing his help, I'll be good.

"Gia." His voice has me pausing in the doorframe, and I prop my hands against the wood to hold myself up. "What?"

"I don't think you should be alone. You might get sick and—"

I look over my shoulder at him, but I do it too fast, and it makes everything spin. The room is tilting, or maybe I am.

Cade catches me before I fall, his hands swooping beneath my armpits, and then he lifts me and carries me to the bed.

"Go away." I roll to my side and pull my knees against my stomach. "I remember you, Cade. I remember meeting you before." I close my eyes. "So, please, leave me alone."

He curses beneath his breath. "Whatever you think—it's not that bad. Well, probably not that bad."

"You were in the McCullens' underground casino. No one gets in there without being connected to them." My stomach starts to squeeze. The nausea is hitting hard and fast.

It's funny how you can have trouble walking when you're drunk, but the second you feel like you're going to throw up —*bam*, you can sprint like an Olympian to get to a bathroom.

And in a split second, I'm on my feet, making a woozy beeline for it.

I barely make it.

It's as if my muscles are convulsing, and I keep vomiting until my stomach is empty—and Cade is holding my hair back. Damn him.

"You okay?"

I cover my mouth as I sit up a minute later and peer at him over my shoulder. He's on his knees behind me, and as much as I shouldn't care, I feel embarrassed that he witnessed that.

"Please go," I choke out, but he doesn't move. He doesn't even flinch. Instead, he hands me a wet towel and runs his palm up and down my back.

I close my eyes and press it to my face, wanting to hide from him. Hell, from the world.

I try to stand a few moments later, and he holds on to my elbows and helps me up.

It's not fair. I want to be mad at him, but he's making it hard.

I brush my teeth and rinse the disgusting taste from my mouth before heading back into the room and sinking onto the bed.

"Take off your clothes," he says as if it's the most natural comment in the world. My lips open, and I'm ready to use every ounce of energy I have left to stand and smack him, but he adds, "You should get comfortable and sleep."

I relax almost instantly. And because I'm exhausted, I begin lifting the soft V-neck sweater his friend got me over my head.

His hands rush to mine, covering them, and he pushes the material back down. The muscles in his face lock tight.

"What?"

"Are you crazy?" His lips crook at the edges into a half-smile. "I didn't mean in front of me. I, uh, think me seeing you naked wouldn't be a good idea."

"And why not?"

He raises a brow and retracts his hands, but he doesn't answer my stupid question. Instead, he asks, "Can you manage on your own?"

"Yes." The alcohol is starting to recede, like water pulling back after the waves crash on the sand. Anger bubbles in its place.

"We'll, uh, pick up our conversation after you've gotten some sleep. Or maybe at the next hotel."

"Or maybe never at all."

"What's that supposed to mean?" He scrunches his brow and takes a step back.

"You really expect me to believe anything you say now?" I reach for the hem of my sweater and peel it off, regardless of what he wants. I suddenly want to torture him—to frustrate him. He's a liar. A fake. A man I can no longer trust, even if my heart freaking sings when he's in the room. Even if the desire inside of me is like a tight fist in my stomach—pumping relentlessly.

His eyes darken and drop to my chest, to my bra, where my nipples press against the thin lace fabric. Why did his friend buy such sexy undergarments? These things were made to be seen, not hidden. And Cade is seeing me right now like no man ever has.

"Gia." His gaze shifts to my face.

I stand and move closer to him. My palm rests on his chest, and his heart is beating so quick, matching my own.

"You're dirty, Cade. Like the cops, judges, and politicians Rory has on his payroll. You're just as bad." I reach around behind my back, prepared to unsnap the bra, but his hands fly to my forearms and stop me, pinning my arms to my sides.

I can see the pulse in his neck. The controlled but tight strain of his jaw muscle. And we're so close now I can feel his hardened length against me.

I should hate how this moment makes me feel right now—the prickly burn of desire between my legs.

He's no better than Rory, I remind myself.

I look up into his eyes, his body still pressed close to mine as he holds me in place.

"You know, the day I met you was when I got this tattoo." I pull my right arm up between us and show him my wrist.

He wraps his hand around my forearm, angling my wrist in his direction for a better view.

"Who died?" He keeps a hold on me as our eyes meet.

"My mother. I think so, at least. Well, maybe. I'm not sure."

He raises a brow, probably confused by my choice of words, but then he starts to trace his fingers over the angel wings with his other hand. "It was pink and swollen when we met, right?"

I blink away the memory of my mother and focus on him again. "How can you remember the details now—especially something so specific—when you couldn't before? Eight years is a long time ago."

"My memory's both a blessing and a curse." He drops my hand and motions for the bed, but I don't sit, even though I want to. Even though my body is weak. "I wasn't myself the night we met, so the details were muffled. But I remember most of that night now." He swallows. "I remember you."

Before I realize it, I'm sitting back on the bed, and I pull the sheets up to cover my chest. Something heavy is coming, and if this man is actually about to open up to me—he's right, I can't be standing for it.

He shoves his hands in his pockets and releases a breath before his eyes cut back to mine. There's pain there. His blue eyes are darker, more intense. He's carrying a weight around, and I know how that feels.

"I'd never done drugs before." His lips tighten for a moment. "I dated someone once who did, and it didn't end so well, and I . . . well, I don't like anything that takes away my sense of control."

Figures.

"But that night in the casino"—he clears his throat—"was the first time my father introduced me to that world. He frequented the place when he needed to make some less-than-legal business deals."

"With the McCullens?" My stomach drops, and I don't think it's alcohol-related.

"Not with them. I never met Rory or Richard, but I remember seeing them on occasion from that moment forward—well, until I took over the company and ended such business deals." He taps a closed fist to his mouth for a moment before continuing, "My father was meeting with a judge to get some permits passed that were being held up by a bunch of red tape. I guess the McCullens were—maybe still are—a middleman."

I nod, sort of understanding, but I don't like the direction this conversation is going. My hand slips under the covers and to my abdomen, where the discomfort continues to grow. "And what does this have to do with drugs?"

He sinks on the bed near the bottom, and his eyes drop to the tattoo inside his own arm. "I was always desperate for my father's approval, but I never wanted to be part of anything illegal. I didn't like the line he was trying to force me to cross that night. I refused to go into the meeting. Instead, I sat down at one of the poker tables and waited." He shakes his head and squeezes his eyes shut for a moment, and I can tell he's angry with himself. Maybe he's not such a bad guy.

Or maybe I'm clinging to hope because I need him.

"Someone offered me something at the card table. It looked like a blunt." His eyes flash open. "It reminded me of a woman from my past. And something inside me snapped. I became so pissed at everything in that moment, and so I took it. It was probably laced with heroin or something. I don't know. I was fucking out of it."

"You ordered a drink from me. Before you smoked, probably." The memory is foggy, but it's there. His face is hard to forget.

He nods. "I noticed your tattoo as I told you my order, and then I looked up into your eyes—"

"And I remember thinking you looked like a good guy. And for some naïve reason—and because I was still fairly new to Rory's world—I thought maybe you'd help me. It was a dumb idea, but I was seventeen and hopeless." The night comes back to me like a watershed, and emotions dump all over me, raining down in swift, sharp movements.

As he stands back up, his large hand sweeps up to his face as if ashamed to look at me. "When you handed me the napkin with your note, I was already fucked up, and I honestly thought your request for help was code for you wanting to have sex. And even on drugs, I wouldn't hook up with a minor. Then my father came out of his meeting and flipped when he realized I was high."

He laughs, but I can tell it's an attempt to hide emotion.

"My father said he expected that kind of shit from my brother, but not from me . . . and we left."

"So you're not bad?" I sit up higher, feeling more invigorated. Maybe my plan can still work.

His shoulders slouch as his blue eyes dart to mine. "I did shit I'm not proud of after that night. I did what Dad wanted. Deals I shouldn't have made. But I've been trying to be different from him. I'm looking for—"

"Redemption?"

"I don't know if I believe in redemption." His gaze falls to the floor. "But I want to do what's right. I want to help you."

I rise without thinking and stand before him. Maybe he's as broken as I am, but he hides behind a rough shell.

I forget I'm only in a bra and pants, but he doesn't even glance at my chest. His eyes find mine as I reach for him and slide my hands up his muscled arms, then grip both his biceps. "That must have been difficult for you." I press my lips together as I consider my next words. "It's not easy for someone like you to open up."

"Yeah? And how can you tell?"

"Because I think we're alike. It's not exactly easy for me to open up either." I swallow the emotion in my throat. "So, thank you for telling me the truth and not sugarcoating it."

"Don't do that." The muscle in his jaw tightens as he shifts back a step, and my arms fall to my sides, like leaves swooshing down in a storm.

"Don't do what?"

He grips his temples with his middle finger and thumb for a brief moment, before catching my eyes again. "Don't let me off the hook. I don't deserve it."

"Maybe I should be mad at you, but you're not your father, just like I'm not mine. So, I believe you when you say you want to be different than you were in the past."

My hand rests on my abdomen, and I can't tell if it's the nausea from the alcohol coming back to bite me or if it's butterflies.

"I should let you get some rest." He turns to leave, but I reach out for him, my hand landing on his hard back, wishing the layer of clothing didn't separate us.

He stills at my touch.

"We're both a little messed up, aren't we?"

"You're not—not at all. You're"—he turns to face me, and my arm goes back to my side— "incredible."

My lips part in expectation, in need. And he wants me too. I can see it. His brow creases as if unsure, but then he lowers his head, slowly, until our lips are almost touching.

My eyes close, and my body begins to warm the moment his lips press to mine. It's a soft kiss.

Lips to lips.

My chest rising.

When his hand finds the small of my back, and he pulls me flush to his body and tips my chin up with his other hand, deepening the kiss, I nearly wilt against him. His hand glides up my back and beneath my bra, but he doesn't unsnap it. No, he just runs his fingers along my flesh, sending a cascade of shivers over every inch of my skin, right down to my toes.

The kiss intensifies, and he groans against my mouth, moving even closer to me—so strong and powerful, his kiss, his desire . . . that I fall back onto the bed. His chest rises and falls, his gaze tight on mine as I observe him, waiting for him to come to me, and he does.

"Fuck," he whispers, and I shift farther up on the bed so he can brace himself above me.

When his mouth claims mine again, this time his tongue slips inside. It's like tiny pulses of heat flash between my legs, making me so sensitive.

His hard length presses against me, and I buck my hips up to let him know I need more.

I want to live in this moment for as long as possible and make everything outside disappear. All of the evil. All of the hate. I want it gone. I just want him.

But the moment is cut short so fast I don't have time to realize what's even happened.

Cold. That's all I feel when he lifts himself off me abruptly.

I sit, and he stands, bringing his hands into prayer position, tapping them at his forehead.

"I shouldn't have done that." He curses beneath his breath

as his hands drop back to his sides. "I'm trying to be a good guy here. For once in my fucking life."

"Kissing me doesn't make you a bad guy."

He gives me a half smile and steps closer to the bed, and the proximity gives me hope that he'll come back to me and relieve this pressure he's built up inside me.

It physically hurts right now.

"You and I both know this would have led to a lot more than a make-out session." He clears his throat, his cock still pressing hard against his jeans. "You've been drinking. How about we discuss this tomorrow?"

I rise before him, but he steps back as if he's afraid he'll lose control, and—*shit*—I want him to.

"I really need to get out of here." There's a definite grit to his voice. His face muscles are taut, his shoulders pinched back and tense.

But, damn it, maybe he's right. I have been drinking, and I don't trust my own judgment right now. And I should respect him for helping me acknowledge that.

"Good night." The words roll off my tongue and take a second to reach him, because he doesn't move.

Jesus, I want him to kiss me again.

I want his tongue in my mouth and his hands on my bare skin.

But . . .

His eyes flicker down for a brief moment at the swell of my breasts, the bra not hiding my desire. And then he gives a forced nod and leaves.

I wait for the door to close before I fall back onto the bed and cover my face, wondering how the hell I can feel so much for a man I barely know.

And how will I ever say goodbye to someone who seems to steal my every breath when we're alone?

11

CADE

Fucking chills rush through my body. This woman is making me absolutely nuts.

My cell vibrates in my pocket as I cross the living room and head to my bedroom.

I assume it's Jessica because it's the burner phone. But when I check it, I'm surprised to see Corbin's phone number on screen. I grumble before I answer it, knowing there's only one way Corbin got a hold of this number.

"What did Jessica tell you?" She always liked Corbin better than me. Pretty much everyone likes my kid brother more. I'm the asshole. Maybe always will be.

"Man, what the hell did you get yourself into?" His voice is off, so I assume he's been drinking. He's in Sin City, after all.

"Nothing I can't handle." I shut my bedroom door so Gia can't hear and then sink down on the bed. My elbows rest on my knees as I press a palm to my forehead. "You might want to stay in Vegas until this all blows over, though." I'm trying to be optimistic and assume we'll get this handled and fast. But who the hell really knows?

"You don't have to ask me twice, but is this really for some chick you met last week?"

Gia's pouty lips come to mind. "It's complicated."

"And the company? Are you seriously taking a break from work?"

"We have capable people there who can handle things." I swallow, hoping I'm right.

"Shit, I know that, but it's about damn time you do. When was the last time you took a vacation?"

I honestly don't have a clue, not that I'd consider this to be leisurely time off. "Just hang tight in Vegas until you get word that it's safe to come home. I assume you talked to Grace?"

"Yeah, she told me about the babies. We're going to be uncles, man."

"How much does she know about what I'm into?" How much did Jessica tell her?

"Grace doesn't know a lot. But Noah will make sure she's good."

True.

"Well—" There's a beep. I hold the phone out to see who's calling. "I gotta go."

"Yeah, okay. Be safe. Don't die." I can almost hear his smile through the phone. "It's not every day I get to use your line."

"Be safe, too." I end the call and switch lines. "What's up?"

"We have two problems," Jessica says right off the bat.

A humorless half-laugh escapes me. "Only two?" Hell, I'd call that good news.

"Cade," she bites my name out like it's sour on her tongue.

"Well?"

"For one, Mya is in Brazil. And Jerry McAllister just walked into Rory's club."

I don't know which fucking problem to tackle first. She could have at least given me a second to digest one before slamming the second at me. "Jerry. Like, our friend Jerry? Detective Jerry McAllister?"

"Yup."

"You think he's making some sort of bust?" That'd be too coincidental.

"He's a homicide detective, so I don't think so." There's a hiss over the line. "What exactly happened at the club last Friday when you guys went there?"

I think back to the night I met Gia, the night all of this started. "Corbin said Jerry picked the club out. And when I was talking with Gia, he got a private room with one of the dancers. He didn't want to leave with us when I insisted, either."

"It doesn't make any sense. I don't believe Jerry's cheating."

"I don't, either." I scratch at the base of my skull, trying to think. "Which means—"

"Which means Jerry's not there for a lap dance tonight."

"Given his line of work, he'd know the place is run by the mob."

"So, maybe he purposely chose that place—"

"Because the man never stops working." A fucking stone drops in my stomach at the realization there's more to all of this than we anticipated. Jury is still out on whether that's a good or bad thing.

"Can you ask Gia if she recognizes him? I'll text you his picture."

I glance at my closed door. I don't want to wake her,

especially after what happened between us tonight. "Yeah, I will. In the morning."

"You, uh, don't think he's dirty, do you?" It's one of the few times I can actually hear worry flowing through her words.

"Absolutely not."

"It'd be nice to have him as an ally." She's silent for a moment, and I know what she's thinking because I'm thinking the same thing. "He'd probably tell us to back down, though, so maybe we won't say anything to him. Not right now, anyway."

"Agreed." I stand, prepared to hang up, but shit, there's still more we have to talk about. "Tell me what you know about Mya."

"Mya took a vacation all right, but to Rio de Janeiro. And this isn't her first time. She's been there twice in the last four weeks."

"Fuck."

"This can't just be about breaking a story on Rory. If Mya's in Brazil, there's a hell of a lot more going on. I looked into her, and the woman is legit—like, she thinks she's Lois Lane or something, always breaking stories on some heavy shit. Her dad probably has to send her on regular vacations." She pauses. "So if you don't get Gia to open up about it and soon, then—"

"She needs to trust me more, but I think she's coming around."

"We don't have much time if we're really going to try to wrap this up quick enough for you to get back to your boring-ass job."

"Give me a day or two. I'll see what Gia's been up to; hopefully, it can be useful somehow." I place the phone on speaker and toss it on the bed. "Any movement on Rory's people yet?" I take off my clothes, stripping down to my boxers.

"The plan worked. Well, for the most part. He dispatched two teams, one to our false lead in Austin and the other to Chicago."

"So what's the issue?"

"Gia's dad is still in New York. You'd think he would have gone, too, right?"

"I don't even know what to think anymore."

She clears her throat. "Just get some rest tonight, and I'll be in touch in the morning. And find out what Gia says about Jerry. I just texted you his photo."

I look at my friend's picture. Mid-forties, with a kid from a previous marriage and an amazing fiancée. A man I've always trusted.

There's no way he's dirty. No fucking way.

"'Night." I end the call and shrug the stress from my shoulders. I'm not sure if I want to take a cold shower or sleep the night away.

I choose option two and get into bed, running through everything in my head. Each thought, image, and even certain smells are cataloged in various parts of my mind for easy access. Sometimes I wish I could be like other people—you know, normal. Normal people don't remember absolutely everything.

But, then again, maybe I wouldn't have remembered Gia.

And I know for damn sure that when this is all over—crazy memory or not—she's not someone I'll ever be able to forget.

* * *

"WERE YOU TALKING TO SOMEONE?" I ASK AFTER GIA COMES into the living room.

I could have sworn I heard her speaking, but she's staring at me like I'm certifiable.

"No."

"Gia," I rush her name out, knowing damn well she's lying to me, and we don't have time for that.

"I was mumbling to myself. You know, thinking about what might happen next." She brushes past me, heading to the sitting area.

"Fine." I force the doubt from my mind, saving it for later, and take in the sight of her. She looks okay. No apparent hangover, which is impressive.

Her skin has a glow to it, even. Her long hair is damp from a shower, and from where I'm standing, I can smell the lavender soap she must have used.

"Well, uh, how are you feeling? Stomach okay?"

She settles on the couch, wearing a pair of black jeans and a white, oversized sweater. "I'm so embarrassed I got sick in front of you."

"It happens." I shrug, but she blushes.

I reach into my jeans pocket for my phone and pull up Jerry's picture. "Before we get going, Jessica needs your help." I hand her the cell.

She zooms in on the image as I try to get a read on her. Her brows pinch inward, her lips pursing together in a tight line.

"He was at the club with me for his bachelor party. Have you seen him there before?"

Her chin lifts and her hazel eyes meet mine. "Yeah, I remember him." She hands me back the phone and rises to her feet.

I cock my head. "And?"

"I've seen him with Tracey, maybe twice. She's one of the dancers. But he's normally with Rory."

"Normally?"

She nods. "Yeah, but he usually comes to the casino, not the club." She rolls her tongue over her teeth, and now she's the one giving me a questioning look with raised brows, her eyes narrowed. "Who is he?"

"A friend. Also, a detective," I grumble. "And I doubt he was questioning Rory, so unless he's undercover—"

"He's on Rory's payroll."

I don't buy it, though. First, Mya's father disappoints me by being a cheating ass. And now . . .

No. My straight-edge friend can't be corrupt. Fuck that.

"I need to call Jessica. Is there anything else you can tell me that might help?" I'd like to bring up Mya and the art classes right now to get the conversation over with, but I don't want to hit her with too much all at once.

A small smile tugs at the corners of her lips. "I know a lot about Rory, enough to put him away for three lifetimes, but anything I'd say would only put a target on our heads."

"Isn't there one already?"

"True, but I don't exactly want to draw the attention of every criminal in New York quite yet. Snitches aren't shown much love in the city."

"I told you I'd keep you safe." And I mean it, down to my last breath.

A knock on the door has Gia taking a step back.

"We're ready to roll," Owen says once I've let him in. "Miami, here we come."

CADE

"A two-story view of the bay? You're not using your credit card for this suite, are you? My dad could definitely track us that way." She spins away from the window and faces me, her hands landing on her hips, sunlight pouring in behind her, making her look like an angel or something.

"This might be my first time on the run, but I'm not an idiot." I tuck my hands in my pockets, continuing to study her, unable to stop myself from wondering how she'd look with the sun splashing over her naked body.

"What are you thinking about?" Her dark brows arch as she angles her head, observing me—maybe even reading my mind.

"Just hungry." Damned if I couldn't hide the deep huskiness of my voice when I said that.

"Me too, but do we have to eat in the room? Can we grab a bite at a restaurant in the hotel?" Her face lights a bit as she smiles. "I saw they have a rooftop bistro. I bet the views are even better than they are here."

"That's only one more level up."

"True." She faces the windows again. "But it'd be nice to

eat outside and get some fresh air. Miami reminds me of home."

I join her by the window. "Owen checked out the hotel and said we should be good." We already updated Gia on the status of Rory's men on the ride here. And for the rest of the trip, Owen regaled us with his "stories of adventure," as Gia likes to call them.

She sighs and glances upstairs to where Owen's room is. The water is running, so he's probably in the shower. We're all staying together this time since there are three rooms.

"Thank you. And I think I know what we should do after dinner tonight," she says almost casually, despite the depth of thought in her eyes. Her tongue peeks out of her mouth like a delicious tease, and she rolls it over her lips.

"Gia," I drag out her name.

"What? I was talking about fighting. Maybe we could kill some of our stress and tension by sparring. You could show me some moves. Teach me."

"You want to spar with me?" I ask in surprise. She had brought it up the other day, but I didn't think she was serious.

"I really do want to learn to protect myself. Don't go getting any dirty ideas."

Too late for that. The muscles in my torso tighten as I imagine her sweaty and pinned beneath me.

"How about I protect you so you never need to throw a punch?" I suggest.

"You won't be around forever."

She's right, even if I don't want to admit it. "Fine." I hate surrendering. "You should be able to defend yourself when I'm gone."

Triumph spreads across her face, and I rake my fingers through my hair. I need to knock this damn desire free from my body that's taken hold since the day we met.

How many days now has it been since I've fucked?

Too. Damn. Many.

And having someone like Gia around me all of the time is like asking an alcoholic to hold a shot of whiskey.

She's become my top-shelf brand, and I want to do a hell of a lot more than simply taste her. I want to—

"Thank you," she says in a soft voice.

I nod. "Sure." I start in the direction of my bedroom. "I'll meet you back here in an hour, and we'll head to dinner."

"Cade?" At the sexy sound of my name on her tongue, I stop before my door. Why does she also have to have such a hot accent? And when she gets angry, it becomes more noticeable—and God, it goes right under my skin in an I-want-to-screw-you-until-the-sun-comes-up kind of way.

"What?"

"Everything will be okay, won't it?"

She's asking for reassurance. She's asking for me to make her feel better. But right now, all I feel like is one more asshole in her life. Because I want to fuck her, regardless of what the hell is going on right now. And what kind of person does that make me?

A person like Rory.

Like my father?

"Yeah, everything will be okay," I lie.

* * *

"Do you really think we can trust her?"

The server lifts my empty plate from the table, and I wait until she's gone before answering. "Of course," I say, because I don't want him worrying about my own doubts or the weird conversation she was supposedly having with herself this morning.

"She's the daughter of an assassin. Not just any killer, either. I looked the guy up. He was a beast when he was Irish Special Forces. I can only imagine how lethal he is now, without limitations. How is she not dirty, too?"

"Why the hell are you just now asking me this? You didn't seem to have any issue when you were getting her drunk last night."

Owen takes a swig of his soda. "And why do you think I was really liquoring her up? I was trying to get a read on her and see if she'd talk."

I lean back in the chair and look over at Gia, who is resting by the pool. No one is swimming right now since the sun isn't out and the temperature has dropped. Gia looks both classy and sexy in her sleeveless black top. Plus, the ass-hugging jeans are a bonus.

"And did you learn anything?"

"Yeah, that she's dangerous."

"Dangerous?" I finally look away from her and back at him.

He nods and sets his drink down. "Yeah, she could get you killed."

"Well, no shit. That's why I hired you guys."

"That's not what I'm talking about. She's a distraction for you. I've seen what women like her do to men. She's making you weak."

A slow anger creeps through me at his comment. I don't view myself as weak. Not even a little.

I squeeze the back of my neck, working at the tension—realizing that maybe he's right on one count. I've been off my game since I met Gia.

"You ought to be tucked away somewhere safe, while Jess and our team troubleshoot this problem."

He knows full well that won't happen, so I don't bother to

answer. He might have been a SEAL, but I'm not some timid guy in a suit. I can handle my own.

"Just so you know, I wasn't only hired to keep Gia safe," he adds.

"And what bullshit instructions did Jessica give you?" I finish off my tumbler of whiskey, relishing the warmth as it burns its way down to my stomach.

I look over at the metal sculptured palm trees that surround the pool that still have Christmas lights wrapped around the fake leaves.

Then my view darts to Gia.

And she's heading our way.

Jessica didn't pack her any heels. Why would she? So, Gia hit up a nearby store before we came to dinner. She picked out a ridiculously tall pair. When she was modeling them, asking for my opinion, I swear she was purposely trying to get me to pull her into my arms right then and there.

She's testing my limits. My patience.

But she was raised in the shadows of mob bosses. Maybe she can handle someone like me. Maybe I'm not giving her enough credit. She might be young, but she's probably experienced.

"Jess said I'd better bring your ass back alive. It's a top priority."

"I don't need you to worry about me," I grit out and direct my attention back his way.

He raises both palms in the air and smiles. "Jess and your sister are best friends. What the hell did you expect?"

"But I hired you guys to protect—"

"Hi, Gia," Owen cuts me off.

"I think I'm ready to go back to the room." She braces a hand on the back of the chair she occupied during dinner and waits for one of us to respond, but I know what she wants—and I'm not sure if it's the best idea.

Her eyes land on mine. I'm fucked.

I'll be rotting in hell for this. My corpse has a predesignated spot, anyway. Bought and paid for.

"Maybe you should stay here and relax," Gia says in a rush after Owen stands.

His brows dart inward. "Not what I'm here to do."

"Well, I'm going to teach her some self-defense moves," I say.

Owen claps his hands and rubs them together. "Great idea. I'd be happy to help."

"I think I'd rather it just be the two of us if you don't mind." Her lip lands between her teeth, and she waits for Owen to respond.

He looks at me, his eyes darkening. "You have an hour."

"Great. Thanks," she says once Owen sits back down.

"You sure you want to do this?" I ask once we've made our way to the elevator and begin the quick descent to our floor.

"I have to start sometime. The sooner the better." Her shoulder brushes against my arm, but I check my desire to look at her, knowing all I'll be able to do is envision what she'd look like up against the mirrored wall with my body pressed tight to hers and my mouth at the crook of her neck.

Once we make it to our room, I instruct, "Meet me in the living room in five."

"Okay."

"Did Jessica pack you anything comfortable?"

"Yeah, even a sports bra."

I blow out an uncomfortable breath.

I go and change a minute later. Sweats and a tee this time.

I don't need her warm hands on my skin when I need to keep my cock in check.

I shove the couch out of the way and catch sight of her padding toward me in bare feet, with tight black yoga pants and a white tank top that dips way too low.

"Gia," I say her name with a gruff voice as desire claws at me from the inside.

She holds her hands palms up and shrugs. "This is all I had."

"Sure." I flick my wrist for her to come closer, which, in my mind, is still a really bad idea.

"So, teach me." She sweeps her long hair up into a ponytail and smiles.

She seems different tonight. Looser. Less on edge. Maybe being so far away from Rory and her father has made her feel like she can breathe.

But we're not out of the woods yet.

"The first rule of self-defense is to try and avoid ever being in a fight."

She chuckles. "Wow. Shocker."

I roll my eyes and motion for her to turn around. "Press your back to me."

She follows the command, and I try to remain focused on what I'm supposed to be doing right now.

"Always know your exits and your way out, and try to stay away from any enemy, so he or she can never get their arms around you." I swallow and step closer. "But, if they put you in a bear hug," I say while pulling her tight against me, "you want to lower your center of gravity and drop down as much as you can, squirming to make it harder for them to keep a hold on you."

I get a whiff of her shampoo. It's the same one I used, but

on her, it smells like wild orchids and the expensive kind of champagne you break out for New Year's Eve.

"Should I try it?"

"Go for it."

She starts to struggle, her ass moving from side to side, rubbing against me, and I'm impressed that I manage to keep from swearing at her movements. "You've got to become dead weight," I instruct.

"Okay."

"That's it." She's slipping from my grasp. "Stand up straight again, and I'm going to squeeze tighter this time. I want you to step on my foot first, then drop down."

She strains her neck to look over her shoulder at me, her brows pinched together. Her mouth too fucking close. "I don't want to hurt you."

I laugh. "I'll be okay. Promise."

She nods and faces forward. "Okay." She then makes her best effort to hurt me, and after ten more minutes, she nails the move. And I've managed to keep my erection at bay.

It only took thoughts of my asshole father to keep me like that, but hey—a win is a win.

She faces me, her cheeks red, her eyes sparkling. Her hands rub together, and she smiles. "I like this. It makes me feel powerful."

She really has no idea how much power she does wield.

"We'll try the choke hold now." We get into position and go through the moves several times. "Remember, you only have three to eight seconds before you start to lose oxygen."

She scowls. "Unfortunately, the memory of that is recent."

When I saw Rory's hands wrapped around her throat the other night, I wanted to snap his neck then and there. I've never wanted to hurt another person so much in all my life. I maintained my control then, but now I'm wondering if maybe I should have just killed the son of a bitch.

Could Jerry keep me out of jail for murder? Probably not.

I shut out the possible thoughts of Jerry being dirty because it'll fucking sour my mood. And I've got to admit I'm enjoying myself right now, which I didn't think would be possible.

It was torturous at first to be so close to her. But I like seeing how much this means to her, and how excited she gets every time she masters a move.

Having that cloud of gray lifted from her might be worth the throb in my balls from the lack of orgasm.

"Put your back against that wall." I gesture to the other side of the room. "We should work on the move Rory used against you, but are you sure you really want to?"

"Yes." She nods, but there's a change in her eyes once she's in position. Her breathing has increased, her chest rising and falling more than before.

I brace the wall instead of touching her neck, my hands positioned over her shoulders.

I don't know if I can re-create the scene when that asshole wrapped his hands around her throat.

"What's wrong?" Her hand rests on my flexed bicep, and I close my eyes.

"Maybe we'll save this move for another day." I'm about to push away from the wall, but at the feel of her other hand on my chest and over my heart, I keep my palms in place.

"Why don't you kiss me instead?"

I lower my head until it's touching her forehead. "Gia." How many times can I utter her name like a warning before I lose my resolve?

"Aren't we at least going to talk about last night?"

I back up a few steps to add some distance between us.

117

Her hands fall to her sides, disappointment on her face, mirroring one of the women in her sketchbook—something she risked her neck to save.

That's something we still haven't talked about. But we're both fairly good at avoiding the heavy stuff.

"I want you." They're the three words I had wanted to hear the night we'd met at the bar, and now, they're three words I need to forget she just said.

"No, you don't." I drag a hand down my face and pinch the skin at the base of my throat as I contemplate how to get her off this idea of there ever being an *us*.

"Why not?" She folds her arms across her chest, which only further accentuates her breasts. "Is this because I'm a virgin?"

Fuck. Me.

A rock—no, a goddamn boulder drops into my stomach, and it sends shock waves throughout every nerve cell in my body.

"You must have known, right? At least suspected. I mean, I've barely done anything with anyone. With my father being the way he is, and Rory wanting me . . . no one was allowed near me." She attempts to close the gap between us, but I lift my hands up in the air like she's dangerous—like Owen is right about her.

The thought of her being a virgin never crossed my mind. And now I'm wondering how I could have been so stupid.

"Gia, you should go shower and get some rest." I can't even entertain finishing this conversation right now.

"Cade, I want my first time to be with you."

I turn my back to her.

"We barely know each other, but I'm finally free—who knows for how long. I want to experience life." Emotion floods her voice. An entire ocean of pain swallows her words. "I want you." Her hand is on my back, but I don't move yet.

"I can't be your first. What you're asking for shouldn't ever happen." I shake my head. "You deserve your first time to be with someone who gives a damn."

"You're lying. I know you care. You wouldn't be here with me right now if you didn't."

"I didn't mean it like that." I curse beneath my breath, turn and face her, my body rock-hard, my want for her obvious. But I'll carve the word *no* into my chest if it'll convince her to back down. "I'm not good for you."

She steps in as if challenging me and lifts her chin, her eyes defiant. "Why don't you let me be the judge of that?"

I don't say anything, and my silence encourages her to continue.

"I've read a lot of books. It was my only escape, and so I've learned how to do things."

"Things?" I grin, and my sudden amused state pisses her off, because she's scowling, folding her arms now like a kid who's not allowed on her favorite amusement ride. And God, would I love her to ride me.

"Jesus, Gia. What the hell are you talking about? I'm not some character in a book." I scratch at my jaw. "And besides, I'm much more original than whatever bedtime stories keep you up at night."

Her eyes draw together, sharp and focused on me. "That's a low blow." Her shoulders start to sag, registering defeat. "I guess I am too young for you."

She shifts away, but without thinking, I grab her wrist and spin her back around, unable to stop myself.

Her hands land on my chest, and neither of us speaks for a minute. I'm trying to come up with another excuse to talk myself off this cliff.

I want to say fuck it and fly.

Her mouth tightens. "What if you were my second?"

I blink. "Second?"

"Yeah. I can go find someone else, and then—"

"No," I say, effectively ending the discussion. My brows lower as I brush her cheek with the back of my hand. "Tell me why you want me to be your first." I'm giving in. I can feel it.

She closes her eyes and lifts her chin, offering me better access to her lips. My balls tighten, the expectation and need mounting. "Because you're the first person I've ever wanted to be with."

That's a pretty simple answer. Maybe even truthful, but still . . .

"But *why*?"

"I knew the second our eyes connected last Friday night— hell, even eight years ago when you first looked into my eyes. I think I've always wanted you." Her eyes flash open, and they're glossy. "I've been waiting for someone like you my entire life."

I let the moment hang between us for a second, before I do the only thing that feels natural and right.

I cup the back of her head and pull her toward me so my mouth can claim hers, so I can be in the exact position I've wanted to be in since we met.

A soft moan escapes her as she increases the pressure against my lips, and her fingertips climb my chest, her hands slinging around the back of my neck.

My tongue finds her, and I reach beneath her ass and guide her up, lifting her legs so she's wrapped tight around my hips.

I break the kiss to ask, "Are you sure?" I want her to say *yes*, but I'm worried, because she should say *no*.

I set her on the couch and look down at her.

Instead of responding, she lifts her tank over her head and unsnaps her bra, tossing it onto the floor.

"I'll take that as a *yes*." I stare at her tits. Her nipples are hard, and her flat stomach lifts as her back arches. She slips her hands down to her hips and works at the material, forcing her pants and thong down to her ankles.

I drop to my knees, ready to worship this woman like she deserves.

A virgin.

I've never been with someone so innocent, and I've never wanted to before. I like experienced women, women who know what to do in bed.

But Gia . . .

I help her finish the job and toss her clothes over my shoulder. She's completely naked on the couch, and for a virgin, she's not even the least bit timid. Her hand finds her center, and she touches herself. And I fight the urge to take control.

"Cade." She shifts up again, bucking her hips in obvious need.

I edge closer to her and kiss the inside of her thigh by her knee. My fingertips glide up the outside of her legs with just the right amount of pressure against her flesh.

Her hands dive into my hair once my mouth reaches her clit, and my tongue moves over her sensitive flesh. She gasps and presses against my mouth, and I force myself to make this last for her—to go slow, so she can enjoy it. I have to assume it's her first time for this, too. I don't want her to ever forget it.

Her quads tighten as my fingertips bury into the flesh of her ass—her perfect ass, which she keeps lifting up into the air. I shift my hands to her hips since she can't stop squirming, and I hold her firmly in place.

She's getting close.

Her panting increases and she drags out my name in one long cry.

She grinds against my face, taking over, and she tastes so goddamn sweet, so good, that my cock is nearly ready to explode just from her getting off, which has never happened to me before.

After she settles down, I trail my lips along the top of her thigh down to her knee.

I lift up, my palms on the couch on each side of her toned legs, and I find her eyes.

"I want you inside of me," she murmurs, her eyes half-lidded. Her body sated.

I bring my hand up and palm her breast.

"Not tonight," I say.

"What?" Worry eases into her voice and covers her face.

"You're a—"

"Virgin." She shakes her head as she reaches for my hand, covering it. "You don't need to be gentle if that's your concern. I want you to enjoy it, too. You can do whatever you want to me."

I smile. "Believe me, I did enjoy it." My other hand goes back between her legs, and she immediately parts for me. "And in a moment, I'll be getting you off again." My jaw tightens as I observe her, loving how she feels, loving the way she moans when I make her come. Hell, I love absolutely everything about this woman. "But we shouldn't—"

"Yo." Owen's voice shatters the moment, disrupting the bubble we're in.

Reality hits.

And I remember where we are and why we're here.

Christ. Talk about timing.

Owen taps hard at the door. "I need in. Now."

Gia gasps, and her cheeks turn brighter than I thought possible. I gather her clothes and hand them to her.

I cross the room once she's dressed, then slide the chain out of place to open the door.

"Gia's father just landed in Miami," Owen says. "We need to go. Now."

13
GIA

My stomach folds in on itself at the sight of the sleek white object before me. Owen said it's a Lear Jet 45XR and that it's the perfect size for us.

"Where's the pilot?" I ask.

"You're looking at him." Owen pats me on the shoulder and winks before climbing the short steps into the plane.

I've only been aboard two planes in my life: one from Rio to Florida, and then the connecting flight to LaGuardia in New York. They were massive compared to this thing. I'm not sure if I can go aboard, but my father is nearby, and if I don't want Cade and Owen to die at his hands . . . maybe Owen's right. We need to get the hell out of the country.

"He's not serious, is he?" If my stomach was knotted before, it's a freaking twisted mess now.

Cade nods. "He did a brief stint as a pilot before joining the SEALs."

I still can't believe we're about to head to Cuba.

"Whose plane is this, anyway?" I call out to Owen once I'm inside.

He comes out of the cockpit wearing mammoth-sized

headphones draped around his neck. "A buddy of mine. He's a spook." Owen points to the seatbelts and tugs his arm down in front of him, motioning for us to strap in.

He's been performing checks on the plane, but I had thought he was bored while waiting for our pilot to show. I had no idea he was capable of actually flying.

"CIA?" Cade's sitting across from me in a creamy leather chair. There are four seats, and they look more like Lazy-Boy loungers. Two chairs face the others, with plenty of leg room between them. "You didn't mention that."

"Does it matter?" Owen shrugs. "He's hooking us up with one of his safe houses in Havana, too. We needed something quick that couldn't be traced to either of us."

"True." Cade's brows drop lower, as if in thought. Maybe this whole situation—the gravity of it all—has finally hit him.

"It'll be wheels up in five." Owen glances at me while placing the earmuff things on. "Hopefully I remember how to do this."

"Not funny." I wait for him to settle back into the cockpit before redirecting my attention to Cade, a man whose face was between my legs not even two hours ago, giving me the first orgasm of my life. Well, the first from another person, at least.

I'm not exactly sure what I was thinking when I practically begged him to take me. But I don't regret it.

"You want something to drink to help ease the tension before we fly?"

"What? Did you raid the hotel minibar before we left?" I smile.

"I did, in fact." He digs into the black leather bag by his feet and retrieves two little blue bottles.

My insides tense immediately, remembering the horrid hugging-the-toilet-bowl experience last night. I couldn't even get myself to have wine at dinner earlier. "I think I'll wait."

He nods and puts them away before clasping his hands together on his lap. He's in loose-fit jeans and a white tee, and his corded forearms draw my eyes.

We didn't have time to shower before we left, but I did manage to swap my clothes for some jeans and a long-sleeved black tee. My hair is still tied up, strands loose and wild, so I push them away from my face and try to settle back against the leather and calm down.

As nervous as I am to get off the ground, staying here would be more nerve-racking.

"Did I tell you how I first discovered what my father does for a living? How I ended up in New York?" My voice breaks through the sound of the swooshing noise once we're in the air. My ears are already closing, making it harder to hear, and the sounds of the plane remind me of the white noise app I use on my phone to help me sleep at night.

Cade's shoulders lift at my words, and his turquoise eyes take hold of mine. "No."

It was a dumb question, because of course I never told him. As acid rolls around in my stomach, I want to look away from him and down at my lap, but I can't seem to rip my gaze free of his. "My mother never told me much about my father when I was growing up, and most of what she did tell me made their love sound like some modern-day Romeo and Juliet story." Memories drop through my mind like paint pouring slowly down a canvas. Some memories are bright orange, but most are midnight black.

"How so?"

Shivers roll over my skin as I speak, as I open my heart up to this man. "My mother lost both of her parents in a car accident when she was five. She was sent to live with her only relative in New York. Her uncle wasn't a great guy—that's all she told me." I press my lips together for a moment, and my forehead pinches tight. "My parents' families didn't approve of their relationship. Mom said things became more dangerous for her in New York, especially once they found out they were having me. So, my father decided it'd be best for my mom and me to start a new life somewhere else. Somewhere safer."

My eyes finally fall shut as my hands clench on my lap, my fingertips biting into my flesh as the pain pricks my insides. "Now, of course, I know the truth. My uncle worked with cartels in South America, and his family and the McCullens were rivals."

"Is your uncle still around?"

"No. He and his family were long gone before I wound up in New York. I never met any of them."

"How exactly did you end up back with your dad? Did you ever see him growing up before then?"

I open my eyes to look at him, and he's leaning forward with his elbows on his knees as he studies me.

Am I really capable of doing this, of telling him the truth of my past?

My stomach wrenches, but I take a steady breath.

"Well, my mother told me that, if anything ever happened to her, I should find my father. She had a picture of him, with his name and last contact information, hidden in a shoe box in her closet." My vision begins to blur a little at the last memory of my mother. "She talked about him when I was younger, telling me how much she loved him, and that he'd come to us when he could—someday." My chest constricts, so I unbuckle the strap.

"You okay?" He removes his belt and crosses over to me, taking the seat at my side.

At the warmth of his hand on mine, my gaze sweeps up to look into his eyes. "He finally showed up, but it was only because I told him my mother was gone." I swallow. "Taken."

His other hand brushes over the back of my cheek, catching a tear. I can't go into more right now.

"I wish I never called, though. I wish I'd never ended up in this life." I sniffle, trying to keep the other tears at bay. "I didn't know how dangerous being in my father's life truly was until I discovered what he actually does."

"How'd it happen?" he asks, his voice low and smooth, but there's true concern on his face as he slowly lowers his other hand back to his lap.

My attention settles on our hands, on our now laced fingers, which form some kind of tight, unified fist.

"I was supposed to be at school, but I skipped class and came home one afternoon." I swipe my other hand down my face, holding it over my mouth for a brief moment before I can continue. "I heard something in the basement. I thought maybe it was a cat, so I went down the stairs to check it out."

So.

Much.

Blood.

That's mostly all I can ever remember. That's mostly what I see when I stand before a canvas and try to paint with color —everything becomes dark red, dripping like a fresh wound.

"Some guy was on our concrete floor, held down by packing tape. And his eyes immediately caught mine when I hit the last step. My dad lifted the blade he was holding when he saw me." The pressure in my stomach intensifies as I relive the moment when my world fell apart for the second time. "I took off. Terrified. And that was the first night I ran away."

"Jesus, Gia. I knew things must have been bad, but—"

"Which is why he can't find you." I pull my hand free from his and stand, but we hit some turbulence, and the plane takes a sharp right. I lose my balance and fall on top of him; he secures me on his lap, my legs draping over the sidearm. "He won't hurt me, but you—"

"Shh." He presses a quick kiss to my lips, which catches me off guard. He pulls back and cups my face with both palms, holding me in place as he stares deep into my eyes.

"We're both going to be okay. You hear me?"

I force a nod, but how can he know for sure?

Then he pulls me in tight, and my face rests at the side of his throat as he holds me.

His heart races, matching mine beat for beat.

And right now, there's nowhere I'd rather be.

"Welcome to Casa de Santos." Owen opens his arms, his back to our temporary home. Not that I can make out much in the dark, but it must have a beach behind it because it sounds like waves are rolling in.

"And you really don't think my father can find us in Cuba?"

"He might find us. I mean, hell, I don't know how the fucker—" Owen cuts himself off. "Eh, how your *dad* found us in Miami either. But it's not as easy to travel to Havana, so we'll be alerted if he steps foot on the island."

"Well, *we* got here without anyone knowing, didn't we?" I challenge.

"Yeah, but only because of my government contacts." Owen smiles as he slings a bag over his shoulder and heads to the front of the house.

"You ready?" Cade's hand rests on my shoulder, and I

take a breath. We're still hanging back at the end of the driveway. We took a cab to a street three blocks away and then walked the rest of the distance. Owen is thorough. He didn't want a cab driver knowing our location.

I should feel confident in his ability to protect us, but I have such a bad feeling in the pit of my stomach—and even having a man like Cade and a former SEAL at my side doesn't seem to take it away.

"Yeah, I think I'm ready." I look up at him, but I can only make out his face because I've adjusted to the darkness after having walked outside for the last fifteen minutes.

"We don't have to do this, you know." His hand finds mine, and he holds it, gently tightening his grasp.

"Do what?"

"Bring down the mob."

I laugh, and a bit of my nervous energy melts away. "Why? What do you suggest? We run away to some little beach and live out our days drinking fruity cocktails while rolling around in the sand?"

I pull my hand from his grip, nearly choking on my own words—on their meaning.

There won't ever be a *me and him.*

It's not in the cards for us.

"If your plans are to remain naked while on that beach, you just might convince me." He closes the small gap between us and rests his hand on my back, pulling me against him.

He can't possibly mean what he said. From my research, he was only in one serious relationship in the last decade, and that was to the governor's daughter. Other than that, he's been spotted with a different woman on his arm each week.

A man like him wouldn't settle down with someone like

me—the daughter of a mobster. Hell, I'm the reason he's in danger.

Plus, he'd never give up his life in New York, and I don't ever want to go back.

But why am I even going down this road of *what-ifs* right now?

"No, Rory has to go down. It's the only way to keep you safe. And the same with my father. He has to be stopped, too."

He may love me, but he's a murderer.

And murderers belong in hell.

"I'll do whatever you want," Cade says in a low, gruff voice, and there's a hint of desire that sweeps through his speech.

"You want to kiss me, don't you?" I smile, our mouths close, but not quite touching. I'm not sure how we went from talking about Rory and my father to this, but when it comes to us, we just might both be a little crazy.

"I want to do a lot more than that." His lips brush across my cheek until they touch the shell of my ear, and his breath has my nipples hardening, my stomach muscles tightening.

"But you'll need your energy for it," he says into my ear as my skin flushes. "A lot of energy."

14

GIA

I'VE BEEN AROUND ENOUGH WEAPONS IN MY LIFE, SO I'M NOT too startled by what I'm seeing, but still—I'm a bit in awe at the sheer volume. The room looks military, for sure. One wall is lined with firearms of all sizes. Bulletproof vests, other tech unknown to me, and computers that look like they double as heavy duty briefcases sit on top of shelves on the other side of the room.

"Wow. An MK23 MOD 0 45-caliber handgun with a suppressor and laser-aiming module." Cade lifts one of the guns, eyeing it. The way he handled the gun back at my apartment suggests he's used one before.

"Say what?" I murmur.

Owen comes up alongside Cade, his eyes fixated on the gleaming metal. "You know your weapons."

"I may not have served like you, but I know a few things. How else do you think I let off steam?" Cade looks back at me, his eyes telling. I'm pretty sure there's one more way . . .

My stomach tightens at the thought of him letting off some steam with me.

Cade repositions the gun on the shelf and faces Owen, his

stance wider, his shoulders square. "Who are you, really? I know you said this place belongs to the CIA—well, one of their dummy shelter companies—but I doubt you could get us access just because this guy is a friend."

Owen's attention shifts to me for a moment, and I can see it in his eyes: distrust. I can't exactly blame him, given who I am. I'm sure he's been itching to ask me why I waited ten years to finally roll over on Rory. Maybe I've been asking myself the same question, but it's not like I didn't try to get away before.

But did I ever try to get any of the McCullens, or my father, locked up?

The word *no* echoes through my mind when Owen looks back at Cade.

"Are you still government?" Cade's question sounds accusatory.

Owen works for Scott & Scott Securities, right? He can't be a civilian and government—aren't those words a contradiction?

"All you need to worry about is that I'm on your side. And, if her dad shows up here we have enough tools at our disposal to start a small war." Owen winks at me, catching me off guard, and a little of his sudden frost starts to dissolve. "Of course, I'm under strict orders not to let the Cubans know I'm here, so we gotta be discreet with our weaponry."

But he's right. He's on our side, thanks to Cade, and I'm not sure if any of this would have been possible if Cade didn't have a friend like Jessica.

How was I ever planning on doing this before Cade galloped into my life on his white horse? He may think he's the dark character in a fairy tale, but to me, hell no—he's the prince.

Owen motions to the door. "I've got something else to show you."

A few minutes later we're at the other side of the huge restored Spanish mansion and in the garage.

"This bad boy is a 1951 Chrysler DeSoto." Owen smooths his hand over the top of the moss-green vehicle. "This beast is built like a tank, even though it's fastened together by makeshift parts, including everything from pieces of a refrigerator to a Russian-built diesel engine." His eyes sparkle as he lifts his palm from the hood and crosses his arms.

Cade looks over at the other vehicle behind us. "I think we'd better stick with the DeSoto. We might attract too much attention from the locals if we drove around in the Ferrari."

"Agreed. Although I wouldn't mind giving it a test drive." Owen flashes me his white teeth before pushing away from the Chrysler to open the garage door. "You feel like exploring the city? No point in sitting around here."

"It would make me feel less like a prisoner," I say.

The house has plenty of room to breathe, but I hate the feeling of being trapped.

My teeth sink into the inside of my lip as I wait for Cade to respond, hoping he'll say *yes*. We slept in late after being up most of the night traveling. We also slept in separate rooms, which was kind of a bummer. Maybe he doesn't want Owen to suspect anything is going on between us.

"You're the expert. If you think we can go into the city, then I'm good with it." Cade eyes Owen.

"Yeah. I don't see why we shouldn't enjoy ourselves," Owen says.

"Thank you!" I smile. "Let me grab my purse. I'll be right back."

Cade nods.

Our shoulders almost touch as I pass him, and there's a little spark. It's a quick magnetic pull between us that sends vibrations down my spine.

The door scrapes shut behind, and I rush for the spiral staircase that's off to the side of the living room.

Once in my room, and the door is shut, I grab my burner phone and power it on.

I don't have much time, so I dial Mya's number with nearly trembling fingers. "I'm in Havana," I say the second she answers.

"What are you doing in Cuba? I thought you were going to stay in Florida for a bit," Mya says.

I wonder where she is because it's dead silent in the background.

"Plans changed. My father showed up in Miami."

I've been keeping Mya up-to-date as much as possible. It hasn't been easy.

Cade almost caught me on the phone yesterday before we left for Florida.

I should tell him what's going on, but I'm afraid he'll try and talk me down. I need to wait for the right time to spring everything on him.

"Shit. Sorry about your pops. But being in Cuba might work out even better. I'll just have to make some adjustments. We weren't expecting for this all to go down so soon. It's crazy, right?"

My heart skips. The excitement of finally being so close to the truth—to answers—is overwhelming. "You really think we can pull this off?"

"That's why you chose me, right? Plus, you knew I'd be a sucker for breaking a story on the mob. We both get what we want."

Mya's taken a lot of risks in her line of work, and she's

still alive. Maybe she has a death wish—who knows? When I offered information in exchange for her help, I warned her what could happen if she writes a story about the McCullens. Her response had let me know I picked the right person: *If it isn't risky, the story probably isn't worth it.*

"Gia?" Cade's voice is like a rumble from beneath the floor. Strong and powerful.

"I have to go, but before I do, did you learn anything new?" I step closer to the door and yell back, "Be right there!"

"I'm in the records department at the police station," she says. "I found the case file that I think is connected to your mom."

My eyes fall shut. My breathing slows. Time stands still as I grasp the importance of her words.

It's no longer a dream, but reality.

"I need some more time to go through everything, but this is it, Gia."

I drop to my knees in one fast movement, growing dizzy. My eyesight is hazed by a sheen of emotion, by my soon-to-fall tears.

Finally . . .

There's a rap at the door, and my shoulders flinch. I end the call without saying goodbye. I slide the phone across the floor and under the queen-sized bed.

"You okay?" Cade's on the other side. He knocks again.

I need to pull myself together.

I need to lie.

"Yeah, I'm just, uh, emotional about everything. It's all a bit much," I say, knowing my broken voice and the pooling in my eyes will give me away once he sees me.

The knob turns, but the door is locked. "Can you let me in?" he asks in a soft voice.

My mother's brown eyes flash into my mind as I stand and let him in.

His large hands are hidden in his pockets, his head bowed before he lifts his gaze to find mine.

And something inside me lets go in that moment. Maybe it's the news from Mya, or maybe it's something even more.

I cup a hand to my mouth and stumble forward. He catches me in his arms in one swift movement, holding me tight as I cry. As I let go.

"Sorry," I say after pulling back a minute later, wiping at my face.

"Never apologize." His brows pull together, and his lips part, but he doesn't say more.

I stare at him, curious as to what he's thinking, and we both stand there, watching each other, but neither of us speaks.

The muscle in his jaw is clenched tight, the veins noticeable in his neck, and I wonder if this is hard for him—dealing with emotions.

It's hard for me.

I've had to bottle up my fear of the McCullens for so long that everything I've lived and experienced feels more like memories from some movie and not part of my actual life.

But the violence, the blood, the pain—it was real. It wasn't scripted.

And then my insides start to shake, and a tightening pain in my gut roars to life.

Guilt. A five-letter word that should be tattooed on the inside of my other arm.

"I should have gone to the police," I whisper, closing my eyes. "I'm as guilty as Rory. As my father." The realization that started gnawing at me in the weapons room now pours into every crevice of my mind, of my soul.

"What?" He reaches for my hand, but I pull back and head to the window, observing the water as it bleeds onto the sand before retracting.

"Gia." He wraps his arms around me, his chin resting on my bare shoulder.

It's a sweet moment. Almost too sweet for people like us. But I don't want him to let go either.

"I've been living a lie, haven't I? And it took me getting away to realize it."

"What are you talking about?"

"I was silent. I saw and heard things, and I didn't do anything. I didn't speak up. I didn't report my father for murder. I was too afraid." I close my eyes. "Because of my fear and my desire to live, others died."

Cade turns me around to face him now, but I won't open my eyes. I can't look at him.

"It's like I killed those people myself. Every time my dad took a life—"

"Stop." His finger touches my lips.

My shoulders roll forward, the shame weighing me down.

"No. It's true. I'm the one who needs retribution, not you." My teeth sink into my lower lip as I finally open my eyes and level my gaze with his. I expect—no, need—for Cade to be my judge, juror, and executioner.

The pad of his thumb glides over my mouth, and then he leans forward and kisses my salty lips, trying to silence my words. But it's a quick kiss before he says, "Maybe we can help each other find a way back into the light."

He doesn't challenge me. He doesn't tell me I'm wrong.

No, he gives me the truth.

And I fall forward and press my face to his chest.

Eight years ago I asked this man to save me . . . never expecting him to actually do just that.

* * *

"THIS CITY IS VINTAGE ON STEROIDS." CADE ADJUSTS HIS shades as we walk through Plaza de Armas. We take in the sights, people, and the architecture.

Stopping in front of one of the book vendors, I pick up a copy of *Little Prince* and flip through the pages before returning it.

"Gracias." I nod at the old man who observes me from his stool, probably hoping I'll buy something. I start to turn away, but Cade's hand captures my wrist, and I still at his touch.

"I can buy it for you if you'd like," he says into my ear.

"Do you have pesos on hand?"

"Good point, but he might take dollars."

"We're trying to blend in." Although I doubt Cade or Owen could ever blend in here.

Everywhere we go they stand out, especially Cade. His confidence, and the way he holds his chin up as he walks, his jaw tight—he could probably part the Red Sea with a look.

Cade releases me, and I continue to browse before facing the white marble statue at the center of the square. I'm not sure who it is, but I assume he's someone important. Being here reminds me of home: the culture, the soft tunes floating in the air around us—the bright buildings that jump from one shade to another as we walk by.

Color.

My art instructor wanted more color in my life.

And here it is.

I just never expected it to be with someone like Cade at my side.

Owen's behind Cade now, and I didn't even realize he'd

been gone. "I exchanged some bills for pesos. You guys up for a cup of joe?"

I smile at Cade. "See."

"What? It's his job to be prepared," Cade says.

"Come on. This place is supposed to have the best coffee." Owen points to a building up ahead.

"Well, I could definitely use a good cup. My mother used to make the best coffee." I was too young to drink it. But I knew based on the aroma it had to be the best tasting in all of Brazil.

Once we have our coffee we sit at a table in front of the café, which is open to the square.

I cross my legs and lean back and close my eyes, allowing the sun to absorb my problems.

"This is good," Owen says, dragging out the last word.

I open my eyes, and there's foam on the top of his upper lip from the latte. "You got a little something." I point to his mouth, and he smiles and wipes it off and licks his finger.

I don't know Owen that well, but he seems to enjoy life and have fun. It's hard for me to picture him ever being military. He doesn't fit the straight-edge image I have in mind. Although, back in that war room, he did start to look the part.

Of course, my dad was Irish military. And so . . .

People have layers.

My eyes go to Cade's lion tattoo, and the sun splays over his arm, making the red ink flare.

He has a lot of layers. I never thought I'd get a chance to peel any of them back, but maybe there's time.

"What exactly do you do at your company?" I ask him.

He grumbles and adjusts his sunglasses as if the topic makes him uncomfortable. "Mostly we buy struggling companies and sell them for parts."

"Hm." I take a sip of my drink, relishing the bold flavors that pop in my mouth. "Not sure what to think about that."

"There's a reason both his sis and brother bailed from the business," Owen says.

"Listen," Cade begins while placing his elbows on the round, black wrought-iron table, leaning forward, "every company would have gone out of business, regardless of my interference. And some we saved. But the others, well, they benefited financially from our deals." He lifts his broad shoulders, defensive. "What we do now, at least, is not as bad as it sounds."

I raise a questioning brow to give him a hard time and flick my gaze to Owen, who appears to be loving every minute of Cade's discomfort.

Owen fights a laugh. "I don't know, man. Jess says differently."

"Yeah, well, Jessica fucking hates me." Cade scratches the back of his neck.

"She can't hate you that much since she's helping you," I say, setting my drink on the table.

"No, she does," Owen says. "But she used to wish his corpse would rot in hell. It's a vast improvement."

My lips part, but Cade doesn't seem the least surprised by his words.

"She's best friends with his sister. And let's just say he hasn't always been brother of the year. Word is he was a major tool."

"At least he's speaking in past tense." I fight a tremble of laughter that rises in my chest. "At least you're not a tool now."

Cade's mouth forms a tight-lipped smile. "True." He removes his sunglasses, which is dangerous for me because I'm not sure if I'll be able to hide my feelings once he's looking at me. Every time our eyes connect, it's as if time stands still. Like we're dancing alone in the middle of a stage, and a thousand people could be watching, and I wouldn't even know. I wouldn't care.

I suck in a breath as he does just that—look at me in the way only he can. It's not like he's undressing me with his eyes. No, it's like he's looking right into my soul.

"So, where's your brother?"

Cade's the one taking a breath now, and for the second time, it looks like he's uncomfortable. "He's in Vegas." His Adam's apple moves in his throat as he fights to counter whatever emotions are seizing hold of him. I'm learning to read him better, even though he tends to hide behind a six-by-two concrete fence.

"What's so bad about Vegas?" I've never been, but it can't be as bad as the *Hangover* movies, right?

"He's racing. *Illegally.*" Cade rolls his eyes and secures his sunglasses back in place.

"Why does he do that?" I ask.

"And that's the million-dollar question." Cade raises his palms in the air. "No goddamn idea."

Owen pushes away from the table and stands. "It's obvious. The adrenaline rush."

"Of course an adrenaline junkie like you would say that." Cade starts to rise, but Owen pats the air, motioning for him to stay seated.

"I'm going to grab us some takeout to bring back to the house. You guys wait here." Owen nods my way and starts through the plaza, and now Cade and I are finally alone. There's so much more I'd like to ask him about who he is and what his life has been like, but I hate when people ask me questions, so I decide not to be a hypocrite.

"My sister's pregnant."

His words, his admission of something so important, catch me off guard. It takes me a second to look up at him. "Congratulations."

"She'll make a great mom. Twin boys." He reaches for his mug. "And her husband was a SEAL, like Owen. He gave it up for his daughter. Had a rough time adjusting, but Noah seems to make my sister happy."

"And if he didn't, why do I get the feeling you'd break his legs?" I wince at my choice of words. That's the mob in me speaking.

"Hell, yes," he says matter-of-factly.

Is it strange that I like his response?

What the hell has living in the world of the McCullens done to me? How have I not realized who I've become until I'm away?

I finish what's left of my coffee, wondering if he's thinking about our earlier conversation and my confession of guilt as if he were my priest.

Speaking of . . . "Are you religious?"

"My parents never took us to church. I don't know all that much about it, to be honest."

"My mother took me every weekend. We lived in a village outside of Rio, but we still had our own church. I think that, during prayer, she was always asking for God to deliver my father to us." My hands fall into my lap, and I thread my fingers together. "How could she want to be with him, knowing what he did? My mother was such a good woman."

"Sometimes love is complicated," he says slowly. "I was in love once. I think I was, at least." He pauses for a moment, and his forehead wrinkles as if he regrets his words.

His attention is cast down, toward his tattoo. "Samantha and I were polar opposites."

"Oh? What happened?" My heart rattles in my chest.

"I was in college in California, and she was this wild bartender slash tattoo artist." His chest lifts as he smiles and looks up, but his eyes are hidden by his glasses, and it keeps me from witnessing any real emotion. "She was a couple of years older than me and was always partying and having fun."

"Let me guess—you weren't a partier." He likes to be in control too much to let loose.

"I was focused on being valedictorian. The pressure from my father was intense, but she got me to have fun sometimes."

"She gave you the tattoo?"

His fingers rush down the ink, stopping at his wrist. "She said I was a lion. Powerful." He smiles. "How could I say *no* to that?"

I chuckle, but I know there's a punch coming.

"Anyway, I was prepping for my final exams, and I wasn't paying attention to what started happening to her."

"Drugs," I mouth the word, unable to stop it from slipping free when I put two and two together.

I've seen so many people fall captive to drugs at Rory's hand.

He nods, slipping a hand beneath his glasses to his temple, pushing two fingers against his flesh as if there's a sudden throb there. "I found her on graduation morning."

The nerves fist in my stomach and my heart breaks for him.

"I never made it to the graduation ceremony. I went to her apartment to pick her up to bring her with me . . . and I found her on the floor. The tubing was still wrapped around her arm —her eyes open."

"Oh, God."

"I checked her pulse, I tried to bring her back, and when nothing worked, I called the one person I never should have. Dad was in California for the ceremony." His forehead has a slight sheen of sweat, and the veins in his forearms darken.

"Do you know what the prick did?" His voice deepens, hate searing through each of his next words as he says, "He took fucking pictures of her body before calling the police. He threatened that if I ever messed up or hung out with the so-called wrong person again, he'd share the pictures of Samantha with my mom and sister—hell, the whole world." The chair legs scrape on the concrete. "My father was an asshole who pretended to be a good guy in a suit." He stands. "At least your father didn't fake it."

"I'm sorry," I whisper the words, knowing such an overused phrase probably won't mean much, and so I stand, too, maneuvering around our table to come before him. I reach for his sunglasses, remove and fold them, holding the black shades in my palm before finding his eyes.

There're no tears. But there's fury, bright and almost toxic, and I can recognize it because I know how it feels to hate someone so much.

I can see now why he likes to go shooting. His father is his target.

Because I'm not good at handling situations like this, I say, "I'm still going to give my dad the worst-father-of-the-year award. But"—I gather some of his shirt in the palm of my free hand, tugging him closer to me—"I'm pretty comfortable with giving your dad second place."

He stares at me for a long moment, and I wonder if I blew it—I killed the moment when Cade King bared his soul to me.

But then . . . his shoulders lift, and his head tips back just a touch as rich, velvety laughter flows from his mouth and deep from his stomach.

After a few seconds, he shakes his head and covers my wrist with his warm, sun-kissed hand. I'm still clinging to the cotton fabric of his T-shirt.

Cade's full lips part, about to speak, but then his attention shifts away.

Owen's standing there, eyeing us, or more specifically, eyeing my hand clutching Cade's shirt. "What'd I miss?" The oil is sweating through the brown bag he has tucked under his arm.

"Um." A gargling sound sputters from my mouth as I attempt to clear my throat, dropping my hand from Cade's shirt in embarrassment. "I think I have a better idea for food," I say after I catch sight of the fresh market stands off in the distance.

Cade steps out of my reach, which makes things a little less awkward in Owen's presence. He glances back, following my gaze. "I don't have any idea how to cook."

Copying Owen's signature move, I wink at the both of them once their attention returns to me. "It's a good thing I do."

15

CADE

OWEN'S STANDING OVER GIA'S SHOULDER, WATCHING HER cook, and I'm a couple feet behind taking in the sight.

My attention keeps drifting down her tan back. She bought a dress at one of the markets when we were out today. It's killing me that Owen is seeing her in it. It shows off too much skin. It's silky and thin, with big bright flowers, and almost her entire back is exposed. She's also not wearing a bra.

When she bought it, she said she wanted to look the part, to feel Cuban or something. I can't remember her exact words, because I was too distracted by the little dimple that popped in her right cheek when she smiled so damn big.

I didn't know cooking could be sexy. Then again, she does so many things that turn me on: the way her nose pinches together when Owen says something funny, or how she rolls her bottom lip between her teeth when she's looking at me.

I still can't believe I told her about Samantha, that I opened up about my past . . . a past where I let a woman die because I was too busy trying to impress my father.

I didn't notice Samantha was in trouble, that she was an addict. I was too self-absorbed to find time to notice anything.

Until today, no one other than my father knew about her.

I don't deserve redemption, but I can relate to what Gia's going through. Her guilt.

"So, this special dish you're making is basically chicken and rice." Owen grins and faces me.

I swallow the rest of the Sangria Gia made and head for the pitcher to refill my glass. As much as I wanted Owen as a buffer yesterday, now I'd prefer he disappear. I don't want to share Gia with anyone. I don't know how much time we have, and I need to soak in every minute, to kiss every inch of her skin.

Gia sets her spoon down and presses her palms to her apron, wiping her hands. "This was my mother's favorite dish."

"And it's Cuban?" I approach the full-range gas stove and inhale the garlic and spices.

"There are different variations of this recipe all over Latin and South America, but my mother preferred to make the Columbian version."

"Any reason why?" Owen leans against the kitchen island, his eyes assessing the scene—basically, Gia and me. It wouldn't take a rocket scientist to figure out what was happening between the two of us, though. Hell, he called me on it last night.

"Columbian food is good, so I hear," I say, as she reaches for the wooden spoon again and dips it into the frying pan.

"My Spanish isn't that great—not as good as my Arabic. But I'm pretty sure *arroz con pollo* still translates into *rice and chicken*," Owen says.

Gia mutters something under her breath, probably in

Portuguese, and offers me a taste. She holds her hand beneath the spoon, our faces close together and my eyes on her, as I take a bite.

The flavors hit my tongue, exploding in my mouth, but it's hard to pay attention to how good it tastes when there's so much damn desire inside me, making me want to go ahead and kick Owen out right the fuck now.

"It's good." I rest a palm on the counter.

She reaches for my mouth, touching my lip. "There was some sauce."

I fight the urge to lick my lip and catch her finger between my teeth.

But Gia is right about the food. It's definitely not like any chicken and rice I've ever eaten. It's a hell of a lot better, in fact.

A little while later and after we're almost done eating, she asks, "Did either of your mothers like to cook?"

Owen looks at me, but I don't say anything. "My mom thinks she can cook, but she's not that great. She usually burns her toast."

A soft laugh rolls from her mouth and hits my chest.

"At least your mom tried. My mom didn't even know where the kitchen was." Maybe an exaggeration, but not by much.

I pause for a second as I think about my childhood, sorting through dozens of memories, trying to snatch a good one that revolves around Mom. Nothing comes to mind.

"My mom didn't give a damn about us. I'm pretty sure she only had kids to keep the money and business in the family. My parents' marriage was practically arranged between two wealthy empires, and my dad tried to force me to do the same."

Fuck me. Did I just—

Owen blinks a few times and guzzles the rest of his drink.

Gia's hands slip to her lap. I think I've made her uncomfortable. I'd blame the truth dump on the Sangria, but I was opening up before that. Plus, it takes a hell of a lot more than three drinks to get me talking.

"My mother liked to say that people tend to act one way on the outside when they're really the opposite on the inside." She lifts her eyes to meet mine. "Maybe your mother was not good at expressing her true feelings. Maybe she didn't know how to show her love, especially if she never had a chance to find her own true love." Her emotions swim beneath the surface of her eyes. "I'm sure she cared about you."

Owen clears his throat after a few seconds. "Well, this has been fun, but I, uh, think I better go do a perimeter check." He stands. "I could be a while." He smiles at Gia. "Thank you for dinner. It was fantastic."

"You're welcome," she answers.

Owen makes eye contact with me next, and it doesn't take a genius to read his hard expression.

He's giving me the green light for something, but it's not to hook up with Gia. No, it's to try and get her to open up more, to find out why Mya's in Brazil. But I don't answer to him. He's getting paid by me.

Once he's gone, she stands and starts removing the plates, so I follow suit and trail after her into the kitchen with the rest of the dirty dishes.

She drops the plates into the sink and faces me.

I set what I'm holding on the marble island and back up to take all of her in.

"Are you okay?" she asks softly, concern resonating throughout her voice.

"I'm great. You?" I expel a deep breath.

"Yes," she almost purrs the word, which has my body tightening with need.

"Then take off your dress."

She squints as if it's bright in here. Her lips tuck in, a little shy, unlike how she was last night, and she hooks her fingers beneath the thin sleeves. The dress drops to her bare feet.

I lower my forehead, observing her smooth center. "You're not wearing underwear."

"I wanted to be prepared." She tugs her plump bottom lip back between her teeth, chewing on it.

"And Owen was in the room." My voice grows tense. "Don't do that again," I grind out, maybe rougher than necessary.

"Okay," she whispers and takes a step forward, over her dress.

I hold up my hand. "Stop."

A dark brow arches in question. "What?"

"I just want to look at you for a second." I start at her painted black toenails. The color would normally be fitting for her, but I like the idea of her sporting a red or pink—something bold and bright to match who she is on the inside.

From her slim ankles to her bronzed and toned calf muscles, she's absolutely stunning. And once I reach her full tits, my mouth starts to go dry.

"Do you like what you see?"

I take a slow breath and try to calm my heartbeat, to force myself to do this right. She deserves sweet. She deserves the fucking world.

"You're not saying anything." Her hands clench at her sides, nerves striking her. Her inexperience is obvious.

Can I really do this? Well . . . that's what I should be asking myself. But I'm not.

I stride forward slowly, half expecting her to stumble back as if I'm the lion on the inside of my arm—dangerous.

Fuck. Is she dangerous, like Owen said? Or am I?

Maybe we both are.

I reach out and drag my knuckles up the middle of her breasts before palming her cheek.

She arches against me, her nipples brushing against the fabric of my T-shirt.

"I want this to last as long as possible. I want you to remember everything."

She nuzzles her nose up against my palm before kissing it. "I'm pretty sure I'll never be able to forget tonight. But maybe we could go to my room, in case Owen comes back."

I assume he'll be a while, but the thought of him waltzing in while she's naked, sweaty, and riding me—no, I can't take that risk.

I drop my hold of her and pat my front pocket to ensure I remembered condoms.

"Go ahead. Let me grab your dress and some water." I shouldn't care about hiding the evidence of what Gia and I do. It's not Owen's business, but he's putting his neck on the line for us, so I'll try to respect that.

"Okay."

Her slim waist and an ass I want to sink my teeth into hold my attention as she moves across the room and to the stairs.

Once I have the dress and bottle in hand, I rush up after her.

When I enter the bedroom, the curtains are pulled open, allowing the moonlight to wash over the room and across her body, which is splayed out on the bed, her hand on her stomach, her head on the pillow.

She's a masterpiece. A work of art. And I already know that one time with her won't ever be enough.

"I need you. So goddamn much." With a twist of the lock and the bottle and dress tossed to the floor, I pull my shirt off as fast as possible.

She pushes up, resting back on her elbows, and studies me.

I'm already barefoot, so once I place the condoms on the nightstand by the bed, I unbutton my jeans and slide them and my boxers down in one swift movement. Her gaze drops below my hips to where my hand is, to where I'm pumping.

My eyes adjust to the light, and I notice her thighs squeeze together, so I kneel on the bed and drop over her, caging her with my body. She looks up at me while her fingers caress the edges of my muscled arms.

I would give anything to drive into her right now, to spread her legs apart and take her all at once.

I lower my hips so she can feel my hard length against her, and she immediately meets my body, grinding against me, letting me know she wants me as much as I want her.

I keep one hand braced over her shoulder to keep my weight off her, and then our lips meet.

Slow, I remind myself.

A soft mewl escapes her mouth and her fingertips bite into my shoulder blades. She's hanging on to me tight as if I'm already plowing deep.

I lift up to break the kiss, so I can look into her eyes. "If you want this to last, you need to slow down. I have control, but if you keep rubbing against me like this, I'm going to lose it."

"Mm." She wraps her hands around my neck, tugging me closer, and she bumps her slit against my tip.

She's playing dirty.

"Gia," I warn, as my hand drops down between us and my thumb rolls over her, feeling her wetness.

She gasps when two fingers slide inside of her.

A slur of syllables, or maybe she's speaking Portuguese, escapes her mouth as she tips her head back, still hanging on to my neck, and I thrust my fingers in and out of her again and again. "Please. I don't want to come without you being in me."

I drop my head closer so she can feel my breath at her ear. "Baby, you're going to be coming all night. Don't worry."

And within a minute, her hips are gyrating against my palm, and she's crying as shudders rock through her body. When she lowers her ass back down on the bed, I shift up to my knees and stare down at her.

Her eyes are closed, her breathing heavy. Her nipples are tight and perky like she's cold. And so, that's where I decide to take my time next.

I cup her breasts and massage, the pressure in my balls building.

When her eyes find mine again, there's a hint of a smile there. She's ready to go again.

That's my girl.

She reaches between my legs for my shaft, and I grunt and almost drop my weight onto her as she fists me with both hands, moving up and down.

I release a hand on one of her tits to hold my weight up, and I glance down between us at her hands before catching her eyes.

I lean forward and kiss her, missing the taste of her tongue in my mouth, and my other hand shifts beneath her ass cheeks, digging my fingers into her tight flesh.

"I want to get you off, too," she cries against my lips a few minutes later.

She has no idea how strong I am—that there's no fucking way I'll bust my load for the first time with her in any other way than being inside of her.

"Later," I murmur.

She pouts, and so I nip at her lip and tug at it for a moment as her hands release me and slide up my abs.

She starts rotating her hips again, begging for my touch, and I want to give it to her—but the wait . . . the agony of the wait—is something that will only heighten her pleasure, and so I push back up and slide off the bed into a standing position.

She sits up, her brows knitted. "What are you doing?" Worry flutters across her pretty face.

"I need you as ready for me as possible before I fill you. It's going to hurt."

"I *am* ready."

"You're almost ready." I grab a foil pack, but I'm unable to take my eyes off her as she watches me roll the condom over my length.

My thighs are tight, the muscles tense and almost achy. And I'm going to do something I've never done before. I'm going to give her the control.

Well, in a minute, at least.

First I'm going to drive her goddamn wild.

"I want you to hold the headboard." I tip my chin to the black metal rods that look like a gated fence. "Get comfortable, grab hold of the poles, and don't let go."

"Why?"

"Why do you think?" I join her back on the bed as she settles down and does what I ask.

A guttural moan slips free from her when my mouth presses to her center, my tongue darting up and down, stroking her already sensitive flesh. I need her to be as wet as possible to reduce the pain.

When her hands thread my hair, I shift up just enough to say, "Get your hands back on the headboard." I wait until she's done what I've demanded and continue to torment her with my mouth.

"Cade," she says my name in a frenzied panic. "Cade, please." More panting. "I. Want. You."

She's close. Too close. And so, now is my cue.

"And you can have me." I move next to her, and she sits up. "Right now." And I need it to be now, before I do, in fact, lose my mind. "But I want you to be on top. I think it'll hurt less." I've never been with a virgin, but I'm assuming that if she's in control of how much pressure she can take, it should be more comfortable. And I'm not sure if I'll be able to hold back from pushing too hard.

"But, I . . ." Her eyes are pinned to my massive erection.

"Do you want to stop?" My heart finds my throat.

"God, no. I just don't know how to—"

I grin. "It'll come to you. I promise." I reach for her and pull her on top of me, too damn anxious to wait any longer. I need to feel this woman as much as I need air to breathe. Probably more.

"If it hurts, just—" Before I can finish, she sits on my shaft, swallowing every fucking inch of me in one quick movement, and my head nearly melds into the pillow as she cries out.

"Jesus, Gia," I rasp.

She doesn't move. Her body is completely still, and I'm so deep inside of her that our hip bones are touching.

"Are you okay?" I look at her face, and her eyes are closed. Worry crawls through me, but before I get a chance to digest the moment, her eyelashes flutter open, and she starts to lift up slowly, before crashing down hard. "Holy fuck."

Her palms are on my chest, her fingertips digging in, and she starts moving up and down, faster and faster.

Every sensation, every movement of her body—I feel like I'm fifteen again, losing my own goddamn virginity.

This is . . . *new.*

And unexpected.

She's so damn wet around my cock. Her chest rises and falls, and she leans forward more to connect even deeper.

"Cade," she drags my name out in one long breath, and everything inside of me is burning to be on top now.

I lift her up and pull out before flipping her to her back. She wraps her hands around my biceps and squeezes in preparation, and I thrust inside of her hard and fast without thinking. She bucks up off the bed, and we crash into each other.

And I pull back and do it again.

She's so wet. Much looser now. And she's enjoying it, which means there's no pain—and so I don't hold back. Hell, I can't hold back.

She curses and then bites my shoulder as she comes, her body moving with mine like a dance that only we know.

I fuck her until I can't see straight, and then, and only then, do I allow myself release. I allow myself to give in to what this is—to give in to her.

I remain inside of her, worried about how sore she'll be, and I want to ease out of her, just in case. Of course, as hard as I was pumping before, I'm worried about whether she'll be able to walk tomorrow.

I drop my face to her ear and whisper, "Are you okay?"

She turns and kisses my cheek. "You have no idea just how okay I am."

"Oh, I think I do," I say with a smile and slowly pull out and roll to the side.

I place my hand between her legs, but she flinches and faces me.

"Are you in pain?"

She chuckles. "Not yet, but I'll probably be tomorrow."

"I'll be sure to give you a morning-after treatment." I wet my lips, and she squeezes my hand with her thighs. "Mm. Maybe I don't want to wait for the morning."

And I don't let her.

After another hour of our bodies tangling together in ways that should far surpass the books she's read, I wake to the sound of a vibration beneath the bed.

I glance over at Gia. Her arm is draped over my chest, the silk sheet below her gorgeous round tits, so I move her arm and pull the sheet up beneath her chin to keep her warm.

Rolling out of bed, I look beneath it to find the source of the noise.

A small red light gives way to the object thrumming against the wood floor.

I reach out and snatch the object, then head to the connecting bathroom.

Who would be calling this late at night? And what the hell is Gia doing with a phone under the bed?

I close the door and answer the call.

My heartbeat escalates when I hear a familiar voice on the other end of the line repeating Gia's name over and over.

"It's not Gia. It's Cade," I finally say.

16

GIA

THE MORNING SUN PIERCES THROUGH THE WINDOW, TRYING TO wake the dead—the dead being me.

A groan escapes my lips.

Every fibrous tissue in my thighs aches, as if I did a ten-mile run and—

Cade.

I pop upright, the disoriented state fading fast with the realization that last night wasn't a dream.

I had sex.

For hours.

And he's gone. The room feels empty without his massive presence occupying the space.

I look at my closed door, wondering if he went to his room to sleep so Owen wouldn't know what happened.

Of course, based on my appearance right now it'd be obvious we had sex.

For one, I'm naked. Not that I'm about to go traipsing around the house like this with Owen downstairs. I don't want Cade having a heart attack.

But my hair . . . well, it looks like I purposely screwed it up for some exotic Vogue fashion shoot or a Girls Gone Wild video.

I did go a little wild, though.

And it was cathartic. He made me feel so at ease with my body. How could I not let loose with someone like him?

I'm sore, there's a definite achiness between my legs, but God, it was worth it.

Cade was my first.

Part of me wishes he could also be my last.

But I can't think too much about that right now, so I grab a quick shower, leave my hair wet but brushed, and slip on a pair of jeans and a tee I picked up yesterday. In gold letters, it says, *I left my heart in Havana.*

As I head to the door, I catch sight of my dress from last night on the floor. The memory of being in Cade's arms resurfaces. Heat gathers in my stomach as I think about his broad chest and the feel of his muscles beneath my palms.

It takes me a minute to compose myself and reel in the red in my cheeks before I exit and pad down the stairs slowly, my quads on fire.

At the bottom of the steps, I halt at the sight before me.

Cade's sitting in the floral lounge chair in the living area, with his ankle crossed over his knee, and there's a distinct scowl marking his face.

Owen is hanging back behind the chair, arms crossed, and an equally pissed-off look replaces his normally carefree one.

"Sit," Cade commands.

My shoulders flinch at the tone of his voice.

What the hell happened this morning?

I do as he says, taking a seat opposite him, welcoming the space between us, since his dark mood is occupying plenty already.

And that's when I see it.

A small black object is pressed to his thigh beneath his palm, and I swallow as unease spills through me.

"Is that my phone?"

Cade takes a long, deep breath. The silence is almost too much. His stare nearly cuts through me as I wait for him to speak. I look at Owen when Cade remains quiet.

Owen grumbles then says, "At what point were you going to tell us that this was never about the McCullens, that this was about putting yourself—and us—in some serious shit by trying to take down a goddamn human trafficking organization? A little heads-up about what we were dealing with would've been nice."

"What—how . . .?" I'm all blank thoughts and misplaced words. My stomach squeezes, knotting hard and fast. And Cade is looking at me as if he's disappointed.

"Mya called," Owen says as my eyes sweep back to the phone, his words confirmation that it's mine.

"Were you snooping through my things?" I stand and plant my hands on my hips, staring down at Cade, but his face remains the same: a clenched jaw with normally soft blue eyes that have gone dark.

"Mya called in the middle of the night. I heard it vibrate under the bed." Cade's voice is like hot water pouring over an open wound, but my eyes widen in recognition of what his words mean.

"What—what'd she say?" My emotions are all mixed up right now, but I have to focus on what matters.

Mya must have news.

Cade lifts the phone and tosses it at me. He rises and hides his hands in his pockets, but he can't hide his emotions. He's pissed.

I stand and go to him. When I reach for his arm, he doesn't pull away, at least.

The way his eyes drop to my fingers has me worried that I don't have much time to explain. But, damn it, he still hasn't answered my question.

"I, um, this is still about getting away from Rory." I lift my hand from his arm and back up a step. "It was you who demanded I run. You sped up my timeline to get away. I didn't ask—" I stop myself, knowing that's not the point. I should have told them the truth as soon as we ran, but everything happened so fast, and then I was afraid they'd try to stop me if they discovered the truth, and so . . .

"What's this really about?" Owen asks.

"Her mother," Cade says in a low voice.

Breathe in through the nose; exhale through the mouth: that's what my yoga instructor always says. Yeah, well, right now I can't follow his advice because I'm taking so many short and rapid breaths, I'm lightheaded. "Give me a second."

I drop the phone on the chair, even though I want to use it and call Mya for answers this second.

But I also need them on my side, so I turn before they can say anything and run to my room. There's something I need in order to help them understand.

When I return, their backs are to me and they're talking, but too quietly for me to hear.

I clear my throat to alert them to my presence, and I hold my sketchpad out once Cade faces me. His brows draw tight as he tries to put two and two together.

It's complicated, but I'm going to try.

Cade strides toward me and takes the pad, but he doesn't open it. He lowers it, resting it against his outer thigh as he waits for me to speak.

"When Richard McCullen got sentenced for life, I decided it was finally my chance to try and get free. It was my chance to find my mother." My hand presses to my abdomen to ground myself, to maintain the strength I need for this confession.

His attention flicks to my wrist, to the angel wings there.

I point to the sketchpad, and he lifts it but still doesn't open it. And his eyes take forever to work back up to mine.

"My mother used to sell her art in a café in Rio. She was an artist, too. Her work sold better in an area that mostly had tourists—a lot of *gringos*. Uh, non-Brazilians."

The first image in the sketchpad is now open, and Cade is looking at it. It's a sixteen-year-old girl.

"A lot of those girls worked the streets. I used to sit in the café and sketch what I saw. The faces of these girls—their haunted eyes, their sadness . . . My mother finally told me who they were when I was fifteen. She called them *os tomadas*, which means *the taken ones.* Some were poor and saw it as a chance to make money, but most were forced into the life."

"By traffickers," Owen bites out like he wants to rip someone's face off.

I nod. "There was a trap door in our home beneath the kitchen, and Mother said if anyone ever came to our home to try and take me, I should hide there." My eyes fall shut as the darkness of my past blankets my mind. "She thought we'd be safe since we lived outside the city, but we must have been followed home one time. A dark SUV had rolled up outside. She told me to hide, that she'd be down with me in a minute."

"But the room wasn't big enough for two," Owen says, his voice grave. It's as if he's experienced a massive pain before, too.

"I should've gone out to help her." My voice quavers. "She shouldn't have been taken because of me."

"You both would have been kidnapped. She sacrificed

herself to save you," Owen says, but it's Cade I'm looking at, wondering what he's thinking and feeling.

He's staring down at the last paper, the one of my mother. The one I drew of her once I arrived in New York with my father.

I rest my fingertips on her drawn face, a face that looks so much like mine.

"It's been ten years. That's a long time," Owen says.

"I know, but I've been trying to find her all my life. This is the closest I've ever come to getting answers. I have to know what happened to her. What if she's still alive?" My eyes connect with Cade's.

"Who told you she wasn't?" Owen interrupts my intense focus on the man who made love to me last night, the man whose very soul feels like it's bleeding into mine right now—keeping me safe, even if he's angry at me for hiding the truth.

"After my dad brought me to New York, he disappeared the very next day to go and find her. He had no choice but to leave me with Richard McCullen, I guess."

Owen asks, "And if a notorious hitman couldn't find her, what makes you think you can?"

Cade remains silent, and I wish he'd say something.

"He said he found her, but it was too late. She was dead."

"I don't get it." Owen falls back onto the couch.

"I didn't believe him. I thought—I still think . . . maybe he lied to try and keep me from going back to Brazil. And with Rory taking over the business, I knew I had to find a way out soon, before he—" I let the words die on my tongue when I notice Cade's grip tighten on the pad, the anger flaring hotter within him. "It made sense to try and get away while also discovering the truth about my mom."

"Mya never came to you about Rory. You went to her." Cade hands me the pad, and I close it, pressing it between my palms. "The art classes were your idea." He's not asking questions; he's making statements, and now I have to wonder how long of a conversation he had with her because it sure as hell sounds like he knows a lot.

"Did she tell you that?" I ask.

"I know her. She's the daughter of a friend, and she came snooping around my office for information last Monday."

"She never mentioned she knew you."

"Would it have mattered? She only cared about you getting away, right? It didn't matter how it happened."

"Hey, you only just showed up in my life. Mya and I have been going at this for weeks," I snap.

"Yeah, well, at what point were you going to ask me to take you to Brazil?" Cade's face is unreadable now as he looks at me. "And did you two plan on taking down traffickers by yourselves?" He turns his back and curses beneath his breath. "Are you out of your goddamn mind?"

I drop the pad on the chair to rest my hand on his back. But this time, he jerks away and stalks across the room, an icy path in his wake.

He presses a palm to the glass door, but he could be miles away right now; that's how it feels, at least.

"I approached Mya because she's one of the best investigative reporters in New York, and she covers a lot of international stories. Plus, when we spoke, she said she had a lot of connections to people who could help." I clear my throat to try and get rid of my frustration. "*Again*, you are new to my life. We were going to figure this out before you arrived with your cape."

My defensive walls are locked and loaded, and a burst of adrenaline has me unable to back down, even if it's not the best idea right now.

"What'd you promise her in return for the help?" Owen leans forward, resting his elbows on his knees. "Rory?"

"I was planning to get away as soon as Mya found out who took my mom, but then Cade changed everything."

"Sorry, did I screw up your plan to get killed?" Cade keeps his back to us.

"Well"—Owen shoves up to his feet—"Mya not only found out who took your mom but also the buyer. Both of those men are dead."

My stomach drops, and so do I. I fall to my knees, pressing a hand to my mouth, trying to understand what this means. It takes me a moment before I ask, "Is anyone connected to this alive? Anyone who might know what happened to her?"

Cade's before me now, crouched down and offering a hand to help me rise. His face is still expressionless, but there's less tension between us now.

I gather the strength to take his hand and stand.

"Jess sped up the process and hacked into the Rio police records. The group who kidnapped your mom . . . well, the main guys were killed within a week of taking her, and the rest were arrested right after. Your mom had already been sold before that happened," Owen explains.

"My father," I whisper and release Cade's hand. "He killed them, didn't he?"

"I'm thinking it's not a coincidence," Owen says. "And the guy who, uh, purchased your mother—he died a few days after the others." He scrubs a hand down his jaw. "There's no record of death for your mom."

"So she could be alive," I say.

"I don't want you to get your hopes up." Owen's brows drop. "We don't know anything for sure yet."

"You're going to help me, right? You'll help me find her?"

"I can't promise you anything," Owen says. "We'll look into it, but I've asked Mya to back off. It's too dangerous, especially with Carlos Perozo alive. He's the brother of the man who bought your mom."

"So there is someone connected to all of this." My hands tighten into knots at my sides.

"Perozo took over his brother's business, and from the looks of it, he's even more dangerous."

Carlos could have my mother.

My mother could be alive.

"I know what you're thinking, but we still have to worry about your father and Rory's men coming after us. Let's handle one thing at a time." Owen releases a deep breath. "I need to get back on the phone with Jess. Is there anything else you think we ought to know?"

I shake my head. "I'm sorry," I finally say.

He studies me for a minute, and I can't quite get a read on what he's thinking. "Listen, I'm sorry about your mom and what you went through, and I get you want to find her, but you let others die at Rory's and your father's hands for years until it was convenient for you to do the right thing."

"Owen." Cade's eyes narrow, and the muscle in his jaw ticks. He crosses the room and faces him. "Don't talk to her like that."

"But he's right. You know he's right. This is my fault." I look toward the windows. "I need air." I head to the back door and slide it open. Then I take off in a run. My legs might hurt, my stomach might be a shaky mess, but I need to get away.

The sand is soft between my toes, and there're no people in sight. The CIA must own at least a mile of this beach.

"Gia."

I glance over my shoulder to see Cade jogging behind me.

"Leave, please." I look back ahead, pumping my arms at my sides to go faster, but I catch sight of him out of the corner of my eye not even a few seconds later.

"I'll stay quiet, but I'm not going anywhere."

"Fine," I mutter and continue to run until I see people up ahead.

I stop and face him, my hands on my hips to catch my breath. He's not even the least bit winded.

"He shouldn't have said that to you. He doesn't know you like I do."

"But you're angry with me, too."

He blows out a breath and hangs his head forward. "I'm angry that someone could have gotten hurt. You left us in the dark, which put us all at an even greater risk."

"I was afraid you'd make me back down."

"You're damn right I'm going to make you back down."

"What?"

He braces me by the elbows. "Do you really think I'll let you run off to Brazil and get yourself killed? Are you insane? I care about you. I made the commitment to keep you safe back in New York, and that's exactly what I'm going to do."

"No." I try to break free of his grip, but he won't let go. "Cade," I beg.

"I never said I wouldn't find your mother; I'm just saying you won't be risking your neck to do it."

I sniffle, trying to hold back a sob.

He shifts his hands up to cup my face. "I'll go to the ends of the fucking earth to give you what you want. You know that, right?"

At his words, I stumble forward and into his arms, allowing the tears to scroll down my face.

* * *

"I WAS A DICK. I'M SORRY." OWEN EXTENDS AN OPEN BEER bottle my way.

"Cade send you out here?" I rest my sketchpad on my lap and take the beer.

He plops down in the chair next to me on the patio and directs his focus out on the beach as the dark water glimmers beneath the moonlight. "No."

"Liar."

The side of his mouth curves up. "He's right, though. I was out of line." He swallows some of his beer, and I do the same, even though there's an intense pressure working at my temples.

His fingertips drum his thigh as an uncomfortable silence stretches between us.

"So, uh, what are you drawing?" he asks a few minutes later.

A breeze nips my shoulders and blows strands of hair into my face.

"Nothing. Just staring at a blank page."

"Well, what do you *want* to draw?" He lifts a brow as our eyes meet.

"I was kind of hoping for some inspiration. I thought maybe drawing would take my mind off things, but my creativity is jammed up right now."

"Yeah? I work better under pressure."

"In your line of work, that's probably a good thing." I glance over my shoulder, wondering where Cade is, and Owen reads my thoughts.

"He's on the phone with his brother-in-law, Noah. Checking on his sister."

My lips tighten as I consider how many lives I've

messed up.

"So you and Noah were on the same team in the SEALs?" I don't know much about the military, aside from what I've seen on TV.

"No, we ended up on different teams, but we trained together."

"Cade said Noah left the service for his daughter. What about you? Um, if you don't mind my asking."

Owen presses a hand beneath his chin and pushes up on it, cracking his neck. "Classified," he says. I almost expect him to wink like usual, but instead, I realize he's dead serious.

"Oh." I take a sip of my beer, the tangy sour flavor kicking up in the back of my throat. "Can I try a different question?"

He grins. "You can try."

"Fair enough." I set the beer next to my chair and shift to the left to better face him. "Did your team ever go after human traffickers?"

The rim of the bottle rests near his lips, but he doesn't drink it. He holds it there for a moment before lowering it to his lap. "We're usually only sent on ops that involve American lives. That, or a threat to American soil in some way or another. You take Panama, for instance, back in the late eighties, and—" He stops himself, and a smile flickers briefly across his face. "To answer your question, I've dealt with traffickers before."

"And?" I swallow a lump in my throat.

He rests his head on the back of the seat and closes his eyes. "The objective was a rescue mission, and we rescued the asset."

"And the people who took the, uh, asset?"

"It wasn't about them. We got our person, and we left."

My stomach tightens. "What?" My hands clutch the pad in my lap, and then I press it to my chest as I think about what he said.

"We don't choose our targets. We take orders from the government, and they tell us who to kill and who to keep alive." His head turns, and he opens his eyes.

He's speaking in the present tense, and I'm beginning to wonder if Cade's suspicions about Owen are right. Is he still connected to the government?

"Life isn't all sugar and sweet tea, love. If anyone should get that, it's you."

My head butts against the back of the chair.

Would rescuing my mom be enough for me? If she's alive, that is . . .

I'd want payback. I'm pretty sure I'd be comfortable with blood on my hands if it meant retribution for my mom and all those taken.

My hands tremble as I release my grip on the sketchpad and look at my fingers, wondering if I'm capable of being a murderer, like my father.

"Hey, you okay?" Owen reaches over, and his fingers wrap around my forearm.

"Uh, yeah. I think I'd better get some sleep. It's been a long day."

He nods. "Maybe we'll know more tomorrow."

"I hope so." I leave the beer outside and head for the house with the sketchpad in hand. "Thank you for everything," I say before going inside.

I slide the door closed, watching Owen slouch back in his seat, when Cade's voice flows over my skin, making the hairs on my neck stand.

"How are you?"

"As good as can be, I guess." When I face him, he's

leaning against the column that serves as part of the entrance to the kitchen area. "How's your sister?"

"She's fine."

"Good."

There's a weird awkwardness that fills the room, and I'm swimming in a sea of uncertainty.

"I'm gonna go to bed." I stop at the base of the stairs, my heart climbing up into my throat, but my feet remain firmly in place.

The wood floor creaks behind me, and my eyes fall shut as the air seems to shift and grow warmer the closer he gets.

I don't think either of us is in the mood to have sex after today, and yet, little pulses shoot down my core and between my thighs.

"I shouldn't want you right now," he murmurs into my ear, and a rush of air escapes my lips.

His fingers glide down my arm, evoking chills. He takes the sketchpad and gently sets it on the first step.

"I'd love to draw you some day." He could inspire an entire collection of paintings.

"Me?" A quick and low rumble of laughter from his chest moves straight through my back.

I try to shift around to see him, to let him know I'm serious, but he ropes a hand around my abdomen, holding me tight against him.

In response, I shift my hips in a circular motion, as much as his grip will allow.

The idea of Owen coming in and catching us almost turns me on even more. I never knew I could be like this, but I'm beginning to realize I'm not as innocent as I've tried to convince myself all these years.

"You." He grunts out the word. "Upstairs. Now."

I chuckle as I maneuver an arm free from the caged

position and grip hold of his side—trying to bring our bodies even closer together.

"What'd I say?" His voice is deep, commanding, and almost chilling.

"Mm. You need to let go of me, then."

His hand shifts beneath my T-shirt and up my stomach, and his fingers pluck the material of my bra out of the way before he pinches me, twisting my nipple. It's a strange combination of both pleasure and pain. I sink my teeth into my bottom lip and close my eyes, growing wetter by the second.

A coolness sweeps over my skin when Cade drops his hands and steps back so I can ascend the stairs.

Without wasting time, I rip off my T-shirt and toss it over my shoulder as I dash away.

A few seconds later I jump onto my bed like we're about to have one of those slumber parties I always wished I had friends for—not that I'd ever let them come to my house of horror.

I clutch a pillow to my now naked chest, the bra having come off the moment I entered the room and turned on the light.

He's standing in the doorway, hands in his pockets, and he's studying me with brows raised. "A pillow fight?" He laughs. "You know I'd win."

"Have you been in one before?"

He looks up at the ceiling out of the corner of his eyes in thought. "This would be a first."

"For me, too." I drop the pillow so he can look at my breasts, hoping he'll do whatever that thing was he was doing downstairs to my nipples that made me lose my mind.

"Maybe we skip it, though," I suggest.

He closes the door and peels off his shirt. "Agreed."

I follow his strong hands as they start at the button of his jeans.

His rippled muscles, tight abdomen, and the sexy V above his hip bones . . . I wet my lips in anticipation.

"But first, I want to try something I've never done before."

"Haven't we done almost everything already?" He's standing naked in front of the bed, and I crouch down and jump off the bed.

He faces me and smiles, and I point to his hard cock. "I've never . . . you know."

He arches a brow and reaches for my denim and slowly shoves my pants and underwear down until they drop to my ankles.

"The thing is—right now, I'd like a tasting of my own." He gently nudges me onto the bed and on my back.

He kneels before me, lifts my legs to rest on his shoulders, and positions his mouth near my center.

"I never did get a chance to give you that morning-after cure."

I jerk at the soft lick of his tongue on my flesh. "Mm. You're right. Don't let me stop you then."

A soft vibration from a light laugh tickles me, and my legs tighten. I fight back the impulse to moan too loud.

But then I decide—fuck it.

I am who I am. No sense hiding behind a lie anymore.

Sinner or saint? I'm beginning to think that, when I'm with Cade, I can be both.

And so, I scream his name as I come, as I let loose and let go, so damn thankful that Cade King walked into my life when he did.

He set me free.

But he also woke me up.

GIA

"ONE OF THESE DAYS, YOU'RE GOING TO GIVE ME A HEART attack." Cade's voice is a husky whisper as he drags out his words.

I press the back of my hand to my lips, stifling a chuckle. I love making this man lose his mind with only my mouth.

He runs his fingers through his whiskey-brown hair, smiles, and tugs me up off the ground. We both fall onto the bed.

Our naked and sweaty bodies press together, and I grind against him, unable to help myself whenever we're in this position.

His irises are darker than normal, more like a mix of titanium and midnight blue.

"We should probably leave this room at some point." He brushes a hand down the side of my cheek.

I close my eyes and lower my face so our noses touch. "Do we have to?"

"Trust me, I've loved doing nothing but you for almost two days straight."

Two days of sitting around waiting for news from Jessica

could have been as exciting as watching paint dry, but luckily for me, Cade has kept my mind busy. Well, more like my body.

I guess we should get some air, though.

I huff and push off his hard chest, but he catches me by the elbows, yanks me back down, and kisses me.

I moan against his mouth. Every time we kiss, I feel like it's our first, like it'll always be special.

"Now you can get up," he says a minute later, after having turned my body to a sack of mush with that skilled tongue of his.

I finally stand, and he props an arm up behind his head.

I look at the ink there, remembering the woman he lost. "You, uh, want to join me in the shower?"

"You know what would happen if I did. We'd be up here for the rest of the day. And as much as I like that idea, you need to eat something." He smiles. "Energy, remember?"

I laugh. "Yes, sir." I start for the bathroom and purposely sway my hips to give him the view of my ass I worked damn hard to get with years of yoga.

I peek over my shoulder at him, and he's the one biting his lip this time.

"You really don't want to eat, do you?" He grins, his eyes darkening even more. "Get over here."

* * *

Night turns into morning, and when I wake, Cade's not in bed. I've discovered something since our arrival in Cuba. When I'm with Cade, I could paint a freaking rainbow, but when he's not around, a chill sets into my bones.

After getting dressed, I go downstairs to find the guys, but I don't see them.

There's a faint noise coming from the other side of the house, so I wander down the hall, searching them out.

I soon hear, "You're not a soldier. You can't take the goddamn traffickers on yourself." Owen's voice reverberates through the hall. It sounds like he's in the weapons room.

I edge closer, then hang back outside the door to listen. I'm afraid they'll end their conversation if they hear me, but since I've spent ten years eavesdropping unseen, I'm a bit of an expert at it.

But they wouldn't have left the door cracked open if they were trying to keep something from me, right?

"And if you're not going to do it, I have to. I promised Gia."

"The case is in government hands. There's nothing we can do right now. I'm sorry."

"What?" I yank the door all the way open.

Cade's standing in front of the weapons wall with his hands on his hips.

"What's going on?" I confront Owen and cross my arms.

"Well." Owen wraps a hand around the back of his neck and looks at Cade for a brief moment before directing his focus back to me. There's something off about him. He's super tense in his stance, and there are dark circles under his eyes as if he hasn't slept all night.

"Whatever you're about to say, it had better not have to do with my mother." I steal a glimpse of the open laptop on the table behind Owen, noticing a map of Brazil on-screen. "What the hell is going on?"

"He's about to tell you that we can't go after her."

My gaze snaps across the room to Cade's eyes and then to his now downturned mouth—his words having all but chewed and spat out my heart.

"It's complicated," Owen says, and when I look at him, he

takes a slow, steady breath, as if he's attempting to suppress his anger. "You should sit down."

I stand firm. "I'm good."

Owen heads to the computer and taps at the keys, enlarging the map of my country. "You familiar with TBA? The triborder area?"

"What of it?" I ask. Cade comes up behind me, placing a hand on my shoulder as if what I'm about to hear will require his support.

"This area"—Owen touches the screen—"is where the borders of Paraguay, Argentina, and Brazil meet, and it's basically a melting pot of terrorist assholes. From Hezbollah to al Qaeda—you name it, they're there. The terrorists work with a lot of the local criminals in the region to smuggle and traffic everything from arms and drugs to people abroad." He taps at the computer and changes it to a split screen of two people.

"Who am I looking at?" I rub my hands together now.

"That man," Owen says, while pointing to a tan guy with brown hair in his mid-fifties, "is Carlos Perozo."

My eyes lock on the man on-screen, the brother of the man who purchased my mother as if she were a piece of property. The mere thought has my insides shaking as a bubble of nausea rises into my throat.

"And this man is El Said Hassan. The government has been after him for fourteen years, ever since we learned he was responsible for the killing of American soldiers in Beirut."

And there it is again—the strain in Owen's throat, the bulging of veins there. He's about two seconds away from blowing a fuse as if this is all personal for him.

"Okay," I drag out the word, but I'm still not comprehending where he's going with all of this.

"Thanks to you, since we looked into Carlos, we discovered there might be a direct link between him and Hassan. If we can track the next shipment from Carlos to Lebanon, we might be able to get a location on Hassan."

"And by shipment, you mean people?" I gulp.

Owen's eyes are like a glassy stare, and I can no longer get a read on him. I can only see a reflection of myself there.

"Probably." He scratches at his forehead. "The US has been monitoring the situation in Brazil. Hezbollah is always changing who they work with in that region, though."

"Hezbollah," I repeat in a daze.

"Yeah, the terror organization linked to Hassan."

I look back at Cade, trying to get a read on him, but I only see remorse. Remorse, because he's going to break his promise.

"And Carlos is currently working with them?" I face Owen again.

"Yeah, but chances are it won't be for long. And this is a good lead for the military. We need to act now," Owen says, his voice wavering.

"We?" Cade releases my shoulder and comes around next to me. "You say *we* like you're still government." He lets out a *tsk* noise. "Like you never stopped being military."

Owen's lips flatten, and his Adam's apple bobs in his throat.

Cade stabs a finger at the air. "I trusted you and Jessica to help, not to turn this into something else."

"And we're going to help you. We are who we said we are. I work at Scott and Scott Securities. But—"

"And where else?" Rage cuts through Cade's voice.

"That's classified."

"Fuck classified. I paid you to protect Gia, and that's exactly what I expect to happen. You had no business reporting what you found out to the government. Not right now, at least." He curses beneath his breath and pauses for a moment, processing the news like I am. "But Christ, you're still government, and so . . ." His voice trails off for a moment. "That's how you guys managed to get us here and how Jessica manages to waltz into federal offices, isn't it? Is the company a front for something?"

"First"—Owen takes a step toward Cade—"I'm not about to let some terrorist motherfucker, who killed soldiers, continue to breathe." His chest inflates, and then he exhales a long breath through his nose. "And second, you hired us to take down Rory, and that's exactly what we plan on doing. None of us could have predicted this would happen." He glowers at me. "Maybe if she had told us about the traffickers sooner, we could have come up with a different plan."

"Don't even think about blaming Gia," Cade grates outs, almost in Owen's face now. "I always wondered why you, Luke, and a bunch of SEALs would end your careers after only eight years. It never made sense to me, but now it does, because you never left." Cade's face hardens. He's wearing the look of someone betrayed. He pivots on his heel to face the display of weapons, probably worried he might throw a punch at his friend.

God, I'm burning inside, too, and I want to speak up, but the tension is so tight. I'm worried that if I add more gas to the fire, the room will explode.

"I'm not a SEAL. But what I am is—"

"Classified," Cade mutters, and if I could see his face, I'd bet there'd be an eye roll.

"Let me be very clear: you cannot go after Carlos. If he gets spooked and the shipment to Lebanon doesn't happen, we could lose our chance to find Hassan." He drags a hand down his face and looks at me.

"How do you know for certain Hassan will even be there?" Cade counters. "If the military has been after him for so long, do you really think you'd be able to find him so goddamn easy now? Give me a fucking break. I may not be military, but even I know this is a pretty big gamble."

Owen doesn't say anything, maybe because Cade has a point and he doesn't want to admit it.

Cade faces him again and releases a heavy sigh. "But you're willing to take the risk, aren't you? You're willing to try and find this guy and potentially blow our chances of finding out what happened to Gia's mom."

"We have to take the chance." Owen looks at the ground, his voice somewhat calmer now when he says, "Maybe we can confront Carlos and see what he knows about your mom after the op."

I shake my head, finally joining in on the conversation. "It could be too late. I can't wait any longer. I've already waited ten years."

"It's that or nothing," Owen says.

A discomfort I can't shake remains in the pit of my stomach. "What's going to happen to the women and children being trafficked to Lebanon? When the US goes after this terrorist, will they also save the innocents? What happens to the victims? To the people like my mom?"

Owen presses his palms on the desk next to the laptop, bowing his head. He doesn't have to answer because I already know. The mission will be about the terrorist and no one else.

"Remember the story you told me—yeah, well, I do." My hand touches my midsection. "What if it were your mom?" I ask softly a moment later.

"And what if it were your brother who Hassan killed?" Owen's words slice right through me, and now I know why he's so off.

183

"Hassan is the guy responsible for his death?" Cade's mouth goes slack in disbelief.

It feels like an eternity before Owen looks at us. "No. We still haven't caught the SOB who killed Jason, but Hassan killed someone's son, someone's brother. And he deserves a coffin so deep, it'll put him right next to the devil, right where he belongs."

My breathing becomes shakier, the compassion for Owen's loss conflicting with my own desire.

This terrorist may not be who killed his brother, but I'm betting every mission involving a terrorist is personal for him.

"We're all after our own little piece of revenge, aren't we? In this messed-up world, we're trying to right the wrongs." My voice breaks and Cade is back at my side, my personal protector.

Owen steeples his fingers together and taps his mouth for a moment. "I have a plane on standby. I can't stay here. I'm sorry. Jess is trying to find someone to replace me, maybe someone from a PI agency we've worked with before in Florida since the rest of our team is tied up. We can't take our people off Rory or your father, so we need to outsource for help."

"How are we supposed to trust people we don't know?" Cade asks.

"That's your only option." Owen's hands fall to his sides. "I'm sorry this is how it worked out for you. I really am."

Cade's posture becomes stiff, and I'm pretty sure he's walking a fine line between sympathy and fury. "I don't understand you or Jessica—who you people really are. But what I do know is that, if anything happens to Gia because of your cagey classified bullshit, I'll—"

"Stop," I whisper to Cade when I realize his anger won the battle.

Owen's lips tighten before he says, "I have to go." He closes his laptop. "Take something to protect yourself, and then I need to lock up."

Cade releases a lungful of air, as if trying to let go of his temper, and then he grabs a gun and a box of ammo.

I'm rooted to the spot, unable to face the truth about what this means for my mother. My muscles are rigid, but I want to grab clumps of my hair and yank at it.

"We'll get through this," Cade says into my ear, and my chin dips to my chest. I need to be strong right now. I nod after a moment and follow him out of the room.

Owen locks up after us, and we head to the living room like we're in line for a funeral.

"Everything will work out. Try to be optimistic." He lifts a black duffel bag. "You can't mention any of this to anyone, especially Mya. You shouldn't even know."

"Yeah, okay." A thickness grows in my throat, and I work free a pained breath from deep in my lungs.

"We'll both get our people," Owen says, and I want to believe him.

"I'm sorry about your loss," I say in a rush, but he's already out of sight.

"And I'm sorry about yours," he calls back.

CADE

"I HAD TO REPORT WHAT I UNCOVERED ABOUT CARLOS. I'M sorry."

I lean back against the couch, losing sight of Jessica's face on the laptop screen.

I think about pressing her about who she really is, but I have the distinct feeling she'll throw the same classified response at me. This is the first time we've been able to have a face-to-face discussion since Owen left. She's probably been too busy trying to save the world, but there's only one person I'm focused on saving.

"Are you still helping, or are you bailing, too?"

"I made a commitment to you," she says.

I straighten when I hear Gia coming down the stairs. She was on the phone with Mya, but she promised she wouldn't say anything about what we learned yesterday. And she was also supposed to convince Mya to finally leave Brazil. She still hasn't left despite Owen's less-than-friendly request on the phone the other day.

"What's the status on Pierce? Gia's father is still someone we can talk about, right?"

I'm being snarky, but fuck it—I'm pissed. Maybe I'm selfish for not focusing on the potential takedown of a terrorist, but if Gia's not happy, I'm not goddamn happy.

"Or is her dad considered a terrorist now, so it's classified? I mean, last time we checked, the guy was a killer, but I'm guessing there's some sort of chart you keep up in your office to determine which asshole is the most offensive. Maybe it's color-coded?"

I shove up to my feet and scratch at the back of my neck, trying to force myself to calm down, and when I look back at the screen, Jessica's blue eyes ice over.

"Her dad is still checked into the same hotel in downtown Miami. No movement," Jessica says after a beat.

Gia drops down on the couch and reaches out for my hand, so I sit next to her. Our fingers lace together on my thigh. At this point, I don't give two fucks if Jessica knows something is going on between us.

Jessica's gaze darts to our hands, and she clears her throat as if surprised or embarrassed by the sight of me being so "human" as she'd probably call it.

"And the people Rory sent to Chicago and Austin? Where are they now?" I ask.

"They're back in New York."

"And Rory?" Gia's grip tightens on my hand.

"He's been keeping a low profile. I think he's a bit spooked with you being gone. Maybe he's worried you'll roll over on him to the Feds in return for protection." Jessica crosses her arms and leans back in her chair.

"Witnesses die," Gia says, almost under her breath as her eyes remain cast down on our clasped palms.

"Yeah, well, whoever gave the Feds a boatload of intel on Richard McCullen is still alive and never made it into the spotlight, and that can't make Rory feel too confident that the same thing won't happen to him," Jessica says.

"And what if it was Rory who turned him in?" Gia asks, and her question throws me off guard.

"You think Rory would trade his dad in for his own immunity?" Jessica asks, standing now, the wheels churning.

"He never did get along with Richard. They were always butting heads," she explains.

"You think Jerry is really Rory's contact?" I ask Jessica.

She braces the desk and closes her eyes, processing the idea. "I entertained the thought before, but it doesn't make sense that a homicide detective would be assigned that role."

"Unless they wanted it to look like he was just a dirty cop in order to throw off any suspicion by Rory's men," Gia says.

Jessica huffs out a breath. "I looked into things on my end, and there's no Internal Affairs investigation going on that I know of, which doesn't rule out Jerry being dirty. It could just mean he hasn't been caught."

"Or it could mean he's actually working for someone high up, and he's Rory's handler, or whatever the hell you guys call it," I say.

"These are all hypotheticals, but if it's true, how do we let Rory's people know he's the snitch without getting Jerry caught in the crossfires?"

"I guess you'll need to figure it out." It's time for her to hold up her end of this since she's screwing us over with respect to Gia's mom.

"And if it's not Rory who turned in Richard?" Gia asks.

"Doesn't matter." Jessica grins. "We just need his people to believe it."

"Okay." Gia nods.

"I'll get working on this. We still need to figure out what to do about your father, too."

"I want him taken down." Gia releases my hand and stands, folding her arms, showing confidence in her decision.

"And if he dies as a result of the little war we might start within the McCullens' organization . . .?" Jessica allows the question to hang in the air and waits for her response.

Gia's shoulders drop forward enough for me to notice her internal conflict over the decision.

"He's a killer," is all she says before turning her back to the screen, as well as to me, probably so I can't get a read on her.

"Noted." Jessica is looking at me as if she's seeking silent permission for the potential death of Gia's dad, and damn it, I give it by nodding.

"Okay, well, I've got a guy coming your way the day after tomorrow. We worked with him on a case in Tampa last year. He's former Air Force and runs his own PI company."

I'm not keen on the idea of letting someone I don't know come here, but I'm not a cop and I don't have military experience, so I can't turn down the extra protection if it means keeping Gia safe. Of course, if it's her father who finds us, I'm guessing I'm the only one he'll want to slice and dice.

"The day after tomorrow." Gia faces us, blinking, as if her mind is hazy or on overload from all of this. Yeah, well, mine is, too.

"You think you guys can stay out of trouble until then?"

"We'll manage." I end the call and close the laptop, and Gia heads for the back of the house.

"This has become more than I can handle," she says, stepping outside. "I'm betting you wish you never went to that bachelor party the night we met. It would've saved you a lot of trouble."

"Don't say that." I reach out and tug her around. She keeps her arms tight in front of her chest as if she's trying to shield herself from me, and I'm not sure why. "I'll never regret meeting you."

Her head is angled down, so I tip up her chin. "Look at me," I say when her eyes still don't meet mine.

"It's going to be hard to say goodbye to you when this is all over."

"Who said we'll have to say goodbye?"

"AM I REALLY LETTING YOU DO THIS?"

"It'll take my mind off things. Please." She's sitting in a chair about ten feet away, with her sketchpad in one hand and a pencil in the other.

"I don't feel too manly," I joke as I shift around on the stool, uneasy with all of this.

She chuckles. "You could probably walk around in heels and still not lose that dominant alpha thing you've got going on."

"Yeah, well, that won't be happening." I roll my eyes.

"Maybe hold your wrist with the other hand?"

I do as I'm told, not used to being bossed around, but it makes her smile, and that little dimple appears—so it's worth it.

"Close to your face." She nods. "Yeah, and spread your fingers open so I can see your eyes." She makes a soft humming noise as she angles her head and her pencil moves over the paper.

"I can't believe I'm posing for you."

"Stop talking. I need you still." Her lip tucks between her teeth as her eyes keep flickering to the page and back to me.

"I'm surprised you can't draw me from memory." I smile. "Hell, I remember every little detail about you. The freckle on the inside of your wrist. The few strands of honey-colored hair, mixed with the black. Oh, and the way your nipples pucker—"

"Cade!" She holds her pencil to her lips, trying to silence me like she's my teacher in school. Hell, we could role play that any day of the week. I'll even let her keep bossing me around.

Jesus, I'm getting hard.

"I can't draw when I'm shaking from laughter."

"Babe, you're gonna shake a lot more when I'm making you come and scream my name in about five minutes."

She fights another smile. "You can't rush a masterpiece."

I scratch at my two-day-old beard, and she points to my hands, which have abandoned the desired position. I grumble and do as instructed, knowing full well that I'll be ordering her around soon. I think she'll need to be tied up, too. She can never seem to keep her hands on the headboard.

"You're so hot," she says after a few minutes.

I lift my hands up and stretch. "I know."

More sweet laughter flows from her mouth. I never knew a sound could make me feel so much.

She sets down her pencil twenty minutes later, and thank God for that because my patience is about gone.

I stride toward her, needing my hands on her, but I'm also curious to see her sketch.

"It's not done." She rises to her feet and pulls it away, lifting it above her head, as if that can stop me.

"You're going to make me work to get it?" I tug at her yoga pants and yank them down, and she gasps. "Yeah, there it is. The sweet spot. So fucking wet for me." I thrum her clit and slide a finger inside her.

"Mine," I grunt like a caveman who needs to make sure

he's staked his claim loud and clear. "Are you going to let me see the drawing now?"

She starts to pant, her arm dropping down as I rub harder and faster. "Not . . . yet."

I pull my hand free and step back, and her shoulders shudder as if a chill has swept over her. "How about now?" I arch a brow, playing dirty.

"Finish, and yes. Yes, you can do whatever the hell you want." She grabs my wrist with her other hand and presses it back to her pussy, in desperate need of my touch.

"Don't promise me a blank check." I smile. "But I do like you like this, hanging right on the edge." I lean forward and tug the soft flesh of her earlobe between my teeth. Then I give her what she wants, intensifying the pressure between her legs. "I like to be the one to push you over the edge, too."

Her eyes squeeze tight as she chews her lip and bucks against my hand, losing control. And I love every second of it.

"I swear, sometimes you steal my every breath." She falls back onto the chair behind her, totally satiated.

"And you stole mine a long time ago," I say in all honesty, not letting go of her eyes, even as I crouch down to one knee before her.

She runs a short nail down the center of my chest and then hands me the sketchpad.

"This kind of looks like me."

"That's the idea." She straightens in the seat and looks at the picture.

"And what are you drawing in the background?" I notice the start of scenery behind my head.

"Brazil." She rolls her tongue over her lips for a moment, wetting them. "Two images I never want to forget."

Forget?

"Too bad I don't have your perfect memory; then, I wouldn't need a drawing to remember you after I'm gone."

I swallow at her words, at the truth laid out between us.

I can't accept that things will end once we stop running, but I whisper, "Yeah," and shove to my feet, no longer in the mood to do anything. "Too bad."

I go into the kitchen to grab a bottle of water, but her hand sliding up my bare back stops me from opening the fridge.

"What's wrong?" She places a kiss on my back, right next to her palm. "Aside from the obvious, from this craziness I pulled you into."

I turn to face her, and I'm suddenly so goddamn angry. The thought of losing her, of losing someone I care about, knots my stomach.

I want to punch something.

I want to put my fist through every wall in this house until the walls crumble and there's nothing left—nothing that can come between us.

"No." I stride back into the living room. "I say fuck it."

"I'm not sure what you're talking about." She follows me.

I've lost it. I've finally lost my mind.

I grab her hand and hold it over my heart, letting her feel it pounding in my chest. "I'll build the longest fucking bridge in the world that links us together when this is over if that's what I have to do."

Her hand trembles, and her eyelids fall closed.

"When this is over, I want to be with you. I need to hear you say it, though. I need to make sure we're on the same page."

The skin on her forehead draws tight, and her lips roll inward as if in pain.

"Gia?"

A single tear drops down her cheek, and it has me stumbling back a step, releasing hold of her hand.

I gulp back the ugly truth of her silence, unable to wrap my head around it.

Her lower lip quivers now, and another tear glides down. "Of course I want to be with you." The moment of hesitation that follows her words is like a knife to the back.

Still no eye contact, but she says, "There can never be a me-and-you in the future." The shakiness of her voice betrays her.

"You'll be in New York, and—"

"I don't need a geography lesson," I snap.

Her eyes finally open. "When I find my mother, I'll have to focus on her. I won't have room in my life for anyone else." She lets out such a deep breath that if I had been drinking it would've sobered me. "Being with you, even in this twisted situation, has been everything to me . . . but I—"

"I get it, but this isn't some schoolboy crush because I took your virginity. I'm not telling you what you need to hear. I'm telling you the truth."

She keeps opening my fucking playbook. The one I closed for her, damn it.

I focus on her irises, the bright color dimming as she's about to lie to me. And I know it'll be a lie because there's no way I can be the only one feeling this.

But why the hell is she doing this?

"Don't do this, please. Don't make this any harder than it has to be. You know I care about you." She wipes her newly fallen tears and sniffles. "I'll always appreciate what you've done for me, and I'll never forget you were my first, but don't pretend that someone like you could ever let me be your last."

My jaw goes slack when I realize she's turning this back on me. A slow anger rolls through me, and I try to fight it as I tap a fist to my chin. I need to control the situation, to figure out what is happening.

But she doesn't give me a chance to say anything else. She takes off and runs up the stairs.

I want to chase after her, to tell her she's wrong, but what the hell do I do if she's right about me?

What if I really am a monster on the inside, and I've only been wearing a mask? Maybe I can never be more than an asshole like my father.

19

CADE

"WHO WAS THAT GUY YOU WERE TALKING TO NEAR THE dressing room?"

The man had left, brushing past me as I had made my way to her.

"He was asking for directions." She shrugs and heads for the exit as well.

I blow out a frustrated breath and follow her out.

We've been walking around Havana for the last five hours because she wanted out of the house, and I couldn't exactly disagree with her.

We haven't talked about last night. In fact, we've both done our best to avoid conversation all day today. I'm still trying to wrap my head around her words last night, and as much as I want to pin her to the wall and force her to look at me so she can see in my eyes how much she matters to me, I'm giving her space.

At least, for today.

My patience is running out, though.

Monster inside me or not—I want her, and I won't give

up until she's mine in every way possible, even if I don't truly understand what that even means right now.

In the plaza, I look up at the sky, and it's as if the sun is burning the buildings as it lowers to the ground. "Sure he wasn't hitting on you?" I ask once at her side. "A little odd for him to be asking for help near the women's changing room—don't you think?"

"So what if he was flirting?" She stops walking and faces me.

I almost laugh. "What? You think I'm some young kid who will throw down with a guy for making a pass at his woman?"

Her head angles, and I can tell she's fighting a smile. "Based on your personality—yes."

But the sudden warmth in her eyes disappears in a second.

She's got her walls back in place.

They're walls I learned to break down, which means I can do it again.

"I want to get drunk. I need to get my mind off everything while we wait for news from Jessica."

I assume I'm also classified under the *everything* category.

"I don't think that's a good idea."

She ignores me and points to a bistro up the way where a band is playing near an outdoor seating area. "Well, too bad for you, because I don't need permission."

She nearly skips out of reach, her hair whipping up behind her as she moves away.

A low laugh blasts from deep within my chest and hits the air—if she's purposefully trying to get a rise out of me, she's succeeded.

Two hours later, she begins to dance, and instantly gathers the attention of everyone with a pulse.

I leave the table after a few minutes and reach for her elbow.

My patience is officially gone.

"You need to sit. Drink some water."

"What?" She holds her hand to her ear. "I can't hear you."

She spins away and continues to sway her hips, doing some ridiculously sexy salsa moves that have me considering ways we could use some of her talents in the bedroom later.

"Dance," Gia shouts over the music and comes closer. There's a passionate plea in her eyes that the alcohol has helped to unmask.

I go to her, unable to stop myself, and our fingers lace.

I pull her in so close I can feel her heart beating against my chest, and the way she starts to move her body, grinding against my cock a few minutes later, has me wondering if we'll even make it back to the house.

The thumping of the Cuban music and the loud sounds around us from other people dancing and singing along—it becomes background noise.

All I can see is her.

And I know all I'll ever see is her.

I wrap my arms around her hips and drop my mouth over hers, suddenly not able to give a fuck about our argument last night.

Once back at the house, I pin her to the wall without hesitation and hold her in place, commanding her eyes to meet my gaze.

She's breathing hard, nearly panting, and some nagging in my gut is telling me this is our last time. But I ignore it. How can I not?

"Tell me you're mine." I can smell the tequila on her breath, and it mixes with mine. I haven't drunk this much in a long damn time, and it's not normal for my head to feel so foggy, but she kept pushing the drinks on me, and tonight, I didn't say no.

Her lips part, but she doesn't say anything.

She doesn't have to, though.

Her eyes say it all.

The brightness is there—the lie has been lifted, and I can see how she feels, now more than ever before. She can throw bullshit at me and try to push away all she wants, but I'm never letting go.

I lean forward and say, "I don't have a tie or cuffs, but if I did, I'd be using them tonight."

Her mouth finds my ear, and her breath has my balls tightening even more. "I'll hold on to the headboard tonight. I promise."

* * *

Sunlight hits my eyes like a flare being shot right before me, and I jerk my hands to try and cover my face, but something hard rubs against my wrists, stopping me from moving them.

My vision is off, but I squint, trying to figure out what the hell is going on right now.

Handcuffs?

How much did we drink last night?

I blink a few times, attempting to focus on what I'm cuffed to, while I try to remember last night.

Gia and I were drunk, dancing near Revolution Square, when—shit, where the hell is she?

"Gia," I croak out in a hoarse voice.

After a minute, a semi-lucid state starts to lift some of the fog from my brain, and I realize I'm cuffed to the steering wheel of the DeSoto.

What the hell is going on?

I twist in my seat to look around, my head spinning like I'm on a tilt-a-whirl, but I'm alone.

My stomach is doing somersaults. My body is shaky like it hasn't been since . . .

I'm on drugs. But—how?

I bang my head against the back of the seat and pinch my eyes closed for a moment, needing to remember what else happened last night.

The sudden *tap-tap-tap* on the driver's side door has my body flinching, the noise like a jackhammer in my ears.

A man circles the DeSoto with something in his hands, and it's not until he's holding a lighter in front of the car do I realize what I'm smelling.

Gasoline.

20

GIA

"I MADE IT." I WRAP MY ARMS TIGHT AROUND MYA, ALMOST breaking into a sob.

"Connor promised me his guy in Cuba would come through for us."

"And you're sure we can trust Connor?" I ask after stepping back.

The memory of Cade, lying on his stomach with his arm slung over me as I wiggled free without him noticing creates a rush of guilt down my spine.

My stomach clenches, so I press a hand there, trying to dial down the pain so I can get through this and do what needs to be done.

Mya tips her head in the direction of the hotel door. "Why don't I let you decide for yourself? He's across the hall with his brother, Mason."

"But they're military."

"They're not military anymore. The security business they run specializes in this kind of stuff, and they've helped me out of more than one jam before."

"Owen was supposed to be on my side, but—"

She waves her hand in the air, silencing me. "And if Owen really is still military, or whatever, it'll always be country first. But for these guys, Connor and his team, it's *people* first."

We talked about Connor weeks ago when we were organizing our plan, but we didn't have a date at the time. And now, Owen has left a bitter taste in my mouth about the military, even if my feelings aren't necessarily justified.

Mya shoves her long blonde hair behind her and folds her arms defensively. She mentioned before that she grew up with Connor and his brother, so she knows them better than she knows me. I can't blame her for getting protective, but I have reasons for concern.

I sink onto the couch.

"Listen, these guys are incredible. They inherited their father's billion-dollar empire, and they didn't want it. For real. Helping people is more important to them than money. Hell, they're here on their own dime right now."

It's impossible for me to believe that anyone would be willing to do something without getting anything in return.

Cade's an exception, but can Connor and his brother be exceptions, too?

"Just meet them." Her eyes dart to mine. "Okay?"

"Yeah." I sigh. "Okay."

"I'll go get them. Stay tight."

I stand, head to the window, and pull back the long drapes. All I can see is lush green trees down below. We're nowhere near a major city.

But it hits me—I'm in Brazil.

On the flight here, I was so torn up over leaving Cade that I'd nearly forgotten I was heading home.

My fingers brush over the inside of my wrist. "She has to

be alive." I close my eyes, remembering Mom's smell: orange blossoms and sunflowers.

She always put wildflowers all over the house. Our home wasn't huge, but it was alive and colorful.

The colors stayed put in Brazil when I moved to New York, and my life became dark. Shadows loomed over me.

Being home should make me feel better.

So, why doesn't it?

The door opens a minute later. I turn to meet my new saviors, but my conscience eats at me.

Cade's my savior. He's the only one I ever want at my side.

And I lost him.

Emotion works up into my throat, and I'm worried I'll cry, which is ridiculous because I did this to myself. I planned an escape and probably broke Cade's heart—a heart he claims not to have. But I saw it. I felt it.

She jerks a thumb to the tall, powerful-looking men at her side. Black boots, fatigues, green tees revealing corded forearms—yeah, former military, all right. Well, minus the buzz cut.

"These are the guys. Well, the two in charge," she says.

"The rest of the team is in position in our mobile units. They're waiting for my go." One of the men walks toward me, and I think he's the older brother based on his eyes; they've seen more than the other. "I'm Connor. That's Mason."

I tuck my hair behind my ears and extend my hand. He shakes it with a firm grip. "Hi." A shy smile curves my lips, and even though he's handsome and belongs on some Hot Hunks military wall calendar, he doesn't make my heart flutter, not like Cade.

"We're glad to help." Mason starts across the room, and there's a slight limp to his walk.

My cheeks blush when I look up to see his eyes on me.

"IED, but I'm good. No worries." He winks, and it reminds me of Owen.

More remorse floods me.

My betrayal, my actions, my sins will catch up to me in Hell. But if my mom is alive, it's a sacrifice I'm willing to make.

I owe her. I'll give up my happiness to save her.

I blink a few times and bring my mind back into the room, even if every other part of me is still back in that house with Cade. My heart. My breath. Maybe even my spirit.

"Sorry," I mumble.

Mason shrugs and shakes my hand. "War is war."

"They're really amazing, I promise. Mason saved my ass last year when I was covering a story about the drug cartels in New Mexico and nearly got myself killed."

"Lois Lane here thinks I'm her own personal superhero." Mason chuckles. "But she has a good heart."

"She does." I head back to the couch and sit down, not sure if I can stand any longer on my trembling legs.

It's hard for me to believe this moment is really happening, that the plan Mya and I started weeks ago is finally playing out.

"We weren't expecting to get Mya's call so soon, but luckily, we were between ops." Connor reaches into his pocket and pulls out a phone, even though it didn't ring. "Give me a sec. It's one of my men calling." He goes into the adjoining bedroom and closes the door.

"Did you have a smooth flight out of Havana?" Mason asks.

"Yeah. How'd you manage that for us on such short

notice?" It was a near disaster meeting up with the guy at the boutique yesterday with Cade hanging by so close.

"Javier is a military pilot, but he's also in favor of a regime change in Cuba. He does us favors, and we reciprocate."

I don't bother to ask more, because anything involving the government or military will fly right over my head. I got a heavy dose the other day from Owen, and my mind is still reeling.

I've had to deal with the mob for ten years. And my mom was abducted by traffickers.

But terrorism, espionage, and government coups—too much info is sometimes just *too much.*

"Sorry." Connor comes back into the room a minute later. "Perozo and his team just rolled out of town with five military-style trucks behind him."

I sit upright. "That was fast."

Connor's hands disappear into his pockets, and he stands alongside his brother. "We're going to green-light the mission as soon as the deal with Hezbollah is complete. Once the shipment containers reach Lebanon and Perozo is back, we'll move in."

Owen can still get his guy, and now I can get what I want.

"Based on our recon, we have a pretty good idea where they're keeping their records at the compound," Connor explains. "With technology these days, they won't risk keeping track of anything online, so they'll have the data saved to a hard drive or USB."

"And you really think you can get it?" I rub my clammy hands together.

"This is what we do." Connor nods. "It won't be my first time on an op like this."

"And if my mother's name is there, and we find out where she is now . . . what do we do next?"

"We'll find her," Mason answers.

"What about Carlos? What happens to him?" I ask.

"We won't turn him over to the police. We can't risk that he'll end up right back out on the streets," Mason says.

Confidence starts to flow through me, but the guilt is still there, and it's suffocating almost every other emotion.

What if I had waited in New York and had never run away with Cade? What if I had waited for Mya to find answers? Cade would have never been in danger.

But I would never have known how amazing some moments in life, big or small, can truly be if Cade hadn't been a part of my life these last few weeks.

If he didn't open my eyes, if he didn't open my heart back up after it had stopped working ten years ago, where would I be now?

"Gia?" Mya arches a brow. "You still with us, hon?"

"Uh, yeah." I look back at Connor and Mason. "Thanks for coming up with a way to do this without blowing Owen's chances at getting the terrorist he's after."

"I know Owen. He's a friend of mine. He didn't have a choice, so try not to be upset with him," Connor says with grit to his voice.

"Small world, huh?" Mya smiles.

"Us military people tend to be pretty close-knit, especially when it comes to special forces. Although Frogmen tend to be in their own world," Mason says.

"Frogmen?" My lips roll inward in thought.

"SEALs," Mason answers.

"You're just jealous because you weren't a SEAL." Mya slaps his shoulder in a playful way. The jury is still out on whether or not they ever dated, but based on the way Mason's gaze keeps following her around the room, I'd say he has a thing for her, regardless.

"I could run circles around those guys." He pounds a fist to his chest, and his gaze cuts to his brother. "Don't give me that look."

Connor laughs. "Sure, man. Sure."

My jaw goes slack, and my mind is skipping around so fast with everything going on, I barely even hear my own voice when I murmur, "Is this really happening?"

"Yeah, it is." Mya reaches for my hand and squeezes it, but I'm too focused now on my sketchpad on the end table. I fight the smirk that tugs at my lips as I think about Cade sitting on that stool for me the other night, giving me control over the situation . . . well, for a half hour, at least.

My gorgeous but slightly broken man.

I don't want to fix him, though.

I just want him.

Period.

And somehow, after this is all over, I need to find a way back to him.

"One question," Mason says.

I bury my thoughts as much as I can so I don't cry when I look at him. "Yeah?"

"Will this friend of yours come after you?"

My eyes cut to an image of Cade on Mason's cell. He's in a black suit and red tie. Red, the fitting color for such a powerful man. I'm pretty sure I saw that image online on his office website when I was semi-stalking him after we first met, a night that feels like years ago, not weeks.

"Um," is all that slips free.

I wasn't supposed to sleep with Cade last night.

Get him drunk so it'd be easier to slip out of the house

and meet with Connor's contact—that was the plan. Hot, sweaty, and mind-blowing sex with Cade wasn't.

"You left him the note, right?" Mya asks.

I bite my lip. "I, uh—yeah, I left a card." I put it by the gun because I assumed Cade wouldn't leave the house without it. "But I don't know if that will keep him from coming after me."

"So we should anticipate a guest visitor?" Connor's eyes narrow, and I nod.

"Cade is pretty determined when it comes to going after what he wants." I'm surprised I vocalized that information, but it's the truth.

Cade opened up to me the other night.

And what did I do?

I shitted all over his feelings by twisting the blame back on him.

But I had to hurt him to protect him.

"I'd say it's a fifty-fifty chance as to whether he'll show." I let out a long breath, hating myself for wanting him to come, yet longing to keep him away and safe.

21

CADE

"YOU HAVE FIVE SECONDS TO TELL ME WHAT YOU DID WITH my daughter, or the car lights up."

Begging for mercy isn't something I can stomach, but that's not my issue right now—it's what he's saying. *Where is Gia if he doesn't have her?*

"Five," he begins. "Four."

"If she's not in the house, then someone took her," I yell.

I push through the haziness in my head to try and figure out what the hell could have happened to her.

There's no way one of Rory's men would grab Gia and not touch me, which means— "Fuck."

Her father is back by my side now, resting his hands on the roof and bending down so we're face-to-face. "Where's my daughter?" His tone is even and controlled. He's done this a lot, I'm sure.

"If you don't have her, then I have a pretty good idea where she is." Not that I'll tell him. There's no way I'll let this bastard get to her, but I also need to help Gia, so . . .

"Stop fucking around with me and tell me where she is."

"Is it that far of a stretch to believe she ran away with me?

It wouldn't be her first time running." I stare into his green eyes, hoping to see some humanity there. "She wanted my help. I didn't take her."

He stands upright so I can't see his face now. After a moment, he shoves the lighter back in his pocket and reaches around to his back.

"I need to get inside the house. I can tell you what happened once we're in there." If he really wants to find his daughter, there's no way in hell he'll kill me before he has her, even if I'm now staring into the barrel of a pistol, one with a silencer on the end.

For the first time, I notice I'm in sweatpants and nothing else, which means the prick probably took me from bed. "What'd you drug me with?" I squint again as I look out the open door at the sun rising behind him.

"Doesn't matter." He leans in and puts a small key in my hand. "But you have big balls to think you could get away without repercussions."

I work at the cuffs the best I can while being strapped to the wheel, but at least he's letting me free. He obviously has a motive for cutting me loose.

He's probably sixty-five. Even though he somehow managed to get in the house, a place owned by the goddamn CIA, I can take him.

I get out of the car and my stomach muscles tighten as I think about where the hell Gia is right now.

"She wasn't taken." I swallow back my unease and press a hand to the gasoline-covered car, trying to maintain my balance.

Maybe I'll need a few minutes to get my head back on before I try to get the drop on this guy.

"Then where the fuck is she?" His Irish accent isn't as

strong, probably from years of being in the States, but it rattles through louder when he shouts.

He lowers the gun to his side, and his forehead pinches together. I can see Gia in him, in the haunted look in his eyes.

"I think she took off, but there's one way to know for sure. I need to go back inside."

"Guess she couldn't have trusted you if she ran off in the middle of the night." He cocks his head, eyeing me suspiciously.

My jaw locks tight as I allow the last thirty-six hours to fast-forward through my mind.

Gia knew she was going to leave me.

She knew the second Owen told her she'd have to back off from finding her mom.

How could I have been so goddamn stupid?

"Get inside then, will ya?" With his gun, he motions for me to go into the house.

I move as fast as I can, even though I'm lightheaded and my legs are weak from the drugs.

"If her sketchpad isn't here, then she left of her own free will." My eye catches the stool near the window, and the memory of the night she drew me blows through my mind, leaving pain in its wake.

"You know about her drawings?" he asks from behind.

I shake my head free of my thoughts and start looking around the living room. "I told you I didn't take her." I snatch the burner phone off the floor where I must have dropped it when we got home last night.

A blur of movements, of our bodies pressed together—of us making love—comes back to me.

Ten missed calls from Jessica. She started calling shortly after Gia and I got back after dancing.

The sudden pop and crack of my phone has me retracting my arm in a flash.

"Jesus," I hiss as I shake my hand out. "Did you really just shoot my phone?" I spin around to face the son of a bitch, not sure whether I should be angry or impressed by his ability to aim so well that he didn't even touch my flesh.

His brows draw inward. "Why would she run from you?" He doesn't give a damn about my phone or my question. Only his daughter.

This might be our only common ground.

My lips tighten into a sneer as I stride toward him, my chest puffed out, a shot of adrenaline pumping through me, killing the residual effects of whatever chemical he pumped into me while I was asleep.

"And why'd she run before?" I stand in front of the pistol, holding my ground.

The muscles in his jaw clench as understanding flickers across his face. "She's still looking for her mom."

I release a breath, knowing damn well the sketchpad is gone and Gia is on her way to Brazil, if she's not there already.

I'm such a fucking idiot for believing she'd handle the news from Owen in any other way.

He clicks the gun's safety back on and tucks it behind him again. "She shouldn't have left New York, goddamn it."

This man is a killer, but I can see it in his eyes as plain as day: he loves Gia.

"I'm pretty sure she's heading straight to a man named Carlos Perozo."

His face tightens, a flash of anger darkening his eyes, and he closes the small gap between us until we're only a few inches apart, so close I can smell his breath.

"The brother of the man who killed Sara?"

Sara? Gia never mentioned her mother's name, but it must be her. And with the way he's talking right now, it sure as hell sounds like her mom really is dead.

"Those motherfuckers." He shifts away and scrubs his hands through his hair. "I thought I buried everything from her."

"Buried what?"

"A fifteen-year-old girl doesn't need to know about how her mother died. I was vague on purpose. I was worried that if she found out all the gory details she'd try to do exactly what she is now." He curses beneath his breath. "I told her Sara was gone, but she never believed me." Anger pulses through his words like a vibration rocking the room.

"Maybe if you had told her everything, she wouldn't have gone on this crusade to find her mom."

My chest starts to constrict, and I need to take a sharp breath when it truly hits me that Gia's mother is gone. The pain this will cause Gia is un-fucking-bearable.

My hand balls into a fist, and I press it to my forehead, losing sight of her father, of everything.

"All Gia had to do was wait a few more months."

"What do you mean?" I drop my hand and look at him, and it's as if the mood in the room has shifted, and for some odd fucking reason, I feel like this murderer and I are on the same side. I usually trust my instincts, and something is telling me this man does care about Gia. But this is one time I can't rely on my gut, not with her life on the line.

"I might be a killer, but I never wanted this life for my daughter." He turns his back, his hands going to his hips, and I catch sight of the gun.

Can I move fast enough in my current state to snatch it from him?

"Two months and she would have been free." He faces

me, a bleakness to his eyes. "Do you have an exact location for her right now?"

I think back to the map of Brazil and the information on the screen Owen showed us. The text was small, but there was an address in the upper right corner of the picture. Did Gia notice it too? She must have.

I pull up the image in my head and focus on it.

And never have I been so damn thankful for my photographic memory.

But there's no way in hell I'll let him know where she is, even if something is telling me to trust a killer.

"You know the address." He huffs. "I can see it in your eyes." His brows snap together. "Prove to me you're not someone I should put six feet under. Prove it by helping me save my daughter."

"And why the hell would I let a murderer anywhere near her? How can I trust that you're not the one she needs saving from?"

Within seconds, the gun is fixed my way. He removes the safety and aims the gun toward my left kneecap. "I can get the address on my own or by torturing you. I found you, didn't I?"

"Either shoot me or stop pointing the damn thing at me," I grumble.

He ignores my sarcasm. "I'll find Gia. But it could take a day or two, and she may not have that long."

"She doesn't want to go back to New York. Rory will—"

"Do you think I'd ever let that wanker touch my daughter? Do you think I wouldn't break every bone in his body if he ever hurt her?"

"Why'd you bring her into that life, then? Why surround her with such scum?" I step closer, my chest tightening. "If you care about her, it doesn't make sense."

A *tsk* noise escapes his lips as his gun lowers to his side. "A businessman like yourself doesn't know shit about the way my world works."

"Then explain it to me." I'm so close I could grab the gun.

"Who is she to you?" He tilts his head, assessing me. "If you really helped her escape New York, why'd you do it? What's your ulterior motive?"

"You're right that I'm not part of your world, which means you can't grasp the idea of a man wanting to help a woman without trying to screw her over."

"But you did screw my daughter, didn't you?" The vein in the side of his throat starts to throb, his pulse probably elevating.

If I were a father, in that respect, I can't say I'd blame him for his anger.

But I'm not a dad, and so . . . "Gia's personal life is none of your business."

He might look like an older version of Keanu Reeves from *The Matrix*, but being eye-to-eye with him doesn't scare me, even if he frightens his own daughter.

He drags a palm down his face, and I focus on the Celtic cross tattoo that occupies most of his hand. Maybe he's hoping God will forgive him every time he shoots his gun, or maybe he's praying for perfect aim? Who the hell knows? All that matters is I think we're on the same page.

For now, at least.

We might need each other to get to her, but after that, all bets will be off, and I won't let him near her.

"Let me ask you something," he begins in a low voice. "If you had a daughter, would you let her out of your sight if it meant one of your enemies might find her—maybe rape or torture her?"

217

A rush of air leaves my lungs at his words, at the thought of anyone putting their hands on her.

"There're a lot of people out there who would use Gia to try and get to me. I've been protecting her, not holding her hostage."

His words, the simple truth of what he said, surprises the hell out of me. "And does she know that?"

He remains quiet, giving me his answer.

"Why didn't you take her somewhere else when her mom died? You could have watched over her at a beach in Fiji instead."

He holds the gun tight against his leg, but his eyes remain steady on mine. He's reading me like I am him. "Do you know what happens when someone leaves the mob?"

He doesn't actually intend for me to answer, and so I wait. But impatience glides through my veins, making my heart pump even harder.

"They die."

"Aren't you good enough not to be found?" But if this man had run off with Gia ten years ago, I would have never met her.

"I couldn't take the risk at the time, but now . . ."

"Now what?"

His lips part, but darkness falls back over his face. "I don't owe you answers. I'm only giving them to you so we can get this little dance over with a hell of a lot quicker. You and I both know that the longer we stand here, the more likely Gia will get hurt, or worse."

"And what the hell do you propose we do?"

"We go and get her. What else?" His face tightens with irritation. "Get dressed, so we can get the fuck out of here before your little government friends show up and I have to put them down."

"Do you plan on *trying* to put me down once we find Gia?" I think about where I stowed the gun the other day. I'll need to bring it with me, preferably without him knowing.

He shrugs as if it's the most casual topic in the world. "How about we let Gia decide?"

* * *

I grip Gia's card in my hand and lean back in the seat. We've been on a commercial flight for two hours now. We didn't have time to worry about whether or not Rory could track us. We'll cross that bridge once we've found Gia.

"How exactly did you find us?"

I need to get my mind off the card, off what Gia wrote.

I know she didn't mean what she wrote, that she only said she doesn't give a damn about me to protect me, to keep me from coming after her. But that doesn't mean her words don't fucking hurt, lies or not.

"It's what I do. I find people." Gia's dad polishes off his drink.

If I wasn't still recovering from the binge drinking and the drugs, I'd probably take an IV of whiskey right about now. "And then you kill them?" I ask since no one else is around.

"Mostly." He lifts the glass up so the flight attendant can see him. We're in first class, thanks to my credit card. I figure if Rory is going to find us, maybe it wouldn't be so bad if Jessica is able to track us, too.

"Are they all innocent? Do you ever feel bad?" I pat the card against my thigh, the nerves getting to me.

Having Gia's safety out of my control is damn near maddening.

219

"Will knowing this make you feel better?" He snickers. "And do you think I care about how you feel?"

I shift my attention out the small open window. "Just trying to figure out how a former soldier turned into a murderer, and, you know, how you got her mom to ever fall for you."

"Soldiers *are* killers." He clears his throat, and a silence grows between us for a few minutes before he says, "And her mom didn't know what I did for the McCullens."

For some damn reason, part of me wants to try to understand how he could have Gia in his life and not be a better man because of it. I know I already am.

"I'm sorry to disappoint, but I have no redeeming qualities." He mumbles something under his breath. "And from what I discovered about your crooked father and your lifestyle—neither do you."

"A man can change." I tense at the implication of my words, at the broad generalization I made, which could even include him.

"Not me." He thanks the flight attendant after she refills his drink. "And probably not you."

22

GIA

"THAT WAS FAST." I STARE IN DISBELIEF AT MASON.

"Usually arms deals and such happen quickly to prevent detection and government interference," he says.

"Did Owen get his guy? The terrorist?" My stomach tightens.

He nods. "Yeah."

A flush works up into my cheeks, and my head drops forward.

If Owen can succeed, maybe we can, too. Maybe we truly can right the wrongs of the world.

"I want to go with you guys."

Mya squints at me as if I'm crazy. "No."

Mason looks over at his brother, and my eyes widen as Connor nods.

A nod means *yes*, right?

"No," Mya says again.

Connor starts typing on his smartphone and doesn't look at me when he says, "She can come."

"Are you insane?" Mya sputters.

"I've been called a few things, but that wouldn't be one of

221

them." He drags his gaze up toward us once he stows his phone back in his pants pocket.

"You're a father. I thought you'd be less of a risk-taker." She goes to his side and reaches for his bronzed arm, trying to reason with him.

I wasn't expecting Connor to be a dad. I guess I assumed a man like him wouldn't want to leave someone fatherless. Hopefully that never happens, though.

"Fatherhood makes me smarter and safer." Connor smiles. "Lucky for you."

"But you're letting her go with you guys to the compound —that doesn't sound smart to me." She crosses her arms, not ready to back down.

I should say something, but I'm pretty sure he won't let her dictate his plans.

"I'm not letting her inside. She'll stay in the truck with one of my team members." He arches his shoulders back, and his eyes focus laser-sharp on mine. "Sorry, but I'm not giving in to your request to come with us because I'm going soft. It's because I've learned to know better. I'm damn certain you'll try and sneak out of this room to get close to the compound, to the action."

The truth settles in the air between us.

"I'd rather have my crew keep an eye on you, so I don't need to worry about an unplanned rescue." Connor glances back at Mason as he taps at his black wristwatch.

It's time.

Oh, God.

And no sign of Cade yet. Connor's people haven't heard any government chatter about what we're planning to do, which is almost surprising. I had assumed Cade would have ratted on me to Jessica to try and stop me.

Maybe that means my horrible card worked.

"We gotta roll out. It's close to midnight." Connor opens the hotel door.

"Good luck." Mya wraps her arms tight around me and leans in close to my ear. "We'll find your mom." Once I'm out in the hall, she adds, "Be safe."

Mason salutes her and positions a crooked smile on his face. "Always."

"IT WON'T WORK. SORRY." ONE OF THE GUYS ON THE TEAM points to the computer screen. There's an aerial view of the compound with thermal imaging, or whatever Connor had called it.

Connor braces his arms on the top of the man's seat and looks down at the laptop. "And our backup plan?"

Computer Guy looks over his shoulder at him. "I'm still against the idea of using explosives to infiltrate the barriers."

We're inside a large eight-wheeler truck, not far from Carlos's place. The truck has been converted to something similar to a mobile SWAT unit. Lots of weapons and technology.

Five other guys who I met thirty minutes ago are sitting on the bench-style seats on each side of me. I've already forgotten their names, so I assigned them numbers in my head.

"It would make things a hell of a lot easier if we could get in without waking up every damn guard in the place. Plus, we don't want Carlos hurrying out some secret tunnel if he hears us." Mason comes up alongside Connor, but his attention is on me. His lips part a fraction as his eyes narrow.

"No." Connor shakes his head, and I'm not sure what is

going on between the two right now. He faces Mason and squares his hands on his hips.

"It's the best solution to our problem," Mason says.

"I had her come with us to babysit her, not to use her as bait."

"Bait?" I stand, my hands fisting at my sides as I interpret the sudden silent face-off between the two.

"It'd work," Computer Guy says while looking at me.

"She goes to the front entrance, gets the guards' attention, and they open up for her." Mason goes to the computer screen. "We'll have two snipers positioned here and here. They'll take out the guards, she'll run back to the truck, and then our team will get in with a lot less noise than the alternative way."

Connor curses under his breath and scratches at his chin. "You can say no."

"If it means getting inside, why wouldn't I agree?" But my heart skips into my throat at the idea I'll be putting myself directly in harm's way. It's one thing to talk big about what I'd be willing to do—it's another to actually do it.

"You're sure?" Connor's jaw tightens.

"Yes," I answer.

"Let's do this then." Connor grabs a bulletproof vest off the bench. "I can't give you one. It'd obviously raise suspicion with the guards."

"I get it." *Just breathe.*

"There are two men posted inside the main entrance, and then it looks like two in the back, and one on each side of the compound walking back and forth." Computer Guy touches the center of the image on screen. "As for the three main areas, which we believe to be living quarters, we've got about twenty people. Minimal movement, so it looks like they're sleeping."

"Twenty-six in total." Connor straps the vest on. "Some of those bodies could be captives, so look alive, people, and don't shoot unless there's no other choice."

Mason points to the guys I nicknamed Three and Five. "You're on sniper duty. We'll green-light the rest of you to come, once the two front guards have been immobilized." He motions to One and Four. "You guys take the sides and the guards in the back."

Number Four nods as he begins to pack weapons into the various compartments of his vest and cargo pants.

My heartbeat kicks up higher and higher as I think about my role in all of this.

Connor grips my shoulder, and I focus on the black-gloved hand there. I'm unable to look up at him, afraid he'll see the fear in my eyes. "You can change your mind."

"No." A quiver darts down my body, and I hope he doesn't feel the shudders in my shoulder.

"Okay," he drags the word out, as if still not convinced. "You got us on comms?"

Computer Guy makes an okay sign with his hand.

Everything is happening lightning fast.

Within a few minutes, I'm outside the truck, shaking my hands loose at my sides to try and release some tension.

"We're going to hang back and out of your line of sight, but we'll be here, don't worry. It's a half a mile, straight ahead." Connor hands me a cell phone and positions on his night vision goggles. "Use the light to keep on the path."

I take the phone, the flashlight app already switched on, and I point it at the dirt walkway.

I can do this.

I survived the McCullens for ten years. I can survive this.

"Turn it off once you see the compound walls," he says

and squeezes my forearm. "We're not going to let anything happen to you."

The knots in my stomach twist even more, and I release a breath. "Daughter or son?"

"What?"

"Which do you have?"

I hold the light up to see his face, and he shifts the goggles up. "Daughter." He smiles.

"Okay." My hand shakes, and I lower the light. "You'll get back to her when this is over. We'll all be okay."

"We'll all be okay," he repeats, and I listen to his words in my head over and over as I walk.

Then that voice becomes Cade's.

And when I tuck the light away and reach for the buzzer on the cement wall outside the mammoth dark wooden door, which looks like it belongs in medieval times, I remember my mother's eyes, her smile.

I remember why I'm here.

The taken ones.

I close my eyes as the door scrapes against the dirt and opens inward to the compound.

And I keep my eyes closed when I hear two bodies slam down by my feet.

The gunshots were quieter than the sounds of the fallen men.

I spin around to see the team on approach, moving in like a team of soldiers. "Go back." It's Connor's voice, even though they all look the same in their combat clothes.

I force my feet to move, and I run in the direction of the truck.

My body jolts and my heels dig into the ground at the sudden blare of a siren wailing behind me.

No . . .

I twist around and look back at the compound in the distance.

What if Carlos gets away?

I can't let any more people die because of me. I can't hide anymore while everyone else makes sacrifices.

And so, I go back.

I can barely find breath inside of me as I reach the door and kneel down by one of the dead guards.

I take his holstered weapon and remove the safety, thankful for once that I know my way around guns.

My nostrils flare.

My adrenaline spikes.

I press my back against the wall and move along it, trying to stay hidden in the shadows.

The sirens stop. Someone must've killed them, but it's too late. Our presence is known.

The sound of gunfire is all around, and yet, I don't see anyone. They must be inside the buildings, about twenty yards away from me.

I hold the gun tight in my right hand and nearly trip over a body on the ground.

It's a guard, thank God.

But my mind is focused on only one thing: prisoners. Does Carlos have anyone hidden here? If so, where would they be?

My mind is spinning, and more gunshots have my shoulders flinching as I move to walk through the open courtyard toward the sound of guns blaring within the buildings.

The popping of bullets slows as I edge around one side of a building.

I suck in a sharp breath when something—someone— grabs me from behind.

"No!" My arm is knocked down, the gun wrangled free from my hand.

My weapon smacks against the ground, and I cry in panic and twist from side to side, trying to get free.

The man's breath is at my ear as he grips me even tighter, putting too much pressure on my ribs.

He starts pulling me with him as he moves backward.

I continue to struggle, even trying to sink my teeth into his arm, but he's too strong.

I can't let him take me. I can't be this man's insurance plan to try and escape, because I'm sure that's what's going through his mind.

My shoe heels create a line in the dirt as he drags me, his grip a bit looser since he's trying to move us. If I can't get away, at least I can make a trail to our location.

Then I remember I have a voice, and so I scream as loud as my lungs and vocal cords will allow.

But we're nearing the exit, and I'm running out of time.

I dig my nails into his arm, clawing at him like a captured animal.

The night at the hotel when Cade taught me defense moves is a garbled mess in my mind.

Fear cradles my body in a tight cocoon, making it hard to remember what to do.

And then, like that, he stops.

His hands leave my body—for a second.

Then, one massive, calloused hand cups the base of my throat. My chin juts up high as I jerk my head from side to side. My eyes squeeze tight, and little black dots dance up and down before me.

"Release her."

A deep, powerful voice booms through the air, and I know that voice . . .

I'm losing my mind.

But then the deep, husky voice yells, "Let. Her. Go."

"I'll snap her neck," the man hisses over my shoulder, locking his other hand around my waist.

"No, you won't. You're not ready to die, are you?"

It has to be him, but it doesn't make sense. And then I realize that my eyes are still closed and all I have to do is open them. But what if I'm hallucinating? What if he's not really here?

Cade or no Cade—I need to get out of this.

I stop struggling for a minute. I need to concentrate, to focus.

And when I'm brave enough to open my eyes, I find Cade standing beneath a lamppost twenty feet away, the light casting a shadow over his face.

Having him rescue me is the stuff of fairy tales, not for women like me.

But here he is, holding a gun, and I'm damn sure he's prepared to use it.

He'll need my help if I'm going to get away unscathed. With a renewed sense of confidence, I telegraph the moves in my mind, knowing what I need to do now.

"I'll let her go once I'm safe," the guy says before cursing in Portuguese.

"Not gonna happen." Cade steps out of the shadow, his eyes narrowed right on me, and he gives the slightest head nod that this asshole holding me probably doesn't notice.

He's signaling me to make my move.

I think about the hell I've endured.

And then I think about the man standing before me, who came here for me . . .

I slam my heel into the man's boot, drop my weight, and twist my body to the side as fast as possible.

I collapse to the ground in a crouched position at the sound of gunfire echoing through my ears like a never-ending bell.

I scramble to all fours and look over at the body on the ground.

He's still alive. Why didn't Cade kill him?

The man's grabbing hold of his arm and cursing.

I flinch at the feel of Cade's hand on my shoulder. "You okay?"

I squeeze every emotion down my throat, the thickness making it hard to swallow. "Yeah," I whisper, then watch as he straddles the man and reels his arm back, knocking the guy hard in the face with the butt of his gun.

I lean back on my knees and stare at the now unconscious man. My hand flies to my mouth when I realize it's Carlos Perozo.

Cade kept him alive because he recognized him.

"You might need him for information." He stands and tucks the gun in the back of his pants, as if he's made for this life, as if shooting a human trafficker is a typical day of the week.

He's at my side now, his arm extended, but I'm still too stunned to take his hand.

I release a long, thankful breath and finally allow him to pull me up.

He holds on to my forearms for a moment, probably wanting to both hug me and yell at me.

Before I can open my mouth to apologize, there's a parade of cuffed men heading out of the main quarters. There are only about eight guys, so I have to assume the rest are dead.

"There weren't any captives here," Mason says as he approaches. "But we got the files."

"I take it this is Cade," Connor says casually, as if he's not too surprised, then he kneels beside Carlos. He flips his body over and slaps cuffs onto his wrists. "And why are you inside the compound?"

He's not asking Cade. No, he's directing his question to me.

I pull back from Cade's grasp and stand at his side, not sure what to do or say.

I wipe my dirty palms on my jeans, buying time to explain why I stupidly rushed into danger like one of the women in a horror film who should know better.

But my body goes stiff a moment later.

I can feel it in my bones.

I can feel him.

I reach behind Cade as fast as possible, grab the gun from his pants, and lock my arms in front of me. "What the hell are you doing here?"

My dad's in the compound with a gun in his hand, and he's walking toward us.

"Put the gun down." Cade's command has me looking over my shoulder at him, the sudden sense of betrayal causing confusion to swirl around inside of me.

Did Cade bring him to me?

No, he wouldn't.

"He had my back when I was trying to get you free from Carlos. He was waiting to make a move, in case I needed the support." Cade rests a hand over the one that's holding the gun, but I can't lower my arm.

Hell, no.

"I won't go back to New York." My hands tremble. My body shakes.

It doesn't dawn on me until a few seconds later what

231

Cade even said. He's working with my dad? What the ever-loving fuck?

"Leave," I yell.

"Listen, I think we're all a little tense here, so why don't we finish up what we started and work this out afterward." Connor stands in front of the barrel of my gun, trying to serve as the voice of reason.

"I'm not here to take you back."

Connor's tall frame blocks my father from my sight, but his words penetrate through the air, as hard as ever.

"Give me the gun." Cade lifts his hand from mine and opens his palm. "Now."

23

GIA

My fingertips dig into my thighs as the truck moves over the bumpy road, heading toward the hotel where Connor plans to drop me off. He wants to get out of Brazil as fast as possible in case Carlos has any government friends who might try and stop him from bringing Carlos out of the country.

My dad is sitting opposite me, with the back of his head against the wall and his eyes closed. His cheeks are hollow, and his skin is weathered, with age spots smudged into splotchy patches beneath his eyes.

He's getting old. When did that happen?

We still haven't spoken since I turned the gun over to Cade.

I haven't talked to anyone, in fact.

I keep running through everything that happened in my mind, trying to digest it all.

My scalp prickles and goose bumps bloom over my skin at the feel of Cade's eyes on me.

Our eyes connect, and his Adam's apple moves in his bronzed throat.

Slow and steady breaths, his chest lifts and falls, and I can't stop looking at him, even when he rips his attention away.

If someone had injected me with a steroid, I wouldn't be surprised, because I feel like I'm on something. Unstoppable.

Maybe tonight didn't go quite as planned, but we came out on top with no one hurt, and that's what matters.

"You okay?" Mason sits next to me. "We can drop these guys off at the hotel, and you can come with us."

As much as I want to take Mason up on his offer, for my dad, at least, I know I need to deal with this situation on my own. I can't run forever, and that's what would happen if I stay in this truck and leave Brazil tonight.

"No, I'm good."

"If you change your mind, let me know."

I close my eyes, and my stomach wrenches as I remember the feel of Carlos's hands on me and the sound of Cade firing a gun shortly after.

I would have loved to see that man die, but Connor may need to pump him for more information. And, just as importantly, I wouldn't want Cade becoming a murderer because of me.

"I'm sorry, by the way," I say as we near the hotel.

"For what?" Mason asks.

I clutch the bench on each side of my thighs. "For running into the compound."

He nudges me in the side. "Hey, I would have done the same thing, if it makes you feel better."

I force a quick, closed-lip smile. "Thanks."

Connor pulls my attention away from his brother when he hollers, "We're here."

I have to face my father now, and I'm not sure how to do that.

Dad heads to the exit without even making eye contact, which suits me fine.

"You ready?" Cade's gravelly tone makes me wonder how pissed off he is at me.

Maybe my father forced him to come? That would make the most sense. Then again, could anyone force Cade into doing something he didn't want to do?

"Yeah, I guess," I murmur, placing my hand inside his warm one, and I almost shut my eyes at the feel of his touch.

My knees wobble as I stand, but once I'm upright, he lets go of my hand.

"Let's go see Mya. She's probably worried about you." His fingertips splay against the small of my back as we walk to the exit.

He hops out first and holds both arms up in the air, offering to lift me down.

I take a hesitant step back, staring down at him as he waits for me.

"Gia." For the first time, I hear something different in his tone when he says my name. It's like a plea, and it catches me off guard.

It takes me a moment, but I crouch down and press my hands to his shoulders and he lowers me.

My lungs contract. I try to remember to breathe.

I can't seem to drop my hands from him, and he's not in a rush to let go of me either.

Someone from behind fakes a cough, and so I stumble back out of Cade's arms and face Connor and a few of his men.

Connor points to the other truck that was following us, the one with Carlos and his guards packed inside. "Once we get those assholes to safer ground, we'll take a look at the files. I'll be in touch soon."

"My mother's name is Sara Oliveira." I know Mya told him, but I need to look into his eyes when I say it. I need to believe Connor will do everything in his power to find her.

Connor and Cade exchange a look. It's dark outside, despite a few lampposts off in the distance near the hotel, so I can't get a read on whatever unspoken message is passing between the two of them.

"We'll call. Don't worry." Mason pats my shoulder and offers me a half-smile like he's trying to reassure me without setting me up for disappointment. Maybe they don't think they'll find her, but they don't know how strong my mother is . . .

"Thank you." I scan the faces of the men who helped bring Carlos to justice tonight. "Everyone." Emotion starts to catch in my throat, and I reach out for Connor's forearm. "Kiss your daughter for me."

"Will do." He climbs out of sight, and I wait until the trucks are gone before turning in the direction of the hotel.

My dad and Cade trail behind me. And it's so damn weird.

It's one of those moments when you can't decide if you're actually asleep or dreaming inside of a dream.

It can't be real, can it?

Silence swallows the air, suffocating even the sounds of our heavy footsteps as we head to the hotel.

Once inside, the fluorescent lighting has me blinking a few times, as black spots appear before my eyes.

My arms go tense at my sides when we begin to rise in the elevator. It's as if we're all stuffed inside a coffin together. The space is too small.

I can smell everything, too. Cade's sexy, natural scent, plus blood, and maybe something that smells like gasoline. I need to get out so I can suck in a breath of fresh air. The two of them consume all of the oxygen.

I drag my attention up the mirrored doors to Cade's face.

My lips twitch and flatten as his eyes drop to my mouth.

The last time we were together, he was deep inside of me, and now—now what happens? Where do we go from here?

The doors part and I barely make it halfway down the hall when I see Mya darting in my direction. "Oh, thank God. Connor called and said you were good, but when he told me he left you alone with these guys—" She cuts herself off and flings her arms around my neck.

"I'm okay, but if you squeeze any harder, I might not be."

"Oh, shit. Sorry." A nervous laugh falls from her lips as she drops her hold on me. "Hi, Cade."

He scratches at the back of his head as if this situation is making him uncomfortable. Well, yeah, me too.

"We should get inside," he says instead of a greeting.

Mya nods, but she doesn't take her eyes off my dad. She sneers as he moves past her and goes into our room.

This can't be happening right now.

Once inside, Cade goes over to the small sink next to the mini fridge and starts to scrub at his hands, as if washing away the fact he shot a man tonight.

I stand by the door. Part of me wants to escape.

My dad removes a gun from the back of his pants and rests it on his lap once he's seated on the couch.

"Um. No." Mya marches in front of him and holds a hand out. She's fearless, and I admire the hell out of her. "No guns in here."

"I'm not going to shoot anyone, but it's not so comfortable sitting on the thing." A slow smile rolls over his lips so fast I wonder if I imagined it.

I take quick breaths as I absorb the scene.

My dad. Cade. Mya. Me.

No one is being tortured or killed.

Progress?

"You should have never gone after Carlos like that," Dad scolds me.

I take a few steps farther into the room, still unsure of what might happen.

Cade tosses a towel into the sink and faces me. "Your dad's here to help."

His words have my knees buckling, disbelief pulling at me like the strings from a puppeteer who can't decide on the choreography.

"No. That's not true. Don't believe him." I cross my arms, a coldness spreading through my limbs and settling in the pit of my stomach.

"I wouldn't be here with him if it weren't the case," Cade says.

It's like someone went into my head and vandalized it. It's all fucked up in there.

I don't know what, or whom, to believe right now.

When I still don't speak, Cade diverts his attention to Mya and my dad. "We need to be alone." He's not offering them a choice, but there's no way my dad—

"I'll get a room." My dad's back on his feet, tucking the gun away before I have time to be shocked.

"Uh, Gia? You okay with this?" Mya stands before me and squeezes my shoulders.

I stare at Cade now, transfixed by his blue eyes. "Yeah."

"You sure?" she presses. "I can stay."

"No, you can't." There's an icy edge to his voice, and it has Mya stepping back. The woman can face down drug lords, but Cade is able to knock the wind from anyone's sails.

Maybe not mine, though. I know his heart.

238

"If you need me, I'll be in the suite across the hall where Connor was staying." Mya releases an unsteady breath.

My jaw goes slack as my dad leaves, and a tingling in my chest spreads like fire into my arms and fingertips.

When it's only us, Cade hides one hand in his cargo pants pocket and looks down at the carpet. Yeah, the khaki fatigues aren't a look I ever thought I'd see on a man like him.

Cade, a rugged hero?

The man can't help it—he's always sexy. And even in a moment like this, I'm still inexplicably drawn to him. My thighs squeeze tight as a burn throbs between my legs. How is that possible after a night like this?

The adrenaline, I suppose.

I don't cross the room and go to him, though. I can't get my stubborn self to move, and so I stay rooted halfway between the door and the living area, standing eight or so feet away from him.

"You ran." He doesn't look up, but the tone of his voice is hard and unforgiving.

"I know, but—"

"You left."

I fumble for the right words as knots of unease wedge in my throat.

He lifts his hand from his pocket, and he's holding something.

My card.

I take an immediate step forward. Just one. I'm not ready to move more than that yet.

"That was for your protection. I didn't want anything happening to you." I fight back the pull of emotions that are luring me into a sudden sob.

He flicks the card, and it flits around, drifting from side to side, until it lands on the floor.

"You shouldn't have left me." He levels me with his gaze, and my insides tremble, the need to run to him overpowering. All of my senses are in overdrive, and all I want is to be in his arms.

"I'm sorry." I shake my head, my mouth pinching tight.

"Don't do it again." The words rumble from deep in his throat, and then I do it.

I go to him.

I throw myself against him, frantic with the need to be near him. I plant kisses all over his neck before he seizes my face, forcing us to be nose to nose.

"I missed you," I cry.

His irises become a darker blue, almost a charcoal gray, and his breathing grows heavier. The want and need are there, but it's more than lust. Whatever it is, I feel it, too.

He doesn't say anything back, so I press my lips to his.

His tongue twines with mine, and he deepens the kiss before walking backward, still maintaining his grip on my face.

We stumble into the adjoining bedroom, and then he releases me to lock our door. "We still need to talk." He rushes out the words, but I don't want a voice of reason right now. I want to lose control.

Carlos is in cuffs.

Connor will find my mom.

And right now, Cade is with me. He came for me, even if he shouldn't have, even if I wanted to keep him safe. He still came.

"Later." I rip my blouse over my head and toss it to the floor, going for my bra clasp without hesitation.

"Are you sure we shouldn't talk first?" His hands are fisted at his sides, but he keeps his composure. Always in control.

"No talking."

But there's a grim twist to his mouth and a pensive look on his face that has me wondering whether this is a good idea. I press the heel of my hand to my chest, trying to steady my heart so I can hear my thoughts clearly.

But he grabs me and gently tosses me over and onto the bed.

I rush to get my pants off as his drop to the floor.

"I can't wait," he grinds out and positions himself on top of me.

"Then take me." I buck my hips up, more than ready for him.

I'll always be ready for him.

He kisses me again, a rough, almost bruising connection of his mouth to mine.

But it's when he lifts his head and finds my eyes that my heart stutters. The head of his cock presses against my opening, but he doesn't move.

His eyes close. "I need to hear you say it."

I grip his biceps and rock my hips up, needing him to fill me. "What?"

"That you'll never run again."

Ohh. "I'll never run."

"We face problems together from now on. You got it?" He opens his eyes, and the color has warmed again. He's back.

"I promise." He nearly kisses my words as they fall from my mouth, and then he buries himself deep and hard inside of me. I growl out some sort of strange cry.

He thrusts in and out, filling me more and more with each and every movement.

And this man . . . God, this man could go all night. His strength and stamina—I'm no match for him. I orgasm too fast, my body totally spent.

"Flip around and grab the headboard," he commands even though my legs are jelly. But he's still hard as a rock.

I do as I'm told.

He moves in and out, slowly at first.

He squeezes my flesh, twists my nipple, and I gasp as my thighs clench again, every time we connect.

My body quivers and my knuckles start to hurt from holding on to the headboard so tight, but I can't let go. He's driving into me with everything he has now, and I'm getting so lightheaded from the desire sweeping through me yet again, that if I even loosen my grip, I might pass out.

He bites into my shoulder, and I press my ass back against him, knowing I'm hitting that sexy V above his cock.

"Fuuuck." He releases, his warmth filling me, and I lose control again.

We're both breathing wildly.

He rolls me over a minute later, and I'm wet and sticky and covered in his come. My hand plops across my chest.

He looks at me, and our noses almost touch. "You wanna grab a shower with me?"

"You do kind of smell." I half-smile.

"Well, I haven't had a chance to really clean up since your father kind of doused the car in gasoline."

My mouth falls open. "Explain."

"I told you we had stuff to talk about."

"Well, him almost killing you is important information that you should have led with." I bite the inside of my cheek, hating that this is all my fault. "I'm sorry."

"Hey, some people get to bond with their girlfriend's father over drinks, but your dad—"

"You did not just use the words *bond* and *father* in the same sentence!"

He grins. "I wouldn't go quite so far as to say we bonded,

but there was something we discovered we're both very passionate about." He sits upright and ropes a hand around the back of his neck. "You."

"You still have a lot of explaining to do." I get off the bed and start for the bathroom, assuming he'll follow. He does have a weakness for my ass.

There's a sting on my flesh a moment later, and I shriek and turn around. "Did you just slap me?"

His teeth sink into his bottom lip as he lowers his attention down my body. "I couldn't resist."

"I'll pay you back for that." I start to pivot around, then halt halfway. "Wait. Did you say *girlfriend* earlier?"

He grabs me and pulls me against him, my back to his chest, his length already springing back up, hard and ready.

"Like you said, we have a lot to talk about."

* * *

"JESUS CHRIST." CADE SITS UPRIGHT AND RUBS HIS EYES.

"Who is it?" I call out, forgetting where I am. The banging on the door is incessant and obnoxious, and I'm tired as hell.

"It's your father."

My world spins. Everything starts to go black again. The color drifts from my sight and darkness swarms all around me.

My dad.

He's here.

But . . .

"He's going to know we had sex." I tuck the sheet beneath my chin in a panic. "He'll kill you."

Cade reaches for my cheek and palms it. "Sweetie, I'm

pretty sure he figured it out back in Havana, and he didn't kill me."

"He didn't kill you. Right." I release a ragged breath. "Okay."

"But you should probably get dressed, so we don't tempt him into shooting me in the leg. He's still a father and all."

"Hurry," Mya hollers.

She's with my dad? Seriously?

"We don't have much time to prepare. Rory's on his way," Mya adds.

Holy shit. "How?" I scramble out of bed.

Cade pulls on his pants so casually I want to scream.

"What?" He shrugs.

"Didn't you hear her? Rory's coming."

Cade smiles. "Yeah, I know."

I drop my shirt over my head but don't put on my jeans. I'm too astonished to do anything until answers come my way. "How do you know?"

"Your dad and I came up with a plan. Jessica helped out, too."

My spine straightens. My body goes stiff. "You're serious right now, aren't you?"

"Would I joke about something like that?" He raises a brow.

Indecision pulls at me. This doesn't feel right. "My dad must be tricking us. I don't believe he's on our side."

He stalks toward me and grabs hold of my hands. "Look at me."

I swallow and nod.

"Good. Now focus on what I'm saying." He leans even closer, so our mouths are almost touching, and then he does it. He presses a soft and slow kiss to my lips. When he lifts his head, there's a smile in his eyes.

"What was that for?"

"To calm you down."

"Oh." Maybe it worked. I'm not quite as tight. "Okay. I'm focused now."

"I trust that your father is on our side. I know it sounds crazy."

"Because it is," I snap, the tension springing back in place. He doesn't know the man. My father is a liar.

"Gia." His large hands tighten around mine, and I take a deep breath. "I left New York to protect you. I followed you here, even when you tried to push me away. I think it should be clear at this point I have your best interest at heart. So, when I tell you that your father's objectives align with ours, you need to believe me."

I wrangle my hands free and spin away.

"Guys!" Mya's voice cries through the door.

"Give us one goddamn minute," Cade shouts, effectively silencing her.

I cup my mouth and his hands find my shoulders and gently grip them. "Your father has been lying to you, but it was because he thought he was protecting you."

"And you believe him?" I whip around, and his arms go to his sides.

"I'm pretty good at reading people."

"Oh, yeah? Read me." I circle an index finger around in front of me. "What does my face say to you right now?"

He huffs a frustrated breath and turns away.

"Tell me." I grab his bicep, trying to get sight of his eyes again, angry that he'd believe a murderer over me.

"No."

"Tell me," I say, my voice cracking.

He looks over his shoulder at me with a hard expression. "You're scared. That's what I see. You're so scared you can't even see straight." He shirks his arm free of my grasp, grabs his T-shirt off the floor, and slowly rolls it down over his hard abdomen.

"Yeah, I'm scared my dad is going to ship me back to that prison of a life in New York." I grit my teeth together.

"No. You're afraid you've been lying to yourself for the last ten years."

"About what?" My head jerks back like I was smacked. I don't understand. But when his eyes land on my angel wings tattoo, the heaviness in my stomach turns to lead.

"Wait," I whisper the word as he grabs hold of the doorknob.

"You need to hear the truth." He swings the door open, and I blink a few times, realizing I'm still without pants.

Once fully dressed, I go into the living room. My father is next to the TV stand, and he extends a coffee my way.

"I'm good." I roll my eyes and look to where Mya's sitting on the couch next to Cade. He's got a coffee in his hands, too, and I can't help but wonder if my dad laced it with poison.

"What the hell is going on?" I lean against the wall by the bedroom door and cross my arms.

Dad looks down at his watch. "Rory is on his way from the airport."

"What?" My head's pounding, the pain growing in my temples. "And I assume you're the one who told him where we are?"

"Of course." My dad sets aside the coffee I turned down and takes a sip of his own.

How is everyone so damn casual right now?

"Rory wouldn't have come himself if I didn't tell him I needed him here."

"And why would we want Rory here? Why have him

come unless you're planning on bringing me back to that hell?" I shove off the wall and stare at him in disbelief.

"It's the only way to ensure you never have to go back. Well"—Dad looks over at Cade and then back at me —"unless you want to, of course."

New York with Cade?

How is that possible?

"I'm two seconds away from running out this door." I stand before my father as if we're in a showdown, but he doesn't look angry. He looks tired. Sad, even.

Cade doesn't have to say anything, because when I look over at him, I can see it in his eyes. *No more running.*

I hiss, but say, "I'm listening." I don't have to believe him, but for Cade's sake, I'll give my father a chance.

"Mya, let's give them a minute alone." Cade rises and motions for her to follow.

"No. Don't go," I plead.

He stares at me for a long moment but finally settles back onto the couch.

"No lies. Just the truth. You owe me that much after chaining me to a life of death and fear." I head to the window before swiveling around to face my dad. But all I see is a pair of dull, lifeless green eyes looking back at me.

His shoulders sag, and for some reason, he doesn't look like the boogeyman anymore.

"I've always been honest. I just didn't tell you everything." He starts to walk toward me.

His hands slide into the pockets of his slacks, and he angles his head but keeps his eyes on me. "Your mother's name won't be on that USB drive."

I swallow, knowing exactly what he's going to say next— understanding why Cade looked at my tattoo, but still, I refuse to believe it. "No." My hands ball into fists at my sides, and I bury my fingertips into my palms as tight as possible until my own nails cause me pain.

"I'm the one who buried her," he says in a low, throaty voice.

"You're lying." I take short, quick breaths.

He steps closer, and I can't move anymore with the window to my back. My emotions catch in my throat, a bubble of pain ready to explode.

"Your mother was a fighter. And as soon as those pigs bought her, she fought so hard against them they ended up killing her." Pain edges through his voice, sadness overtaking his face. "She was willing to die, rather than let those bastards near her body. You need to understand. You need to know that what she did took courage. She refused to be a prisoner."

"No. Fighting to live—to see me again—would have been courageous." But that's not fair . . . and I hate myself almost immediately for what I said.

She was in an impossible situation. There's only one person who was weak. The man who took her.

My hands tremble as they cover my face, and my dad wraps his arms around me and pulls me against his chest, and I don't even have the energy to fight him. I sob into his chest until there's nothing left inside of me.

When he lets go, I wipe away the rest of my tears and look over at Mya and Cade. His palm is to his forehead, his eyes shut, and Mya's softly crying.

I turn away from everyone and plant a palm to the window, lowering my head against the glass. "I'm being selfish," I whisper. "I wanted her to still be alive so I could have my mother again."

The truth grips hold of me, and I want to let it go. I want to go back to being naïve, to being hopeful she's out there. "I want you to take me to her."

"I told Cade where she's buried. After all of this is over, he can take you."

"This doesn't change the fact I still don't trust you." My voice quavers, emotion threading heavier than normal through each of my words. "Why do you want Rory here?"

"So I can bury him, too."

When I face him, I see the slight twitch in his jaw. It's obvious that he's angry. He hates Rory. How could I have not known this until now?

Cade's on his feet, and he's working at the tension in his neck, his eyes cast down at the floor. I'm not used to his silence, but I guess he's decided to give my father the driver's seat in all of this insanity.

My shoulders hunch forward, my body aching to rest and let go of today. But that's not possible.

"Why now? Why do you want to stop him now?" If I'm going to trust him, he needs to prove he's worthy of it.

"We don't have much time," Mya says from behind.

"I know, but I won't agree to any plan if I don't know what the hell is going on."

"You don't need to. This is on me. None of you are leaving this room, not until it's over." Dad turns to face Cade. "That includes you."

Cade nods, his eyes meeting mine for a moment, and I can tell it's hard for him to take orders, but it doesn't look like he has much choice right now.

"I never wanted you in this life, and I'm sorry." My father clears his throat and forces his gaze to mine. "I'm not a good person, and I don't deserve your forgiveness, but I was trying to make things right for you . . . but you expedited things by running." He fakes a laugh. "You're definitely your mother's daughter, all right."

I fidget with the bottom of my shirt, twisting it around my

finger as if I'm that little girl again, looking out the window, wondering if my dad will ever show . . .

And here he is, and it's as if I'm actually seeing him for the first time.

"How will killing Rory protect me? Won't his people want revenge? Won't I be in even more danger?"

"Not with the plan Jessica and I came up with," Cade says.

"The one we talked about?" I think about the conversation we had with Jessica, and it feels like an eternity ago. "Is your friend dirty, or is Rory a snitch?" My forehead tightens as I look back and forth between Cade and my father, waiting for clarity.

"My friend is dirty." A film of unease shadows his face, the reality of the truth unsettling for him. "But that doesn't mean Rory's people have to know that."

"I don't understand."

My dad reaches out for my shoulder, resting a palm there, and I don't flinch, which is surprising. "I'm the one who turned the McCullens in. Richard is in prison because of me."

My eyes widen, and my stomach falls.

"Rory should have been locked up, too." His brows pull together. "I anonymously provided the Feds with everything they could ever need to imprison both Rory and his father, and yet, Rory never got sentenced."

"You're the snitch?" My thoughts are growing fuzzy, and nothing in my world makes sense right now.

"I was trying to get you a way out of this life, but when Rory took over, I realized I had to come up with a new plan." Dad turns his back and retrieves his gun.

It's big and black, and I have no idea what kind it is, but if it's meant to kill Rory, I don't even care. I'm okay with murder. In this case, I'm okay.

"We think Rory made a deal in exchange for his freedom," Mya says. Apparently, my father caught her up on everything while Cade and I were rolling around beneath the sheets last night.

It's like a punch in the gut, being the last one to figure everything out.

"So what do we do?" I ask.

Cade looks at his watch. "Jessica will be forcing Jerry to phone Rory's main crew a few minutes after Rory's arrival. He'll be letting them know Rory's working with the Feds."

"But you said Jerry's dirty."

"Which is why I don't feel guilty about having Jessica hold a gun to his head to make the call."

My fingers fan against my breastbone, taking this all in.

"Nobody likes Rory. His own people can't stand him, and you know that. They won't be too shocked to learn of his betrayal. They loved Richard, and they'll turn on Rory with even the slightest doubt planted." Dad twists a black cylinder to the end of his gun.

"So, why do you need to kill him?" Not that I'm against it.

"To protect you," Dad says. "To prevent anyone from bothering you after all of this is over, his crew needs to think Rory's an informant—which he is. But to keep you safe, Rory needs to die."

"What if something happens to you in there?" My stomach lurches at the thought of losing another parent, which is crazy, because I've spent ten years trying to get away from this man. Ten years hating him.

"There's a chance I'll get caught in the crossfire if Rory or his guys start shooting at each other. Rory might try and do something stupid."

"Tell her the truth. She deserves that." Cade's words have my attention switching to him.

"What?" I mouth the question while looking back at my dad.

He lowers the fully assembled gun to his side and cocks his head, eyeing me.

"I should go. They'll be expecting me."

Realization barrels at me like I've been shot. "You want to die, don't you? You don't plan on coming back, do you?" My lower lip trembles, and I rush to him and throw my arms around his neck.

He's a killer.

And he belongs in hell.

But he's my dad.

"I love you," I whisper into his ear, even if it doesn't make sense.

He holds me tight against him with one strong arm. "I'm so proud of you. Your mother would be so proud of you, too," he says with a strained voice. "Bury me next to her, will ya?"

A quick kiss on my cheek, and then he pulls back and starts for the door.

"No!" I rush toward him, but he doesn't look back.

"Gia, stop," Mya calls out, trying to reach for my arm as I go past her.

The door slams shut, and Cade wraps his arms around me, holding on to me as I fight to break free.

I drop my weight into his arms, sliding to the ground, and he goes down with me.

"He has to do it. Let him do it," he says into my ear as new tears flood my face.

"No," is all I can say.

I can't lose two parents in one night.

"You'll never be safe with him alive. He doesn't want

someone using you against him," he says in a rush to try and get me to understand, to calm me down. But it's not working.

"He's going to die because of me, just like my mom did." I close my eyes, but finally, stop resisting.

"He wants you to be free to live your life."

I tuck my knees to my chest and rock in place, trying to maintain my sanity, but I think I've lost it.

"I've got you," he murmurs. "Always."

"Shit," Mya says, and I look up to see her hurrying to the door. "Did you hear that?"

A few minutes later, the fire alarms sound, and the hallways grow loud with commotion.

"We gotta get out of here." Cade stands and reaches down to help me to my feet.

Mya opens the door and people are running down the hall. "Wait," I rasp, my voice hoarse.

"I'll get it," Cade says before I can move, reading my thoughts.

"Thank you," I say once he retrieves my sketchpad.

I clutch it to my chest and join the frenzied people in the hall, but we walk slowly. We move cautiously.

We know there's no fire.

We can only hope Rory is dead.

But my dad just might be, too.

2 4

GIA

"They're beautiful. She'd love them."

I set the bouquet of flowers down before the tombstone and remain squatting. "Sara Cardona." I smooth my hand over the carved name.

My life has been made up of so many half-truths that I need to figure out who I even am.

I've gone my entire life thinking I'm Brazilian and Irish, only to find out my mother was Columbian. If my father didn't tell Cade everything in that short span of time they were forced together, almost two weeks ago, I could've died thinking I was someone else.

"It makes sense."

I look over my shoulder at him, my eyes welling with tears.

"If your dad wanted to keep you and your mom hidden twenty-five years ago, of course he'd change her last name and have you guys live somewhere that's not a predominantly Spanish-speaking country." He holds a palm up. "I know, I know. They could've clued you in on the fact you're Columbian, at least."

My stomach twists and I push to my feet and look over at the two graves on the left side of my mom's. Her parents. Grandparents I never knew.

"They died when she was so young," I mumble under my breath, wondering how I could have been so clueless.

"I guess they figured you'd be safer living the lie than risking what could happen if someone discovered the truth."

My lips roll inward, the emotions still fresh, even if some part of me came to terms with losing her a long time ago. The moment I'd burned the ink onto my skin, I had known the truth. But right after, I slipped into the quicksand of denial.

"He wasn't a good man," I say when I look at Dad's gravestone, next to my mom's. "But I guess he loved us."

My father had given Cade a combination that unlocked a safe in New York. Cade had his brother open it since we haven't returned yet. Corbin said it looked like a safe of memoirs: pictures, baby items, and so forth.

I'm not sure why he kept them from me. Maybe he thought I wouldn't ever be able to let go if I was reminded of Mom. Instead, it created an emptiness inside me.

I back up a few steps and let out a breath. It's been a long two weeks.

Rory is dead.

I'm no longer wanted by the mob.

Cade's family is back in New York—and they're all safe, including him.

But both of my parents are buried in front of me.

"You want to come back again tomorrow?" He reaches for my hand and squeezes it.

A slight breeze rustles the tree branches in the distance, but the warmth of the sun washes over us, warming me. It's as if the sun is cleansing us both of our sins.

"No. They're not beneath the ground." I sniffle. "They're in my heart."

25

GIA

HE'S BEEN ON HIS COMPUTER ALL NIGHT. I'M PRETTY SURE HE snuck out of bed after I fell asleep. I can always tell when he's not next to me. I don't sleep as well.

"Are you almost caught up?" I clasp my hands together behind my back, stretching.

He pushes away from the kitchen table and closes his laptop. "I've been away for weeks." Laughter rolls from his lips as he spins around and grabs me by the hips. "It's going to take me a while to get caught up on the emails, let alone everything else."

"Well, it was your idea to come here. You could be back in that big tower office of yours, barking out orders and making your employees quake with fear."

His chin lifts and a pair of stormy blues settles on my face. He raises the hem of my tank top and presses his mouth to my stomach. His thumbs smooth over my skin alongside his lips. "Is that how you picture me at work? A dictator?"

"I know how you are in bed, so I can only imagine what you're like there." My teeth sink into my bottom lip when his hand travels up to my breast and palms it, his mouth still making my stomach flutter as his four-day-old beard rubs against my flesh.

"You don't like when I'm in charge in bed?" His fingers pinch my nipple, and I arch my hips forward, giving in to the pressure that pulses between my legs.

"I didn't say that."

"I'd be happy to let you take control tonight." A huskiness moves through his voice, and a shiver licks up my spine and splinters out through my veins.

"You're such a liar."

I can feel his smile against my skin, his mouth still planting kisses all over my abdomen.

He drops his hand to my hip bone and pulls back to look at me. "What can I say? I'm a changed man. Maybe it's the air here."

"Rio can do that." I grin.

We've been in Rio de Janeiro for five days now. We came after a week in Columbia, where I spent time learning more about my mother's true roots.

He had his brother ship his laptop and work to him. He seems hesitant to go back, and I'm sure it's because of me.

Even though Rory's dead and most of his crew are in county jail, thanks to the exposé Mya wrote last week, he probably assumes I'm not ready to face the city.

"What are you afraid of?" I'm ruining the moment, but our time in Brazil has already been filled with so many moments that maybe it's time to face reality.

I just have no idea what my new life is supposed to look like.

"I'm not afraid of anything," he says.

I shuffle back and out of his reach and head to the sink to fill a pot of water for coffee. He rented us a beautiful little house on the outskirts of the city, and it has a killer view of the Christ the Redeemer statue.

Warm hands rest on each side of my ass cheeks. Maybe I should have put pants on before coming out here. I knew that only a tank and panties would distract Cade from having any real conversation.

Maybe I didn't realize I was ready to have it until now, though.

My head falls back, my ear almost touching my shoulder when he slides his hands around to hold me. "I think you're avoiding going home."

"No," he says into my ear. "I can work from anywhere. Hell, you can sit on my lap while I'm on conference calls."

I chuckle. "Well, that wouldn't end well. I'm pretty sure you'd be unable to focus with me grinding on you."

"What? You can't be good and just straddle me?" His lips twist into a knowing smirk, his eyes turning robin's egg blue, light and free.

He's right about one thing: he's a changed man.

We both changed.

And I refuse to let the deaths of my parents become a perpetual shadow of darkness over me. My mom would want more for me, and my father—well, he might have been a bad man, but he died so I could live, so I should do exactly that.

"Ahem." I turn and drape my arms over his shoulders. "You're the one who wouldn't be able to stop yourself from behaving."

"Never." His lips meet mine for a brief kiss. "I'm always in control, remember?" He smiles and touches his forehead to mine.

"So then tell me why you don't want to go back to New York."

He grumbles and backs up, releasing me. "We need a vacation."

I wave a hand at his laptop. "And you've barely slept on this so-called vacation. As soon as I'm asleep, you work. You're going to burn yourself out. It's not fair to you. I've messed up your life enough. You should head home."

He leans back against the kitchen island, studying me from a few feet away, and I copy his move but fold my arms. I'm not backing down on this.

"First of all, you didn't screw up my life. We've been through this. You brought me back to life."

He's said these words to me before, and the honesty and almost poeticness of it gets me every time, especially from someone who claims to be carved from ice.

"Secondly"—he shoves away from the counter and comes back to me, as if the small distance is too much to bear—"I'll do whatever makes you happy. And being here makes you happy, right?"

My eyes fall shut as his question sweeps through my mind.

"I used to think it would. I used to think that, if only I could make my way back here, everything would be okay." My breath catches in my throat at the touch of his hands on my shoulders.

"And now?"

"Now, I only care about being wherever you are." Maybe it sounds cliché, like something from a Harlequin novel, but it's true.

"And what if I feel the same?" His thumbs caress the sides of my bare arms, then one finger slips beneath the strap on my shoulder.

"Then I think we should get back to New York. I also think that, maybe, you're avoiding your family for some reason." I open my eyes. "You should come clean with Grace and Corbin. Tell them who you really are."

His lips lift, and his eyes focus on mine. Like flecks of gold glistening beneath the sun, there are bits of amber within his blue eyes. "And who am I really?"

"You're a good man."

He huffs out a breath and lets go of me. I can tell he's going to back away, so I grab his biceps, demanding his attention.

"You have a family, Cade. Maybe your parents are screwed up, but you need to hold on tight to your brother and sister and never let go. You're lucky to have them, and they need to know how you really feel—that you care about them."

"They know," he grumbles.

"But they don't know everything." I swallow, knowing what I'm about to say will completely eviscerate anything left of his fun, flirty mood. "They don't know about Samantha and how your father blackmailed you."

"What good would come from telling them?" he bites out.

"It's a start at truly building a solid relationship. You're never going to be the brother they need if you keep your walls up. This would be a giant step in the right direction."

His lips tighten, his face hardening, and I'm worried I'm losing him.

"Why can you be so open with me, but not with them?" I palm his face, the prickliness of his beard tickling my hand.

"Because you and I are . . ." He lets his voice trail off as his hand comes up to cover mine. Then he lifts my palm and kisses it. "You're the woman I love, so it's different."

My heart stutters in my chest, and my stomach drops.

His blue eyes are shielded by his lids now, and he angles

his head down. "Shit, I fucked that up. I was planning on telling you in a more romantic way."

I make a fist and tuck it beneath his chin, tipping his head up, needing him to look at me. "Are you kidding?" A thin layer of liquid forms over my eyes, the tears threatening to fall.

"What?" He finally looks at me.

"I'm not a girl who needs romantic gestures."

"And what do you need?"

I sniffle. "You." I sling my arms around his neck, and he holds me against him as I whisper into his ear, "I love you, too."

26

CADE

"Wow." Corbin scrubs a hand through his hair and rises to his feet. "He's even more of an asshole than I realized."

My shoulders arch back, and my spine stiffens at the realization of what I've done, of what Gia helped me understand I needed to do.

The truth about everything is exposed, and my past is no longer a secret.

"I'm so sorry." Grace crosses the room to where I'm standing in front of the desk, and she reaches for my arm. "I wish we could have been there for you."

I shrug. All of these emotions are still a little foreign to me, and I'm not fully equipped to deal with them.

She rests a hand on her growing stomach and rubs her belly. "Thank you for finally opening up, though."

I nod, still not sure what to say.

"And when do we get to meet the woman who's responsible for the new you?" she asks.

Gia and I returned to New York a few days ago, and today was my first official day back at the office. I hadn't planned on inviting Corbin and Grace here to spill the truth of my ugly past, but my hand had lifted the phone and called them, as if on autopilot.

I blame Gia for this.

I fight a smile when I think about her.

It's our first day away from each other since she ran off to Brazil a month ago, and it hurts like fuck.

"We can get dinner soon."

Corbin folds his arms and leans back against the wall of windows. "And you guys are really going to move in together?"

"That's the idea." I didn't want to have a fresh start in a home where I've had dozens of women over. And I want Gia to have a say in where we'll live. She deserves it after living the last ten years beneath someone's thumb.

Plus, she's moving back to Manhattan for me, to a place she never thought she'd step foot in again. I want her to be happy.

Hell, I want her to be more than just happy.

"Have you seen Jessica since you've been back?" Corbin's jaw locks tight, and there's a pinch of anger in the muscles in his cheeks. He's thinking about Jerry, I'm sure. He was closer to him than I was, and it killed him when he learned his friend was dirty.

Jerry's fiancée felt the burn the most, though, when he went to jail.

"She stopped by my place yesterday." I sigh. "I owe her a lot. If it weren't for her, I don't know how this would have all turned out."

"And Owen?" Grace lifts a brow. He's one of her husband's best friends, so I'm sure she's hoping I don't hate the guy.

"I understand why he did what he did." I'm trying to, at

least. If I'm going to be the good guy Gia claims I am, I have to support Owen's actions, which led to the takedown of a terrorist. My own desires can't trump that. But when it comes to Gia's safety, everything feels secondary.

"Did you ask Jessica about her extracurricular activities with the government?" If I hadn't been so busy these last few weeks, I'd still be curious about who the hell Jessica and Owen really are.

Grace smiles. "She's still sticking with that whole *classified* mantra. Even Noah can't get anything out of Owen, so I have to assume that whatever they're into is pretty hardcore."

"This is all surreal." Corbin drags a palm down his face, the skin pulling down from his eyes. "I think I need another vacation just to digest everything I've learned this week."

Both Grace and I look at him.

"What, a month in Vegas wasn't enough?" she asks, shaking her head.

"Are you kidding? A month in Vegas is like work. I need to go somewhere I can just chill. Maybe Ibiza."

"Yeah, uh, no. You and a party city like that—I can't take time off to go over there and bail your ass out of prison. And Gia might speak Spanish, but I'm doubting any amount of smooth talking will get you out of a jam."

His mouth spreads into a wide grin as he rubs at his jaw. The man lives for this shit. "Says the guy who took on the mob, and oh yeah—a goddamn human trafficker."

"That was me being on the right side of the law." My arms flex at my sides. Can't I have a minute to relax? "Just do me a favor and stick around for a while. I'm too young to start taking blood pressure meds."

"Nah, man, you're old," Corbin says, and Grace nudges me in the side playfully.

"Don't remind me."

There's a knock on the door, and then I see Gia peeking through the little glass window alongside it.

My heartbeat picks up at the sight of her.

"Guess you'll be meeting her sooner than I thought." I flick my wrist, motioning for her to come in.

A shy smile lights up her face when she notices I'm not alone. I stride across the room, anxious to get to her. "Hi." I kiss her on the lips without thinking twice about it.

"Hi," Grace says right away and approaches her.

Gia starts to reach out to shake her hand, but my sister goes in for the hug.

Another surprise. Must be the hormones.

"It's so nice to finally meet you," Grace says.

"You, too." Gia smiles and then gets caught off guard when Corbin bear hugs her next.

"Easy there." I roll my eyes at my brother. He's trying to rattle me on purpose by hanging on to her longer than necessary. It's been a while since we've been in the boxing ring together, and I'm thinking he's in the mood for a kick in the ass.

But, shit, that's the old me talking.

Then again, fuck that—that part might always be me, and I'm fine with that.

"Okay." I rest a hand on his shoulder. The smirk on his face when he lets Gia go is evidence he can't help but try and get himself in trouble.

And since maybe I'm like the dad in the family, since our actual dad is shit, I'll cut him a break, for now.

"Well." Grace lifts her shoulders, her eyes smiling, her face bright. "You are ridiculously beautiful."

A soft pink creeps up Gia's cheeks. "And you're having twins, I hear. How do you feel?"

"Oh, you know . . . fat. And bread is like crack, but hey, if the babies want it, I gotta eat it."

Silky laughter floats to my ears, and Gia's eyes blaze to life.

"Well"—I clear my throat—"maybe we'll have dinner this weekend, and you can get to know each other. Obviously, bring Noah." I'm hoping they'll get the hint and leave. I've been away from Gia for eight hours, and I need my hands on her. "And tell him thanks for keeping you safe while I was gone," I add.

Grace smiles. "Like he'd have it any other way." She winks, then we exchange a few more words before they leave.

"I had no idea they'd be here. Sorry to interrupt," Gia says once the door is closed.

"Yeah, well, thanks to you, we had that heart-to-heart you insisted upon."

"Really?" Her lips crook into a smile, and I reach out and pull her against me. "Well, Mr. King, I think you deserve a reward."

"Say that again." I nip at the bottom of her plump pink lip.

With heavy-lidded eyes, she looks at me, the passion there. "Mr. King."

I reach around and grab her ass, her jeans still chilled from being outside. It's been snowing since we got to the city, and I think we both miss the sunny weather in South America.

"I was looking at a loft near here, so I thought I'd stop by and see you."

"Oh, yeah?"

"And I brought you something." She reaches into her pocket and pulls out one of my red ties. "I noticed you didn't wear one today, and I thought maybe it could be useful."

My cock hardens as she steps back and demonstrates, threading the red material through her mouth.

"So no one hears me screaming while I sit on your lap during a conference call."

I start to laugh, unable to stop myself. "You're testing me, huh? Seeing if I was serious."

She lifts her shoulders and looks up at the ceiling as if she's so innocent.

Yeah, right.

I take the tie from her and wrap it around my hand several times. "There's no way I'll risk anyone hearing any of your grunts or moans." I palm her face with my other hand. "Those sounds are reserved for me."

My tongue slips inside of her mouth, tangling with hers, and she arches up against me. Even with the heavy material of her coat between us, her heart is pounding so loud, it goes through the fabric and straight to my chest.

I reach down, adjusting myself, the thickness against my dress pants growing uncomfortable. I pull away before I'm unable to stop myself from yanking down her pants to bury myself balls deep.

She's panting when she steps back. "Okay, well, why don't you hang onto it for later, when you get home."

I tuck the tie into my pants pocket and work at my sleeves, rolling them to the elbows. It's too damn hot in here now.

"Where are you off to now?"

"One more place to look at, and then I'm going to cook us up one of my mom's dishes."

"I could get used to this."

"Good, because I'm not going anywhere."

And I never want her to.

She kisses me on the cheek, and I grab hold of her wrist. She gasps when I pull her back against me so she can feel how hard I still am.

"Be sure to think of me while you're on your next call."

"Oh, I'm pretty sure you're all I'll be thinking about."

I kiss her again, hard and long, to give her something to think about, too.

On the way out, her phone starts ringing, so she digs into her purse.

"A realtor?" I ask.

She shrugs before retrieving it. "It's Mya." With the phone pressed to her ear, she waves to me over her shoulder and opens the door. "Hey, everything okay?"

I head back toward my desk and tuck my hand into my pocket to feel for the tie, anxious for today to end so I can get home and see her in nothing but this.

27

CADE

My brows pinch together as I try to figure out what I'm looking at.

Gia's back is to me, a marker in hand, and she's studying the massive whiteboard in front of her.

We moved into our new place only two days ago, so there are boxes littered all over the floor and stacked up higher than Gia is tall. She insisted we do everything ourselves, instead of letting the movers help.

She's stubborn. What can I say?

"What is this?" I drop my briefcase on the floor in the office and come up behind her. I press a kiss to her shoulder. She's only in a black tank top and a pair of shorts that barely cover her ass cheeks.

She sets her marker down on the cluttered desk by the whiteboard and faces me. "Well."

I want to pull her in for a hug after a long day at work, but there's a shade of fear in her eyes, shadowing her face.

What the hell is going on?

"Gia." I step back to fully assess what's on the board.

At least thirty pictures of women are taped up there. Some

have circles around them, and others have the word *MISSING* beneath in large print.

I look back at her, worry darting through me enough to make my brow nearly sweat.

"You know how I've been meeting with Mya every week since we've been back?"

"Yeah."

"We, um, haven't just been hanging out."

Jesus Christ. I already know what's coming, and maybe I kind of expected it, but I'm still not prepared.

She turns to the side and points to the board. "These are the women Connor and his men have already found, but there are still a lot more out there."

"And what does this have to do with you?" I didn't realize Mya's friends were going to keep their promise and actually track the women down one by one.

"This is what I'm meant to do." She places her hands in prayer position and rests them against her lips. It's obvious she's worried I'm going to say no, which is why she's been keeping this from me.

I want to be angry, but maybe I would have gone off the handle with worry had she approached me with the idea too soon.

It's been seven weeks since Carlos was taken down, but I'm not sure if enough time will ever pass before I won't be concerned about Gia involving herself in something dangerous.

She reaches for my arms, holding my wrists. Her big hazel eyes, so full of compassion, capture mine. "I'm only doing research and helping Connor and his men go through files. But . . ."

I lift a brow. "But?"

"I'd like to be directly involved in what happens to the women once they're safe."

I release a ragged breath, my nerves fraying by the second. "How so?"

Her hands skirt up my forearms until her fingertips bite into my shoulders, urging me closer to her.

"I spent the last ten years of my life coming up with ideas to help my mom once she was found. I knew that it would be difficult for her to move on with her life after being"—she stops for a moment to take a breath, the memory of her loss gripping her—"um, captive for so long."

I fight the urge to close my eyes.

"This is my purpose. This is what I'm meant to do with my life. I couldn't help my mom, but I can help others who were taken." She swallows, her eyes glistening from unshed tears.

"That means you'll be traveling a lot. And the idea of you being away from me—" I cut myself off and back out of her reach. "No. I can't risk something happening to you." I drag both palms down my face.

I bow my head and take a moment to think.

"I would never tell you no." I blow out a breath. "But I'm also not willing to let you do this alone."

"I'm not alone. Mya's helping out on the side, and Connor's security team is taking on a major role in this."

"That's not what I mean." I slowly turn around.

Her soul, her love for humanity, is bright and damn near intoxicating.

"When you need to travel, I'll travel with you."

"You have a company to run. You don't need to do that." She palms my cheek, our eyes connecting. "And besides, someone from Connor's team will be with me. I'll be safe."

"I can work from anywhere, and you know that." I lift her

hand from my face and press my lips to her tattoo. "I'm not going to lose you."

"And I'm not running. This isn't me running. I promise," she says, her voice shaky with emotion.

This move on her part makes sense.

I get it.

But I can't tolerate the idea of her going anywhere near the line of fire.

"So I sell the company," I say a moment later, the realization hitting me hard and fast.

It was a job I was born into, a position I was groomed for, but is it something I want or need to be happy?

Fuck no.

She stumbles back, her eyes widening, her lips parting.

"I buy and sell companies for parts, right? I'm a destroyer." Maybe I've still been living in the shade of my father's lies, acting like his sins aren't on me.

"I can't ask you to do that. Your company is everything to you."

"No." I move toward her. "You're everything to me." I smile. "How many times do I have to tell you that?"

"I just can't let you—"

"Unfortunately for you, I'm not so good at taking orders, so I think I'll make the call on this one."

"How do you know this is what you want? What if it doesn't make you happy?"

"Working together to save these women would make you happy, right?" I angle my head, trying not to lose hold of her beautiful eyes.

"Of course," she answers, a little breathy.

"Then it'll make me happy."

She closes her eyes, and I can tell she's thinking about

resisting again, so I grab her and lift her up off the ground, encouraging her legs to wrap around me.

"Hang on to me, baby," I murmur into her ear. "Never let go, and I promise you you'll never regret it." I brush my lips against her temple. "Maybe there is such a thing as redemption for me. Help me find my way to a second chance."

A soft cry works out of her throat, and she leans back so she can look into my eyes without losing her hold around my hips.

"You've never needed a second chance." She hiccups. "We've just needed each other."

My lips smash against hers, and we drop back onto the couch at the center of the room.

She straddles me and holds my face between her palms. "Now," she says, smiling, "let's see who makes the first move with me in this position. I still say it's you who blinks and loses control."

I grip the sides of her thighs, my cock growing thick with her on top of me.

"Oh . . . it's on."

But then she peels her tank over her head, exposing her full, perky breasts.

"Well, that's not playing fair."

She chuckles. "Who said anything about playing fair?"

And this time, I'm the one groaning as we kiss.

"I want a lifetime of this," she whispers into my ear a few minutes later and squirms around on my lap, loving how much she's torturing me.

"And you'll get it." I tug on her hair to tip her head back so I can see her glowing face.

"But first, you want to do naughty things to me, don't you?"

"Oh, fuck yeah." I lift her up into the air.

I'll gladly be the one to blink. Well, this time, at least.

"Where are we going?" she squeals as I flip her over my shoulder so her ass is near my face, and then I spank her as I walk through our obstacle course of a home.

"Shower sex." I slap at her tight, hard ass again, unable to stop myself.

I help her to her feet once inside the master bathroom and switch on the overhead rain shower.

"I love you, Mr. King," she says beneath the water a few minutes later, her hands gliding over my chest, water trickling down her face.

I kiss her wet lips and run my fingers through her slick hair. "I love you, too, Mrs. King."

It's only been three days since we went to the courthouse and said *I do.*

I wanted to carry her over the threshold of our new home as husband and wife.

Maybe we moved fast.

Maybe people think we're crazy.

But the thing is, we don't give a damn what anyone thinks.

She's my wife.

And now, I have everything in the world I could ever want.

Well, almost . . .

EPILOGUE

CADE

"Beautiful." Gia's mesmerized by the baby in her arms. He's wrapped in a soft blue blanket, his face wrinkled and pink, his eyes closed.

"You're an uncle." Grace's gaze sweeps up to my face after staring lovingly at her other son in her arms.

"That I am. And you were amazing."

An emergency C-section, but thank God everyone's okay.

"Congrats, man." I shake Noah's hand. It's still hard for me to believe my sister is a mom, and I'm an uncle.

Caston and Craig. What is it with our family and C names for boys? But I wasn't going to throw my two cents in and offer up alternatives. Apparently, these were the names of two team members Noah lost in the SEALs.

Gia approaches me. "Do you want to hold him?"

I stare down at the fragile little guy, afraid I might drop him.

"No, I'm okay."

"Oh, come on." She hands him over to me without giving me an option, and I cradle his neck and try to hold on to him tight without squeezing too much.

"You're a natural," my sister says.

I can't stop looking at this little dude in my arms. "Are we ever gonna do this?" I ask a minute later.

"Do what?" Gia reaches for the little hand that has worked free from the blanket.

"You know, make one of these."

"These?" She laughs, and I hear my sister make some sort of amused half-snort.

Without dropping the baby's hand, she presses up on her toes and whispers into my ear, "I think you know how to do the making part just fine."

I eye her. "I'm serious."

"And I am, too."

She's young, though.

Just because I'll be forty in a few years doesn't mean she's ready. But Gia's experienced more in life than most people at eighty . . .

We've been busy focusing on the missing women, though, so would we have time for a child?

My chest tightens, constricting with emotions.

I *do* want a child.

"You'd make great parents," Grace interrupts our eye-staring contest.

"Maybe we'll just see what happens. Not make any plans," she says to me when we're alone in the hospital hall a few minutes later. "We'll stop using protection and go with the flow, let fate decide."

I grumble and tug her against me so her hands land on my chest. "You want me to lose control of the situation?"

She smiles. "Yeah. You think you can handle that?"

A low rumble of laughter escapes my mouth unexpectedly. "Well, I have done a lot of things I never thought I'd do since you entered my life."

"You have, have you?" Her hands slide up around my neck, and she tips her chin up.

"But in this case . . ." I shake my head. "We're making a baby tonight."

She snaps her fingers behind my head. "Like that, huh?"

I chuckle. "Don't you know me by now? I always get what I want."

BOOK NEWS

Did you know Connor Matthews stars in his own book, *The Hard Truth*? It's an exciting and intense second chance romantic suspense.

Haven't read Grace's story, yet, *Someone Like You*? This is a heartwarming contemporary romance. Get glimpses of what Cade was like before he met Gia!

A Stealth Ops World Guide is now available on my website, which features more information about the team, character muses, and SEAL lingo.
Also, check out this handy **reading guide**.

***

Curious what Owen and Jessica are really up to?

The new action-packed **SEAL TEAM** (Stealth Ops) series released Fall 2018, starring Owen, Jessica, and other Navy

SEALs that were featured in both *My Every Breath* and *Someone Like You* + more.

*Someone Like You and *My Every Breath* take place in the "5-yr gap" between the prologue and chapter one of *Finding His Mark*.

Luke Scott's book - *Finding His Mark*

Owen York's book - *Finding Justice*

Jessica Scott's book - *Finding the Fight*

Get alerted about new releases, bonus scenes, and sales by joining my newsletter. Learn more at brittneysahin.com.

FB Reader Group - Brittney's Book Babes
Stealth Ops Spoiler Room

met his match.

The Inside Man - 4/30/20

Stand-alone (with a connection to *On the Edge*):

The Story of Us– Sports columnist Maggie Lane has 1 rule: never fall for a player. One mistaken kiss with Italian soccer star Marco Valenti changes everything…

Hidden Truths

The Safe Bet – Begin the series with the Man-of-Steel lookalike Michael Maddox.

Beyond the Chase - Fall for the sexy Irishman, Aiden O'Connor, in this romantic suspense.

The Hard Truth – Read Connor Matthews' story in this second-chance romantic suspense novel.

Surviving the Fall – Jake Summers loses the last 12 years of his life in this action-packed romantic thriller.

The Final Goodbye - Friends-to-lovers romantic mystery

A Stealth Ops World Guide is now available on my website, which features more information about the team, character muses, and SEAL lingo.

Also, check out this handy **reading guide**.

Bonus Scenes

Pinterest - muses/inspiration boards

CONNECT

Thank you for reading Cade and Gia's story. If you don't mind taking a minute to leave a short review, I would greatly appreciate it. Reviews are incredibly helpful to us authors! Thank you!

For more information:
www.brittneysahin.com
brittneysahin@emkomedia.net
FB Reader Group - Brittney's Book Babes
Stealth Ops Spoiler Room
Pinterest - Inspiration boards